'Layers of intrigue and suspense, with a
brilliant sting in the tale. Loved it!'
Mel Sherratt, author of *Hush Hush*

'Just brilliant! Ridiculously addictive (I DID NOT
put it down) and chock full of twists and turns'
Lisa Hall, author of *The Party*

'Suzy K Quinn is a born storyteller'
Erin Kelly, author of *He Said/She Said*

'OMG! What a book! Brilliantly written
and utterly chilling! Just wow!'
Darren O'Sullivan, author of *Our Little Secret*

'Creepy and addictive with a genuine shocker of a twist!'
Roz Watkins, author of *The Devil's Dice*

'A twist so unexpected I had to turn back to the
beginning to see what clues I'd missed! I thought I'd
spotted the magician's sleight of hand, and all the time
I was looking in the wrong direction. Bravo, Suzy K!'
Ruth Dugdall, author of *My Sister and Other Liars*

'A twisty and menacing look at modern
families. Fantastic; I loved it!'
Ali Knight, author of *Before I Find You*

'Deliciously dark; had me gripped from the get-go'
Rebecca Tinnelly, author of *Never Go There*

From Suzy:

Every page in this book is a connection
between us – author and reader.
I am so grateful you have chosen to make that connection.
I love talking to readers, so feel free to get in touch:

Email: suzykquinn@devoted-ebooks.com
Facebook.com/suzykquinn (You can
friend request me. I like friends.)
Twitter: @suzykquinn
Website: www.suzykquinn.com

Don't Tell Teacher

Suzy K Quinn

ONE PLACE. MANY STORIES

HQ
An imprint of HarperCollins*Publishers* Ltd
1 London Bridge Street
London SE1 9GF

This paperback edition 2019

2
First published in Great Britain by
HQ, an imprint of HarperCollins*Publishers* Ltd 2019

ISBN: 978-0-00-832315-8

MIX
Paper from
responsible sources
FSC™ C007454

This book is produced from independently certified FSC™ paper
to ensure responsible forest management.

For more information visit: www.harpercollins.co.uk/green

This book is set in 10.7/15.5 pt. Sabon

Printed and bound in Great Britain by
CPI Group (UK) Ltd, Croydon, CR0 4YY

For my little girls, Lexi and Laya – sorry this isn't a bedtime story. You can read it when you're older :) xx

Prologue

We're running. Along wide, tree-lined pavements, over the zebra crossing and into the park.

'Quick, Tom.'

Tom struggles to keep up, tired little legs bobbing up and down on trimmed grass. He gasps for breath.

My ribs throb, lighting up in pain.

A Victorian bandstand and a rainbow of flowerbeds flash past. Dimly, I notice wicker picnic hampers, Prosecco, Pimm's in plastic glasses.

No one notices us. The frightened mother with straight, brown hair, wearing her husband's choice of clothes. The little boy in tears.

That's the thing about the city. Nobody notices.

There's a giant privet hedge by the railings, big enough to hide in.

Tom cries harder. I cuddle him in my arms. 'Don't make a sound,' I whisper, heart racing. 'Don't make a sound.'

Tom nods rapidly.

We both clutch each other, terrified. I shiver, even though it's a warm summer's day.

Tom gives a choked sob. 'Will he find us, Mum?'

'Shush,' I say, crouching in my flat leather sandals, summer dress flowing over my knees. 'Please, Tom. We have to be quiet.'

'I'm scared.' Tom clasps my bare arm.

'I know, sweetheart,' I whisper, holding his head against my shoulder. 'We're going away. Far away from him.'

'What if he gets me at school?'

'We'll find a new school. One he doesn't know about. Okay?'

Tom's chest is against mine, his breathing fast.

He understands that we can't be found.

Olly is capable of anything.

Lizzie

Monday. School starts. It won't be like the last place, Tom knows that. It will be hard, being the new kid.

'Come on, Tommo,' I call up the stairs. 'Let's go go go. We don't want to be late on our first day.'

I pack Tom's school bag, then give my hair a few quick brushes, checking my reflection in the hallway mirror.

A pale, worried face stares back at me. Pointy little features, a heart-shaped chin, brown hair, long and ruler-straight.

The invisible woman.

Olly's broken ex-wife.

I want to change that. I want to be someone different here. No one needs to know how things were before.

Tom clatters down the polished, wooden staircase in his new Steelfield school uniform. I throw my arms around him.

'A hug to make you grow big and strong,' I say. 'You get taller with every cuddle. Did you know that?'

'I know, Mum. You tell me every morning.'

I hand him his blue wool coat. I've always liked this colour against Tom's bright blond hair and pale skin. The coat is from last winter, but he still hasn't grown out of it. Tom is small for his age; at nearly nine he looks more like seven.

We head out and onto the muddy track, stopping at a blackberry bush to pick berries.

Tom counts as he eats and sings.

'One, two, three, four, five – to stay alive.'

'It's going to be exciting,' I coax as Tom and I pass the school playing field. 'Look at all that grass. You didn't have that in London. And they've got a little woodland bit.' I point to the trees edging the field. 'And full-sized goalposts.'

'What if Dad finds us?' Tom watches the stony ground.

'He won't. Don't worry. We're safe here.'

'I like our new house,' says Tom. 'It's a family house. Like in *Peter Pan*.'

We walk on in silence and birds skitter across the path.

Tom says, 'Hello, birds. Do you live here? Oh – did you hurt your leg, little birdy? I hope you feel better soon.'

They really are beautiful school grounds – huge and tree-lined, with bright green grass. Up ahead there is a silver, glimmering spider's web tangled through the fence wire: an old bike chain bent around to repair a hole.

I wonder, briefly, why there is a hole in the fence. I'm sure there's some logical explanation. This is an excellent school … But I've never seen a fence this tall around a school. It's like a zoo enclosure.

I feel uneasy, thinking of children caged like animals.

A cage is safe. Think of it that way.

The school building sits at the front of the field, a large Victorian structure with a tarmac playground. There are no lively murals, like at Tom's last school. Just spikey grey railings and towering, arched gates.

A shiny sign says:

4

Steelfield School: An Outstanding
Educational Establishment
Headmaster: Alan Cockrun, BA hons
Semper Fortis — Always Strong

The downstairs windows have bars on them, which feel a little sinister and an odd paradox to the holes in the fence. And one window – a small one by the main door – has blacked-out glass, a sleeping eye twinkling in the sun.

The playground is a spotless black lake. No scooter marks or trodden-in chewing gum. I've never seen a school so clean.

We approach the main road, joining a swarm of kids battling for pavement position.

Most of the kids are orderly and well-behaved. No chatting or playing. However, three boys stand out with their neon, scruffy shoes, angry faces and thick, shaggy black hair.

Brothers, I decide.

They are pushing and shoving each other, fighting over a football. The tallest of the boys notices Tom and me coming up the lane. 'Who are *you*?' He bounces his football hard on the concrete, glaring.

I put a hand on Tom's shoulder. 'Come on, Tommo. Nearly there.'

The shortest of the three boys shouts, 'Oo, oo. London *town-ies*'.

I call after them, 'Hey. Hey! *Excuse* me—'

But they're running now, laughing and careering through the school gates.

How do they know we're from London?

'It's okay, Mum,' says Tom.

My hand tenses on his shoulder. 'I should say something.'

'They don't know me yet,' Tom whispers. 'That's all. When they get to know me, it'll be okay.'

My wise little eight-year-old. Tom has always been that way. Very in tune with people. But I am worried about bullying. Vulnerable children are easy targets. Social services told me that.

It will be hard for him …

As the three black-haired brothers head into the school yard, a remarkable change takes place. They stop jostling and pushing each other and walk sensibly, arms by their sides, mouths closed in angry lines.

Tom and I walk alongside the railings, approaching the open gates.

It's funny – I'd expected this new academy school to be shiny and modern. Not to have grey brick walls, a bell tower, slate turrets and bars.

I sweep away thoughts of prisons and haunted houses and tell Tom, 'Well, this is exciting. Look – there's hopscotch.'

Tom doesn't reply, his eyes wide at the shadowy brickwork.

'This is my *school*?' he asks, bewildered. 'It looks like an old castle.'

'Well, castles are fun. Maybe you can play knights or something. I know it's different from the last place.'

'Castles have ghosts,' Tom whispers.

'Oh, no they don't. Anyway, big nearly-nine-year-old ghostbusters aren't afraid of ghosts.'

We move towards the school gates, which are huge with spikes along the top, and I put on an even brighter voice. 'You're going to do great today, Tom. I love you so much. Stay cool, okay? High five?'

Tom gives me a weak high five.

'Will *you* be okay, Mum?' he asks.

My eyes well up. 'Of course. I'll be fine. It's not your job to worry about me. It's mine to worry about you.'

Tom turns towards the soulless tarmac and asks, 'Aren't you coming in with me?'

'Parents aren't allowed into the playground here,' I say. 'Someone from the office phoned to tell me. Something to do with safety.'

Two of the black-haired boys are fighting in a secluded corner near a netball post, a pile of tussling limbs.

'Those Neilson boys,' I hear a voice mutter beside me – a mother dropping off her daughter. 'Can't go five minutes without killing each other.'

The headmaster appears in the entranceway then – an immaculately presented man wearing a pinstripe suit and royal-blue tie. His hair is brown, neatly cut and combed, and he is clean-shaven with a boyish face that has a slightly rubbery, clown-like quality.

Hands in pockets, he surveys the playground. He is smiling, lips oddly red and jester-shaped, but his blue eyes remain cold and hard.

The chattering parents spot him and fall silent.

The headmaster approaches the corner where the boys are fighting and stops to watch, still smiling his cold smile.

After a moment, the boys sense the headmaster and quickly untangle themselves, standing straight, expressions fearful.

It's a little creepy how all this is done in near silence, but I suppose at least the headmaster can keep order. Tom's last school was chaos. Too many pupils and no control.

I kneel down to Tom and whisper, 'Have a good day at school. I love you so much. Don't think about Dad.' I stroke Tom's chin-length blond hair, left loose around his ears today. More conventional, I thought. Less like his father. 'How are you feeling?'

'I'm scared, Mum,' says Tom. 'I don't want to leave you alone all day. What if Dad—'

I cut Tom off with a shake of my head and give him a thumbs-up. 'It's fine. We're safe now, okay? He has no idea where we are.' Then I hug him, burying my face in his fine hair.

'I love you, Mum,' says Tom.

'I love you too.' I step back, smiling encouragingly. 'Go on then. You'll be a big kid – going into class all by yourself. They'll call you Tom Kinnock in the register. Social services gave them your old name. But remember you're Riley now. Tom Riley.'

Tom wanders into the playground, a tiny figure drowned by a huge Transformers bag. He really is small for nearly nine. And thin too, with bony arms and legs.

Someone kicks a ball towards him, and Tom reacts with his feet – probably without thinking.

A minute later, he's kicking a football with a group of lads, including two of the black-haired boys who were fighting before. The ball is kicked viciously by those boys, booted at children's faces.

I'm anxious. Those kids look like trouble.

As I'm watching, the headmaster crosses the playground. Mr Cockrun. Yes. That's his name. He'd never get away with that at a secondary school. His smile fades as he approaches the gate.

'Hello there,' he says. 'You must be Mrs Kinnock.'

The way he says our old surname ... I don't feel especially welcomed.

'Riley now,' I say. 'Miss Riley. Our social worker—'

'Best not to hang around once they've gone inside,' says Mr Cockrun, giving me a full politician's smile and flashing straight, white teeth. 'It can be unsettling, especially for the younger ones. And it's also a safeguarding issue.' He pulls a large bunch of keys from his pocket. 'They're always fine when the parents are gone.'

Mr Cockrun tugs at the stiff gate. It makes a horrible screech as metal drags along a tarmac trench, orange with rust. Then he takes the bulky chain that hangs from it and wraps it around three times before securing it with a gorilla padlock. He tests the arrangement, pulling at the chain.

'Safe as houses,' he tells me through the gates.

'Why the padlock?' I ask, seeing Tom small and trapped on the other side of the railings.

Mr Cockrun's cheerful expression falters. 'I beg your pardon?'

'Why have you padlocked the gate?' I don't mean to raise my voice. Other parents are looking. But it feels sinister.

'For safeguarding. Fail to safeguard the children and we fail everything.'

'Yes, but—'

'Mrs Kinnock, this is an outstanding school. We know what we're doing.'

I pull my coat around myself, holding back a shiver. It's a very ordinary wool coat, bought while I was with Olly.

I was a shadow then, of course. Hiding behind my husband.

Im hoping that will change here.

'It feels like I'm leaving Tom in prison,' I say, trying for a little laugh.

Mr Cockrun meets my eye, his hard, black pupils unwavering. 'There is a *very* long waiting list for this school, Mrs Kinnock. Thanks to social services, your son jumped right to the top. I'd have thought you'd be the last parent to criticise.'

'I didn't mean to—'

'We usually pick and choose who we let in.' The politician's smile returns. 'Let's make sure we're on the same page, Mrs Kinnock. Not start off on the wrong foot.'

He strolls back to the school building, and I'm left watching and wondering.

When I get back to our new Victorian house with its large, wraparound garden and elegant porch pillars, I sit on the front wall, put my head in my hands and cry.

I try not to make a sound, but sobs escape through my fingers.

Things will get better.

Of course I'm going to feel emotional on his first day.

Lizzie

I've been invited to a party, but I'm on the outside, not knowing what to do with myself. I'm not a skier or snowboarder, so I'm ... nowhere. Standing on the balcony, looking at the mountains, I feel very alone.

Morzine is one of the world's best ski resorts. I've heard it described as 'electric' after dark. Tomorrow, the slopes will be tingling with pink, white and yellow snowsuits. But tonight, they're white and calm.

It sounded so adventurous, being a chalet girl out here. But the truth is, I'm running away. Things with Mum are unbearable again. I thought they'd be better after university, but if anything they're worse. Her need to tear me down is stronger than ever.

It's not about blame.

All I know is that I needed to get away, for my own sanity.

Behind me, Olympic hopefuls talk and laugh in their day clothes, drinking sparkling water or, if they're real rebels, small bottles of beer.

Most of them aren't interested in a twenty-something chalet girl with straight, brown hair and floral-patterned Doc Marten boots.

But ... someone has come to stand beside me. He's a tall,

blond man wearing ripped jeans and a loose, light pink T-shirt. His light tan and white panda eyes tell me he's a skier or snowboarder – probably a serious one, if the other guests at this party are anything to go by.

'It's Lizzie,' the man asks. 'Isn't it?'

'How do you know my name?'

'You're still wearing your name badge.'

I glance down and see my health and safety training sticker: Lizzie Riley.

'You don't remember me?' the man challenges, raising a thick, blond eyebrow.

'I'm sorry, I don't—'

'Olly.' He holds out a large hand for me to shake. 'I'm staying in the chalet next to you. With the Olympic rabble over there.' He points to a rowdy group of young men holding beers. 'You're a chalet girl, right?' He grins. 'Nice work if you can get it.'

'Actually, it can be exhausting,' I say.

Olly laughs. 'Are you thinking about jumping off the mountain then?'

My smile disappears. 'No. Why would you ask that?'

'Just joking.'

We stare out at the peaks for a minute.

A live band strikes up behind us, playing a Beatles cover – 'Love Me Do'.

Olly's shoulders move to the music.

Mine do too.

'You like the Beatles?' Olly asks.

'Yes.' I look at him shyly, hoping this is the right answer.

'Me too! I have a massive collection of Sixties vinyl.'

'You collect vinyl?' I ask.

'No, well … not really. Most of my records are my mum's. She listens to CDs now. It feels like time-travelling when I play vinyl, you know? Like I'm part of the swinging Sixties.'

'Olly!' A tall, red-cheeked man swaggers over, holding out a beer bottle. 'Olly Kinnock. This is supposed to be a lads' night out and here you are chatting up girls again.'

Olly smiles at me, staring with blue, blue eyes. 'Not girls. A girl. A very interesting girl.'

I feel myself blushing.

'Fair enough,' announces the red-cheeked man, thrusting the beer into Olly's hand. 'We'll see you in the morning then.' He returns to his group of friends, who break into guffaws of laughter.

'Sorry about them,' says Olly, putting his elbow on the balcony and, in the process, leaning nearer to me. 'They can be morons.'

'You can go back to them if you like.'

'Actually, I've always preferred female company,' says Olly. 'Girls smell better. But you must have a boyfriend, surely? A pretty girl like you. So tell me to get lost if you want.'

I blush again and stammer, 'Um … no, I don't have a boyfriend.'

'Have a drink with me then.'

Surely he's just teasing me? Handsome snowboarders don't chat up chalet girls. And he really is handsome, with his lean, toned arms and perfect white teeth.

His eyes are serious, holding my gaze.

Maybe he isn't joking.

'Okay,' I hear myself say. 'Why not?'

'It's a date.' Olly takes my hand like he's won a prize.

I laugh, sucking in my breath as his strong fingers close around mine.

'So what are you drinking?' Olly asks.

'Um … white wine?'

'Chardonnay?'

'Sure. Yes please.'

He winks at me. 'I love Chardonnay. Best wine ever. Just don't tell the lads. It's a bit girly. I've been noticing you for weeks, Lizzie Riley. I think we should spend lots and lots of time together. And then get married.'

I can barely believe this is happening. A nobody chalet girl like me, being chatted up by this confident, tanned athlete. I guess I should enjoy it while it lasts. When he works out what a nothing I am, he'll run a mile.

I laugh. 'Are you always so forward with your wedding plans?'

'Only with my future wife.'

'You don't even know me.'

'Yes, but I've been watching you and your purple puffer jacket for ages, wondering how you don't freeze to death in those DM boots.'

'Where have you noticed me?'

'Drinking black coffee in the café, buying a ginger cookie and giving crumbs to the birds on your way out. Always carrying a pile of books under your arm. Are you a student?'

'I'm training to be a nurse.'

'A nurse? Well, Lizzie Nightingale, you'll have to put your career aside when you have my five children.'

'Five children?'

'At least five. And I hope they all look just like you.'

Our eyes meet, and in that second I feel totally, utterly alive.

I've never been noticed like this.

It's electrifying.

And I feel myself hoping, like I've never hoped before, that this man feels the same sparks in his chest as I do.

Kate

8 a.m.

I'm eating Kellogg's All-Bran at my desk, silently chanting my morning mantra: *Be grateful, Kate. Be grateful. This is the job you wanted.*

Apparently, social workers suffer more nervous breakdowns than any other profession.

I already have stress-related eczema, insomnia and an unhealthy relationship with the office vending machine – specifically the coils holding the KitKats and Mars bars.

Last night I got home at 9 p.m., and this morning I was called in at 7.30 a.m. I have a huge caseload and I'm fire-fighting. There isn't time to help anyone. Just prevent disaster.

Be grateful, Kate.

My computer screen displays my caseload: thirty children.

This morning, I've had to add one more. A transfer case from Hammersmith and Fulham: Tom Kinnock.

I click update and watch my screen change: thirty-one children.

Then I put my head in my hands, already exhausted by what I won't manage to do today.

Be grateful, Kate. You have a proper grown-up job. You're one of the lucky ones.

My husband Col is a qualified occupational therapist, but he's working at the Odeon cinema. It could be worse. At least he gets free popcorn.

'Well, you're bright and shiny, aren't you?' Tessa Warwick, my manager, strides into the office, clicking on her Nespresso machine – a personal cappuccino maker she won't let anyone else use.

I jolt upright and start tapping keys.

'And what's that, a new hairdo?' Tessa is a big, shouty lady with high blood pressure and red cheeks. Her brown hair is wiry and cut into a slightly wonky bob. She wears a lot of polyester.

'I've just tied it back, that's all,' I say, pulling my curly black hair tighter in its hairband. 'I'm not really a new hairdo sort of person.'

I've had the same hair since I was eight years old – long and curly, sometimes up, sometimes down. No layers. Just long.

'I might have known. Yes, you're very, very sensible, aren't you?'

This is a dig at me, but I don't mind because Tessa is absolutely right. I wear plain, functional trouser suits and no makeup. My glasses are from the twenty-pound range at Specsavers. I've never signed up for monthly contact lenses – I'd rather put money in my savings account.

'I'm glad you're in early anyway,' Tessa continues. 'There is a *lot* to do this week.'

'I know,' I say. 'Leanne Neilson is in hospital again. Gary and I were up until nine on Friday trying to get her boys into bed. I just need time to get going.'

Gary is a family support worker and absolutely should have

finished at 5 p.m. So should I, actually. But two out-of-hours team members were off sick and we were swamped.

Tessa inserts a cappuccino tablet into her Nespresso machine. 'So you were babysitting the three Neilson scallywags?' She gives a snort of laughter. 'They're like child versions of the Gallagher brothers, those boys. All that black hair, fighting all the time. You never know – maybe they'll be famous musicians. But *you* shouldn't have been putting them to bed. You should be in the pub of an evening, like a normal twenty-something.'

It's a bone of contention between us – the fact I rarely drink alcohol. Also, that I married at twenty years old and go to church twice a week.

'Jesus drank, didn't he?' Tessa continues. 'I thought it would be okay for you lot.'

'Us lot?'

'You young churchy types. You'll be drinking soon,' Tessa predicts. 'Just you wait. You're new to this, but everyone ends up on the lunchtime wine eventually. Now listen – have you done the home visit for that transfer case yet? From Hammersmith and Fulham, Tom Kinnock? The one with the angry dad.'

'No. I sent a letter on Friday. She'll get it today.'

'Get on to that one as soon as you can, Kate. The transfer was weeks late. There'll already be some catching up to do. Have they got him a school place?'

'Yes. At Steelfield School.'

'I bet the headmaster is furious,' laughs Tessa. '"More social services children thrust upon us … we already have the Neilson boys to deal with."'

'I'm not sure a high-achieving school is the right environment for Tom Kinnock,' I say. 'Very strict and results obsessed. After what this boy has been through, maybe he needs somewhere more nurturing.'

'Don't worry about the school,' says Tessa. 'Steelfield is a godsend. They keep the kids in line. No chair throwing or teacher nervous breakdowns. Just worry about getting that case shut down ASAP. The father is a risk factor, but all the dirty work is done.'

'I'm pretty overwhelmed here, Tessa.'

'Welcome to social work.' Tessa gives her Nespresso machine a brief thump with a closed fist.

Lizzie

A brown envelope, addressed formally to Elizabeth Kinnock. The mottled paper has a muddy shoeprint from where I stepped on it.

I study the postmark. It's from the county council, i.e. social services. I know these sorts of letters from when we lived with Olly. *We'd like to meet to discuss your son …*

I should have known social services would want to meet us. Check we're settling into our new life. But we don't need any of that official stuff now. Olly is gone.

My fingers want to scrunch the brown paper into a tight ball, then push the letter deep down into the paper recycling, under the organic ready-meal sleeves and junk mail. Stuff away bad memories of an old life, now gone.

But instead I shelve the letter by the bread bin, resolving to open it after a cup of tea. There are other letters to read first.

I sit on the Chesterfield sofa-arm and slide my fingers under paper folds, tearing and pulling free replies to my many job applications. They're all rejections – I'd guessed as much, given the timing of the letters. If you get the job, they mail you straight away.

I look around the growing chaos that is our new house. There are toys everywhere, children's books, a blanket and pillow for when Tom dozes on the sofa. Really, it's hard enough keeping on top of all this, let alone finding a job too.

The house was beautiful when we moved in over the summer – varnished floorboards, cosy living room with a real fireplace, huge, light kitchen and roaming garden full of fruit trees.

But all too quickly it got messy, like my life.

I have that feeling again.

The 'I can't manage alone' feeling.

I squash it down.

I am strong. Capable. Tom and I *can* have a life without Olly. More importantly, we *must* have a life without him.

There's no way back.

A memory unzips itself – me, crying and shaking, cowering in a bathtub as Olly's knuckles pound on the door. Sharp and brutal.

Tears come. It *will* be different here.

I head up to the bathroom with its tasteful butler sink and free-standing Victorian bathtub on little wrought-iron legs. From the porcelain toothbrush holder I take hairdressing scissors – the ones I use to trim Tom's fine, blond hair.

I pick up a long strand of my mousy old life and cut. Then I take another, and another. Turning to the side, I strip strands from my crown, shearing randomly.

Before I know it, half my hair lies in the bathroom sink.

Now I have something approaching a pixie cut – short hair, clipped close to my head. I do a little shaping around the ears and find myself surprised and pleased with the result.

Maybe I should be a hairdresser instead of a nurse, I think.

I fought so hard to finish my nurse's training, but never did. Olly was jealous from the start. He hated me having any sort of identity.

Turning my head again in the mirror, I see myself smile. I really do like what I see. My hair is much more interesting than before, that mousy woman with non-descript brown hair.

I'm somebody who stands out.

Gets things done.

No more living in the shadows.

It won't be how things were with Olly, when I was meek little Lizzie, shrinking at his temper.

Things will be different.

As I start tidying the house, my phone rings its generic tone. I should change that too. Get a ring tone that represents who I am. It's time to find myself. Be someone. Not invisible, part of someone else.

My mother's name glows on the phone screen.

Ruth Riley.

Such a formal way to store a mother's number. I'm sure most people use 'Mum' or 'Mummy' or something.

I grab the phone. 'Hi, Mum.'

There's a pause, and a rickety intake of breath. 'Did you get Tom to school on time?'

'Of course.'

'Because it's important, Elizabeth. On his first day. To make a good impression.'

'I don't care what other people think,' I say. 'I care about Tom.'

'Well, you should care, Elizabeth. You've moved to a nice area. The families around there will have their eyes on you. It's not like that pokey little apartment you had in London.'

'It was a penthouse apartment and no smaller than the house we had growing up,' I point out. 'We lived in a two-bed terrace with Dad. Remember?'

'Oh, what nonsense, Elizabeth. We had a conservatory.'

Actually, it was a corrugated plastic lean-to. But my mother has never let the truth get in the way of a good story.

'I was planning to visit you again this weekend,' says Mum. 'To help out.'

I want to laugh. Mum does the opposite of help out. She demands that a meal is cooked, then criticises my organisational skills.

'You don't have to,' I say.

'I *want* to.'

'Why this sudden interest in us, Mum? You never visited when we lived with Olly.'

'Don't be silly, Elizabeth,' Mum snaps. 'You're a single parent now. You need my help.' A pause. 'I read in the *Sunday Times* that Steelfield School is one of the top fifty state schools.'

'Is it?'

'Yes. Make sure you dress smartly for pick-ups and drop-offs. I paid a personal visit to the headmaster this morning. To impress upon him what a good family we are.'

I laugh. 'You didn't think to ask me first?'

My mother ignores this comment. 'The headmaster was charming. Very presentable too. He tells me Tom is lucky to have a place there. Make sure you put a good face on.'

'Social services got us that place. I'd feel luckier not to have a social worker.'

'Elizabeth.' Mum's voice is tight. She hates it when I mention social workers. 'Don't be ungrateful.'

'You really shouldn't have visited the school, Mum,' I say. 'Teachers are busy enough.'

'Nonsense,' says Mum. 'You need to make a good impression

and for that you need my help. You never could do that on your own.'

'I appreciate you trying to help. I really do. But can you *ask* in future? Before you do things like visiting Tom's school? It feels a bit … I don't know, intrusive.'

I feel Mum's annoyance in the silence that follows. And I become that needy little girl again, doing anything to win back her favour.

'Sorry,' I say. 'Forget I said that. It's wonderful you visited Tom's headmaster. Look, come and visit whenever you like.'

When I hang up, I think about Olly.

You miss him sometimes. Admit it.

The voice comes out of nowhere and I try to squash it down.

Of course there were good times. But if I want to remember the good times, I have to remember the bad ones.

Do you remember him screaming at you? Calling you every name under the sun? And worse, so much worse … Saying things too shameful to think about.

How I could fall in love with someone who wanted to tear me apart?

Lizzie

'So why the blindfold?' I ask, as Olly leads me over crunching snow.

'Because you like surprises.'

Did I say that?

This has all been such a whirlwind. I'm insecure, certain our romance will be over when Olly finds out he's too good for me.

'This way,' says Olly, and I hear a chalet door creak. 'Welcome home.'

'Home?'

'My chalet.' Olly unties my blindfold. 'Where you'll be sleeping for the rest of the ski season.'

I laugh. 'You'll be lucky.'

As my eyes adjust to the light, I see a cosy sofa area and Chardonnay, a bowl of Pringles and glittering tealights laid on a chunky, wooden dining table.

'I'm calling this evening "Lizzie's favourites",' says Olly, plugging his phone into a speaker. 'Your favourite food. Favourite music. Favourite everything. I've got sea bass.' He goes to the fridge and slaps a wax-paper packet of fish on the kitchen counter. 'New potatoes in the oven. Lots of tomato ketchup in the fridge, because we're both philistines.' He winks. 'Sour-cream Pringles to start. And Joni Mitchell on the stereo.

Oh – and black forest gateaux for dessert. The one you like from the café.'

I smile, shaking my head in disbelief. 'You did all this for me?'

'Just for you. Right this way, madam.' He hesitates when he sees my face. 'Hey. Lizzie? Are you okay?'

'Yes. Really, I'm fine.'

'Lizzie.' Olly pulls me close. 'What's the matter? Did I do something wrong?'

I shake my head against his chest, tears pressing into his shirt. 'No. Not at all. The opposite.'

'The opposite?'

'All this for me. I don't deserve it.'

Olly laughs then, his big, cheery, confident laugh. 'You deserve this and much, much more.' He kisses my head and hugs me for a long time. 'Okay?'

I nod. 'Okay.'

'Let the evening commence!' He leads me to the table, snatching up a purple napkin. 'Your favourite colour.' He grins, opening the napkin with a flourish.

Purple isn't really my favourite colour. It's just the colour of the coat I wear. But I don't tell Olly that.

We eat Pringles, sea bass and new potatoes, drink Chardonnay and listen to Joni Mitchell. Then Olly lights a fire.

'I borrowed a Monopoly board,' says Olly, leading me to the sofa area. 'Your favourite game, right? And mine too, actually. Come on. You can thrash me.'

'Love to,' I say.

'Of course, we could play strip poker instead,' says Olly, flashing his lovely white teeth.

I'm hit by an uneasy feeling that this evening might be too traditional for Olly. The wine, the fire, the board game. What if he thinks I'm boring?

'I have an idea,' I say. 'How about strip Monopoly?'

'Strip Monopoly?' says Olly. 'You're on!'

We make up a few rules, deciding to lose an item of clothing every time we land on the other person's property. Then we start playing.

It doesn't take long before I'm down to my underwear.

'Are you cheating?' I accuse, taking off my bra.

Olly watches me, mesmerised. Then he says, 'You're beautiful, do you know that? Hurry up and roll again.'

'It's your turn,' I protest.

Olly struggles out of his clothes, revealing a beautiful toned body and crazy orange tan lines at his wrists and collarbone. Then he stands to remove his underwear.

'Turn taken,' he announces, standing naked. 'Now roll again.'

'That's definitely cheating,' I laugh, shy now. 'You can't take all your clothes off at once.'

'How dare you!' Olly protests. 'I am a serious rules-body. Well, if you think the game has been compromised, we'll just have to abandon it.'

He lifts me into his arms.

'But you were winning,' I laugh, as Olly carries me outside to the hot tub.

'I declare it a draw.'

Olly lowers me carefully into the bubbling water. Then he climbs into the tub himself and slides me onto his lap, arranging my legs so I'm kneeling around his hips.

'I need to learn more of your favourites,' he says, kissing me fiercely, hand moving up and down between my thighs.

Snow falls on the warm water and our bare shoulders.

I moan, but suddenly Olly pulls back.

'Wait.' He's breathless. 'I don't want to move too fast.'

'It's fine.'

'You're sure? Listen, really I can wait. I don't want this to be some quick thing. You're more than that to me.'

I must look upset, because Olly says: 'Hey. It's okay. Really. I'll get you a towel and you can have my bed, okay? I'll take the sofa.'

'No,' I insist, gripping his arms. 'I want this. Honestly, I want this. It's just ... I've never felt this way either. I've never been ... special.'

'You are special,' says Olly. 'The most special girl I've ever met.'

He kisses me again and I'm lost.

We make love in the hot tub and then again on Olly's bed. He's gentle at times, firm at others. He's considerate, but sometimes teeters on the brink of losing control.

In the morning, Olly makes me waffles covered in syrup and a sugary hot chocolate. Then we have sex again before I sneak back to my chalet to prepare breakfast for my host family.

While I'm whisking up scrambled eggs, my phone bleeps. It's a message from Olly: I miss you already.

I feel soft warmth in my chest, but also anxiety.

This is amazing. The most amazing thing that's ever happened to me. But how can something like this last? Half the things Olly thinks we both 'love', I only like a little bit. Like sea bass, tomato ketchup and syrup-covered waffles with sweet *hot chocolate. I've exaggerated so he'll think we have things in common, scared that boring little me isn't good enough.*

Oh, what does it matter?

I'm probably just a sexual conquest and Olly will forget all about me in a few days.

This can't last.

It's too good to be true.

Lizzie

My chest aches as I run up the stony path. I've forgotten Tom's painkillers. They're not vital. His migraines are stress-related and he hasn't had one since we left Olly. But I'd like the school to have tablets to hand just in case.

You'll never cope alone.

Olly's voice plays in my head sometimes, no matter how hard I try to drown it out.

Maybe some things you can't outrun.

Even when you're running.

I reach the school gates, tan-leather handbag bobbing against my side.

Then I remember the padlock.

There is an intercom by the wrought-iron gates, so I press it.

A woman's voice crackles: 'Hello? Do you have an appointment?'

'Hi. It's Tom Riley's mother. I brought his medicine.' I peer through the railings. 'Hello?' I call again. No one answers.

The main door is firmly shut, a solid lump of wood. A few early autumn leaves scatter the empty playground, crispy green-orange, some dancing up against the brickwork. I notice again the bars on the windows and bite my lip. Why have bars like that? This is a school, not a prison. And that blacked-out window. What are they trying to hide?

After a moment, the headmaster himself strides across the playground. He looks earnest. Almost helpful. But I sense another energy too. Something like annoyance.

'Hello, Mrs Kinnock,' says Mr Cockrun, as he reaches the gate. 'How can I help you?'

'Um … it's Riley. And I have Tom's medicine.'

'Medicine?' His eyes bore into me. 'Why wasn't this mentioned before?'

'It's not essential but—'

'All medicine *must* go through me.' Anger passes across his face for a fraction of a second – it's so quick that I almost don't spot it. The next moment, his earnest expression is back in place. 'Well, come inside and we'll make a record.'

He unlocks the gates and ushers me through, taking a good few minutes to re-secure the padlock.

I follow him across the playground.

When we reach the heavy entrance door, Mr Cockrun says, 'Wait in reception, but please don't let the children see you, Mrs Kinnock. I don't want them knowing a parent is here during the school day. It's unsettling for them.'

I nod stiffly.

'Next time, make sure you bring *everything* at school drop-off,' Mr Cockrun continues. 'All right? It's a safeguarding issue, Ms Riley. Having people come and go.' He gives me a winning smile.

'Parents dropping things off is a safeguarding issue?' I say.

'Yes. And the children really do become unsettled too. It's not fair on them. They learn much better when they understand that school is where *we* care for them and home is where they see their parents. I'm sure you can understand.' He puts a hand on my shoulder. 'We're an exceptional school, Ms Riley. We know what we're doing. Let's have this medicine, then. What's Tom taking?'

I don't know why the question feels intrusive, but it does.

'Painkillers,' I say, passing over the white packet. 'He doesn't take them all the time. Just if he gets a bad headache.'

'I'll pop these in my office,' says Mr Cockrun, heading through a side door. In the room beyond, I see him unlock a cabinet made of orangey teak and stickered with a pharmaceutical green cross. The cabinet is mounted low down on the wall – at stomach level.

Mr Cockrun puts Tom's medicine inside, then locks the cabinet and pockets the key.

The room has a single window, I notice. The two-way glass I saw from the outside.

So the headmaster's office is the room they don't want people seeing into.

As I'm thinking about that, I hear the sound of children chanting coming from a room off reception:

'We are the best.
We rise above the rest.
By strength and guile,
We go the extra mile.'

The double doors leading from reception haven't quite closed, and through the crack I see rows of children seated for assembly: eyes dull, school uniforms immaculate and identical, hair neatly brushed. It looks choreographed – as if someone has positioned them for a photograph.

Like the plain tarmac playground, there's something very soulless about it.

I spot Tom then, blond hair shining.

Normally I would smile at the sight of him, but he's tiny beside one of those black-haired boys. The ones who were fighting.

Tom's body leans away from the boy, his pose awkward.

I feel my heart judder.

Someone spots me looking – a teacher, I think – and pushes the double doors closed.

Then the headmaster returns with a book in his hand. 'Jot some details down here,' he says, offering me the lined pages. 'Don't worry – we don't need a medical history or anything. Just the name of Tom's medication, the quantity you're leaving here, the dose Tom needs and today's date.'

I write, pen-marks jerky.

'You keep the medicine cabinet in your office?' I ask.

'Pardon?' Mr Cockrun takes back the notebook.

'Don't you have a nurse's office?'

Mr Cockrun smiles again, a wide version that still doesn't reach his eyes. 'As I said, Mrs Kinnock, there's method to our madness. Don't worry.' He pats my shoulder. 'We have it all under control. Let me show you to the gate.'

We walk slowly across the playground, me watching my plain lace-up DMs *tap tap* over tarmac.

On my way home, I see a dead bird. There's a lot of blood. I suppose a fox must have got it.

It's right by the hole in the school fence – the one I saw

before, repaired with a bike chain. The hole is very small. Not big enough for an adult to climb through.

There's probably some logical explanation.

Given my past, it would be strange if I didn't get twitchy about odd things. But there's no need to be paranoid.

Lizzie

'*Look, keep still. It's broken.*'

I put my hand on Olly's knee, which bulges at an eye-watering angle under his padded O'Neill trousers.

He's lying on thick snow, one ski boot bent back under his snowboard, the other boot snapped open, his socked foot falling out.

Under the bright morning sunshine, Olly's blue eyes water, tanned skin squeezing and contorting. He has English colouring – sandy hair dusting his ski goggles and an unnatural orange hue to his suntan.

'I'm pretty lucky to have a nurse here,' says Olly, after another wince of pain. 'Have I told you I love you yet today? I do. I love you, Lizzie Nightingale. Remember that, if I die out here on this slope.'

He doesn't realise how serious this is.

'I'm not a nurse yet. Don't try to move.'

Olly, of course, makes a stupid attempt to get up, pushing strong, gloved hands onto the snow. But then his eyes widen, his skin pales and he falls back down. This is just like him. Give him a boundary and his first impulse is to overcome it.

'Please don't move,' I beg. 'God – this is awful. I can't bear seeing you hurt.'

Olly reaches up to trail fingers down my cheek. 'Is it bad that even in all this pain, I still want to do things to you?'

'You know, there are times for jokes. And this isn't one of them.'

'I'm not joking.' He gives me the soft, blue eyes that make my stomach turn over. 'We could have sex right here on the snow. The ambulance will take ages.'

'Olly. You've just broken your leg.'

'I get it. You can't have sex in public until we're married.' He heaves himself onto his elbows and grasps my fingers. 'So marry me, Lizzie.'

'I just said this is no time for jokes.'

'I'm not joking. You're the one for me, Lizzie Nightingale. I knew it from the moment I saw you stumbling along that icy path in your big purple coat, looking like a little elfin angel thing. I promise I will take care of you for the rest of my life.' He gives another wince of pain. 'Even if I never walk again.'

Olly is so impulsive. A risk-taker. I suppose that goes hand in hand with snowboarding. He goes full-pelt into everything. Including love.

In a few short weeks, he's made me feel so special and adored. Lying in Olly's chalet bed, wrapped up in his arms, watching snow fall outside, I have never known love like this – utterly consuming, can't-be-apart love.

He makes me breakfast every morning, constantly tells me how beautiful I am and texts me all day long.

I'm waiting for him to work out who I really am. Just a nobody. And then this holiday romance will come crashing down.

'Just lie down and rest,' I say, stroking his forehead. 'They'll take you to hospital. I'll bring you chocolate Pop Tarts.'

Olly loves sugar. He's a big kid, really. So enthusiastic. And when we're in bed he's like that too – just 'wow!' at everything. 'Wow, you look incredible, wow your body is amazing.'

He makes me feel so alive. So adored. So noticed. The exact opposite of how my mother makes me feel.

How did this happen so quickly?

I'm so in love with him.

Olly lies back on the snow, staring up at the sky. 'I'll heal. Won't I? I'll be able to compete?'

He looks right at me then, blue eyes crystal clear.

'I don't know, Olly. Just try to rest. The paramedics will be here soon.'

Olly reaches out a snowy, gloved hand and takes my mitten. 'You're an angel, Lizzie Nightingale. You have fabulous dimples, by the way.'

I smile then, without meaning to.

'You will stay with me, won't you?' Olly asks, suddenly serious. 'Until the stretcher comes?'

'Of course I will. You fall, I fall. Remember? We're in this together.'

I sit on the cold snow, my mitten clasped in his glove.

Kate

I take deep breaths, lifting knuckles to the door. The red-brick house is identical to its neighbours – except for the large crack in the front door.

Knock, knock.

No answer.

Tessa's words ring in my ears: *Get on to that Tom Kinnock case as soon as possible. He should never have been passed over to us. Get it shut down and off your desk.*

I would peer in the window, but the curtains are closed, even though it's gone lunchtime.

Knock, knock.

I put an ear to the door and hear voices. Someone *is* home.

Knock, knock, knock.

'Hello?' I call. 'It's Kate Noble from Children's Services.'

I knock again, this time with a closed fist.

There are hurried footsteps and a woman opens the door, blonde hair scraped back in a hairband.

'Keep it down.' The woman's eyes swim in their sockets. 'Alice is *sleeping*.'

So this is Leanne Neilson. Mother to the infamous Neilson boys.

She wears Beauty and the Beast pyjamas with furry slippers and looks exhausted, huge bags under her eyes. Her grey pallor is a drug-abuse red flag. Unsurprisingly, the files note that Leanne has a problem with prescription medicine.

Behind Leanne is a tidy-ish living room with red leather sofas and a shiny flat-screen over a chrome fireplace. The voices, I realise, were coming from the television.

'You must be Miss Neilson,' I say, reaching out my hand. 'Lloyd, Joey and Pauly's mum. Can I call you Leanne?'

Leanne Neilson isn't the person I wanted to see today. I should be at Tom Kinnock's house, getting his file shut down and letting his mother get on with her new life.

But social services is all about prioritising highest need.

'All right,' says Leanne, tilting her head, eyes still rolling around, not taking my hand.

'So my name is Kate. I'm your new social worker.'

Leanne blinks languidly, grey cheeks slackening. 'What happened to … er … Kirsty?'

'She's been signed off long-term sick.'

'What do you want?' A rapid nose scratch. 'I've been in hospital.'

'Yes – that's what I wanted to chat to you about. Can I come in for a minute?'

Leanne looks behind her. 'I mean, the house is a mess.'

'It looks okay. Are the sofas new?'

'Leather is … easier to clean. But give it a few weeks and Lloyd … he'll wreck them.' More rapid nose scratching.

'Can I come in?'

'When is Kirsty back?'

'She probably won't be coming back.'

'Another one gone then.' Leanne walks back into the lounge, her hand going to the sofa arm for support.

I close the front door.

'Where's baby Alice?' I ask.

'I told you. *Sleeping.*'

'Can I see?'

'This is like a … roundabout,' says Leanne. '"Can I see the bedrooms? How are things with your partner? How are you coping?" I never see the same person twice. No one ever gives me any help.'

'We don't like changing staff either, Leanne,' I say, following her up the pink-carpeted staircase. 'It's bad for everyone when people leave. But it's just the way things are at the moment.'

'Alice is here,' says Leanne, lowering her slow voice to a whisper, and showing me a clean, relatively tidy baby room with five large boxes of Pampers stacked in the corner.

Baby Alice is asleep in a white-wood cot with a mobile hanging overhead. The room smells fine – unlike the landing, which has a faint odour of urine.

'I know it smells,' says Leanne, as if reading my mind. 'Joey's still wetting the bed. The doctor says he'll grow out of it.'

'How did this happen?' I ask, pointing to a hole in a chip-board bedroom door.

Leanne blinks a few times, then responds: 'Lloyd did that. I've told the housing people. They still haven't been round to repair it.' She adds, 'It wasn't my partner, if that's what you're asking.'

'Has Lloyd started counselling yet?' I ask. 'He should be nearing the top of the waiting list by now.'

'No.' Leanne's face crumples. She looks at me then, brown eyes filled with pain.

I know what she's saying. *I can't cope.* And suddenly I want to hug her.

But we're not allowed to do that with adults.

'Lloyd talked with the last social worker about coping strategies,' I say, following the official line. 'Boxing at his cousin's gym? Has he been doing that?'

'*I'm* his punch bag,' Leanne says. 'He's getting so big now, I can't stop him. I've asked them to take him into care. No one listens. He's going to kill me one of these days.'

'Let's talk about how you can set boundaries. Look into some parenting classes—'

'I've been to them.'

'No. They were organised for you, but you didn't attend.'

'I couldn't get there. I don't have a car.'

'I'll set up some more classes for you. Maybe I can look into having someone drive you there. What about your medication? Are you taking it regularly?'

'Yeah, yeah, I'm taking it.' Leanne's eyes dart to the floor. 'But I lost some. Can you tell the doctor to give me more?'

'You'd have to ask him yourself. Let's talk about your partner. Are you still with him?'

'Why do people always ask about him? What has he got to do with anything? I'm allowed to have a boyfriend. I'm a grown woman.'

'He's living here, isn't he?'

Leanne thinks for a moment, eyes rolling around. 'It's my

house,' she says. 'Why is it anyone else's business who lives here? Look, can't you take Lloyd into care, just for a bit?'

'I can't pick up a child and place them in care just like that.'

'Why not?'

Because they have to be deemed at risk of immediate harm. And Lloyd is more of a risk to others than in danger himself.

Lizzie

'So how was school?'

Tom is quiet, head down, kicking stones. I squeeze his hand in mine.

We're walking home along the country path, me shielding my eyes against the low sun.

My little boy seems *so* small beside me today. It's funny – when he started school in London, he grew up overnight. But now he seems young again. Vulnerable.

He hasn't grown much this year, even though he's nearly nine.

'It was all right,' says Tom. His school jumper is inside out, so he must have had sports today. He never has quite got the hang of dressing himself. 'Were you okay at home?'

I laugh. 'I was fine, Tom. You're such a lovely boy for caring. High five?'

Tom slaps my fingers, but doesn't smile.

'Do you need me to carry your bag?' I ask. 'You look tired.'

He doesn't reply.

'Tommo?'

'What?' Tom turns to me, eyes dull. He looks … disorientated.

'Are you okay?'

He nods.

'You don't look okay. What's up, Tommo?'

'Just tired.'

'How was school?'

'I don't remember.' Tom's words are soft now – almost slurred.

My heart races, but I keep my questions calm. 'Nothing? Not even what you had for lunch? Tom ... you don't look too well. Maybe you should have a lie-down on the sofa when we get home.'

'Yeah.' His feet trudge over stones.

I remember chatting with another mum in London once.

Usually, I kept my head down at the school gates, the quiet, downtrodden wife. But this mum sought me out. Forced me into a conversation.

She told me her son, Ewan, never remembered what happened at school. She said it was common.

I'd nodded, feigning agreement. But actually, Tom always remembered his school day. Our walk home was filled with chatter about reading books, school dinners and gold stars.

'Okay, champ.' I ruffle Tom's hair, the words catching. 'A little rest. And then I think a trip to the doctor's would be a good idea.'

'Yeah.' Tom stumbles a little, his black school shoe turning under itself.

'Tom?' I take his arm.

He gives a languid blink. 'Maybe ... maybe I'm getting a cold. Everything looks blue today.'

I stiffen.

When things were especially bad between Olly and me, Tom became fixated on colours. How grass wasn't really green, but

44

green, yellow and brown. And the teacher's skirt was 'turquoise like Daddy's sweatshirt'.

A sign of stress, the doctor said.

We approach our sleeping house, the curtains drawn. They're made from thick, heavy velvet, and I hung them the very first day we moved.

Heavy curtains are a necessity for anyone running from someone.

'Do you want something to eat?' I unlock the front door. 'I bought some biscuits. You can have a snack and I'll take your temperature.'

'I don't want a snack,' says Tom, heading straight through our messy living room and throwing his coat and bag over the bannisters. 'Biscuits are too brown today.'

Too brown.

He hasn't mentioned colours since we left London …

'I just want to sleep,' says Tom.

'Can't we just have a little chat?'

Out of the blue, Tom snaps: 'Leave me alone! I hate the new school, okay? And I hate you.'

I stare at him, utterly stunned. He's never talked to me like that. Ever.

'Maybe you should go upstairs and rest,' I say sharply.

'That's what I just said,' he retorts.

Clump, clump, clump.

Tom stomps up the stairs, head bowed. Then his bedroom door slams.

I follow him upstairs and find him sitting on his bed, playing with his Clarks shoes. He pulls the Velcro back, then sticks it down. *Rip, rip. Rip, rip.*

'Tom? Please let's talk. I know this is hard.'

Tom looks up, and as he does his head begins to loll around.

Then my little boy slides to the floor, his body totally rigid, twisting, biting, drooling.

'Tom!' I stare, terrified, as he snaps his teeth at thin air. One hand is still locked to the Velcro on his trainer, his body a stiff crescent, fingers refusing to yield. 'Tom!'

I see the whites of his eyes as he shouts, 'School *grey*.'

'I'm phoning an ambulance,' I shout, dashing downstairs two steps at a time.

My fingers are shaking as I dial 999, my words rushed when the operator comes on the line. 'Help, *please*,' I sob. 'My son is having some sort of fit. *Please* send an ambulance. Hurry!'

Lizzie

I have nausea – the sort brought on by overwhelming fear and anxiety.

Oh God, oh God, oh God.

Tom lies on white cotton sheets. They're the same sheets I used to strip down in hospitals before I got pregnant. They should feel familiar and safe, but today everything is wrong.

My eyes are wide, barely blinking. 'Why did this happen?' I ask the doctor. 'He's a healthy child. He's *healthy*.'

Tom stopped convulsing when the ambulance came. He is now drowsy and confused, barely conscious. A seizure – that's what they're calling it. Nobody knows why it happened.

'Could he have taken anything he shouldn't?' the doctor asks. 'Medication, anything like that? It's quite unusual for this to happen with no history.'

'No. We keep paracetamol, cough syrup. He has painkillers for migraines … but Tom wouldn't take anything without asking. He's very sensible for his age.'

'Normal painkillers wouldn't have caused something like this.'

'*Tom*,' I whisper.

'Mum,' Tom says.

'Sweetheart.' I stroke his forehead.

Tom murmurs, 'I want to sleep. *Please*, Mum.'

'You haven't eaten. The sooner you eat, the sooner we can get home to your own bed. With all your Lego.'

'Red Lego. Want to ... sleep.'

'Tom, the doctor wants to know if you took anything. Medicine – anything like that.'

Tom shakes his head, eyes bobbing closed.

When the doctor leaves, Tom sleeps until teatime.

He wakes to eat three forkfuls of hospital meat pie and one spoonful of strawberry yoghurt.

While I'm clearing Tom's dinner tray, a nurse says: 'You'll be discharged later. Just as soon as the doctor comes back.'

I nod, shelving the empty tray in a metal trolley.

'Tom will be in his own bed tonight,' the nurse continues. 'And back at school tomorrow. That'll be nice, won't it?'

'Yes.'

But actually, the thought of school ... it frightens me.

Kate

What's the time? My watch hands point to 7.10 p.m., but the computer says 7 p.m.

The computer is right, of course – I always set my watch ten minutes fast. Col calls this my mega efficiency.

I see Tessa in her office, stuffing Nespresso capsules into her handbag.

'I need you here *first* thing tomorrow,' she commands, striding past me. 'Did you get the Kinnock file closed down yet?'

'Tom Kinnock's mother still hasn't replied to my letter. She's had it over a week now. I need to pencil in an unannounced visit. See how Tom's settling into his new school before I close the case down.'

'Don't forget your twenty-nine other children.'

'Thirty children now, Tessa. And yes, I know.'

'Don't cancel anything you shouldn't.'

There is a secret code in social services. Some appointments absolutely can't be altered. Some shouldn't be altered, but have to be.

It all comes down to greatest need.

'Okay, listen. Why not forget about Tom Kinnock for the time being?' Tessa suggests. 'You have a cast-iron defence if anything goes wrong – blame Hammersmith and Fulham. They should have passed it over sooner.'

'I need to make a start,' I say. 'Get some sort of order. The file has passed through ten different social workers – the notes are an absolute mess. Pages and pages of reports, everything out of order. It needs straightening out.'

'Hammersmith and Fulham sound worse than this place,' says Tessa. 'Can you imagine? Somewhere more chaotic than here?' She snorts with laughter and heads towards the swing doors. 'Well. Night then.'

I put my head in my hands.

At university, I was always 'Sensible Kate' or 'Aunty Kate'. The one with a good head on her shoulders. I never broke down or got overwhelmed. But right now, I'm stressed to the point of collapse.

'Are you all right?'

My head jerks up, and I see Tessa lingering in the doorway.

I feel embarrassed and pat my cheeks. 'Fine. I thought you'd gone.'

'You're not all right, are you?' Tessa backtracks, perching her large behind on my desk. 'You're killing yourself. Staying late every night. This can't be doing your love life any good. What does your boyfriend think about all this?'

'Husband.'

'Oh, that's right. I can never get my head around that. At your age.'

'Col's getting used to my working habits. I used to text him if I'd be home late. Now I text if I'll be home on time.'

Tessa guffaws. 'Sounds about right. But how long will he be understanding for? A lot of relationships break down here. Partners get fed up of being second best.'

'Col and I are solid. We support each other.'

'Listen, with a caseload like yours, you've got to put some of them on the back burner.'

'Tell me, Tessa – how can I put a vulnerable child on the back burner?'

Lizzie

Mum is visiting today. She wants to talk about Tom's first week at school. Make sure he's settling in okay.

Two things will happen.

She will be late.

She will criticise me incessantly.

I've made vegetable soup with organic parsnips and carrots, and just a little bit of crème fraîche, plus (I won't tell my mum this) a squirt of tomato ketchup. Pumpkin seed and olive oil bread warms in the oven.

I have been up early, cleaning, scrubbing, dusting. The house looks great, actually. A real step forward. I've laid the breakfast bar in the big, beautiful conservatory using freshly laundered napkins and antique wine glasses.

But I know it won't be enough. Nothing ever is for my mother.

It's 1 p.m., and Tom waits in a clean shirt, face scrubbed, hair shiny. He tried to get out of brushing his teeth ('I'll do it later, Mum'), but I managed to bribe him with a fruit Yoyo and the promise that he doesn't have to give Grandma a kiss.

Now we're sat on the sofa, listening for the *click click* of my mother's high heels.

A car slows outside. I hear footsteps, then a hard knock at the door.

This is her.

I open the door to a cloud of rose perfume and Mum's glossy, denture-perfect smile. She looks like a Fifties movie star – red lipstick, bright green pashmina and Jane Mansfield coiffed black hair.

'Hello, darling.' Mum kisses me on both cheeks, leaving traces of lipstick, which I surreptitiously rub off. She glides into the house, sharp, green eyes inspecting. 'How is my little grandson?'

'He's much better now,' I say. 'They didn't keep him overnight in the end. They think the seizure could have been a one-off. Just some unexplained childhood thing. Tom, say hello to your grandma.'

'Hello, Grandma,' says Tom, back straight, knees together. 'That's a very nice red bag.'

'Have they put him on any medication?' Mum asks.

I hesitate. 'Yes. Yes, they have. Blood-thinning meds, just in case. He's going to be on them for the next few months and then they'll reassess.'

'So he's on prescription medication?' Mum qualifies. 'It must be serious, then.'

'I … yes. He's still not quite himself.'

'How are you settling into school?' Mum asks. 'Are you keeping up with your school work?'

'Yes,' says Tom. 'It's harder than London, but it's all right.'

'Did I mention, Thomas – I met your new headmaster?' Mum slides leather gloves from her hands and pats his head. 'I liked him very much. Behave well for him, won't you? We don't want people thinking you're from a bad family. How are you doing in class? Still at the top?'

'No,' says Tom. 'Not here. But I don't mind.'

'You need to work hard, Tom,' says Mum. 'Don't be lazy. You were top of the class before. The headmaster is *such* a nice man. Very high standards. He'll be disappointed in you.'

'Tom has never been *lazy*,' I say. 'He's just not competitive. He doesn't care about being the best. That's just not who he is.'

'Not like his father then.' Mum raises an eyebrow. She walks through the living room and into the kitchen, opening and closing cupboards. 'So this is where you're hiding the mess.'

It's true – there's a raggle-taggle heap of objects stuffed inside the lower cupboards. Things I didn't have time to sort through and stuffed out of the way to look tidy.

'You're not coping, Elizabeth,' Mum says. 'I knew you'd struggle alone.'

'I'm doing my best. We've only just moved. You should have seen the house yesterday.'

'You shouldn't have left your husband. And now it's too late.'

That last remark cuts like a knife.

'You're saying I should have stayed with Olly?' I glance to check Tom isn't listening, then whisper, 'You know what he did.'

'Oh, Elizabeth, children don't always tell the truth. You hardly ever did.'

'You should have come to court, Mum,' I say, teeth gritted. 'And heard the full story.'

'This is too much for you, Elizabeth. The house. A young child. Why won't you come and live with me?'

I hold back a shudder. 'I'm not sure we'd get along as adults,' I say. 'We didn't get on well when I was a teenager, did we?'

'You were difficult,' says Mum. 'Always criticising. Trying to start arguments. And so solemn.'

'I looked after you much more than any thirteen-year-old ever should,' I say, meeting her eye.

Mum turns to open kitchen cupboards.

Deflect.

Ignore.

Put it in a box and let it explode another time.

That's how things are in our family.

I wonder if Mum has genuinely forgotten her overdose. And the fall-out afterwards. Or just pretends.

'Would you like a cup of tea?' I ask, changing the subject. Slotting in, being a shadow.

My mother's lips pucker. She manages a few tears. 'How could you say we don't get along, Elizabeth? I did everything for you. I gave up my *whole life*. Stayed with your adulterous pig of a father. For *you*.'

Inwardly I feel tired. It's just so much easier to placate my mother than tell the truth.

'I know. I'm sorry.'

Mum goes to a recent picture of Tom on the mantelpiece. I took it when Tom's new Steelfield School uniform arrived. I needed him to try it on, so let him pose with his school bag at the bottom of the stairs.

The uniform was oversized – and still is – but he'll grow into it.

'Is that his new school uniform?' Mum asks. 'Very smart.'

'Yes,' I say, and then pre-empting a criticism I add, 'It was big on him, but better than too small.'

'What are the children like at your new school, Tom?' Mum asks. 'They come from good families, don't they?'

'He's eight years old, Mum,' I say. 'How can he answer a question like that?'

'The headmaster says the school has an outstanding status,' Mum continues, ignoring me. 'Very high-achieving. I imagine the children are well-behaved. Come from the right stock.'

'Most of the children are good,' says Tom. 'Except Pauly and his brothers. They have a gang.'

I turn to him. 'What do you mean, a gang?'

'Lloyd is the general,' Tom explains. 'Pauly is general number two, Joey and I are the soldiers. We like red – red is our gang colour.'

Colours again.

'Lloyd's mental,' Tom continues. '*Mental.*'

'Sounds like he needs discipline,' says Mum. 'I'm sure the headmaster keeps him in line.'

Tom nods. 'Lloyd doesn't dare do anything when Mr Cockrun is around. He's too scared of...' Tom stops himself then, as if he's said too much.

'Are many of the children scared of Mr Cockrun, Tom?' I ask gently.

Tom hesitates.

'Children *should* be scared of their headmaster,' says Mum.

'No they shouldn't,' I say.

'Maybe they're not scared,' says Tom quickly.

'But you started to say Lloyd was,' I insist. 'Why is Lloyd scared?'

Tom shrugs. 'I dunno.'

'Speak properly, Tom,' Mum snaps.

'You should stay away from those Neilson boys, Tom,' I say. 'They sound like bad news.'

'What's your teacher like, Tom?' Mum asks.

'She's like a robot,' says Tom. 'She just says everything the headmaster says.'

'I'm sure she doesn't,' Mum retorts. 'Stop being so silly.'

'He's tired,' I say. 'Remember he was in hospital last week.'

There is a silence long enough for Mum's handsome face to crumple. Then she says, 'I don't know why you didn't call me.'

I want to say, 'Of course I didn't call you. You'd have made it all about yourself.' But I don't. I've learned the hard way what happens if I tell her the truth.

'We've been through this, Mum,' I say. 'Tom didn't stay overnight—'

'But it was a *seizure*.'

'Yes. And it was terrifying for both of us. But I'm trying not to dwell on that.' I say the last words through gritted teeth.

Mum cups Tom's face in her hands, then pulls him into a dramatic, perfumed chest-hug.

Tom accepts the hug limply, without pleasure.

'I handled it okay by myself,' I say. 'I'm not as useless as you think.'

'A *seizure*. Oh my *God*, Elizabeth. How on earth could something like that have happened? Could there be something genetic? On his father's side, perhaps?'

My heart races as I wait for the next inevitable question. And then it comes.

'Has he seen Oliver since you moved?' Mum's eyes roam around my living room.

'No.'

'I thought—'

'I *told* you what Olly did.'

'Couldn't you have tried counselling? I always thought your father and I should have given that a go.'

I let out a shocked laugh. 'It went way beyond counselling. Olly has deep-rooted psychological issues. Good God, I wish you'd been there at the court hearing.'

I turn then, realising Tom might be listening. But he's frowning at a school book – something he used to do when Olly and I were together. Shut himself away.

'You don't even give Olly visitation,' says Mum. 'That would give you a few hours to yourself, at least.'

'Olly will *never* see Tom without me being there,' I say, my voice low. 'Not while I'm still breathing. I failed Tom before. I won't fail him again. Anyway, Tom doesn't want to see his father. They can't make him if he doesn't want to.'

Mum shakes her head. 'But you need *help*. You can't do this alone.'

'What time did you book your taxi for, Mother?' I ask. 'How long do we have the pleasure of your company?'

Mum gives me sad, disappointed eyes, and I feel my inner strength dwindling. 'I was hoping we'd have a nice lunch. I've come a very long way.'

My mother was the first shadow I found myself standing in.

At least Olly noticed me from time to time.

Lizzie

'You are absolutely stunning.' Olly lies back on the sofa, broken leg propped up on a coffee table made of wine corks.

His leg is still in plaster, and I know it's itchy, uncomfortable and driving him mad, especially at night. Sometimes he scratches inside the plaster with a knitting needle.

The plaster has been on for a few months now.

Typical Olly – he's made his leg plaster cool, getting an artist friend to felt-tip a multi-coloured effect on the bandage, copied from a Ride snowboard design. He's even cut pairs of Boma jeans to accommodate the plaster.

Olly is indisputably handsome, with blond hair, tanned skin and white teeth. He could dress in a business suit, sports clothes or as he does – in scruffy surfer clothes with hair messy and long around his ears – and still look like a model. I suppose it's the years of snowboarding. He's so fit and healthy.

I'm wearing a floaty, daisy-patterned summer dress, something I picked out from Snow and Rock – one of Olly's favourite shops. It's not my usual sort of thing, if I even have a usual sort of thing, but I feel relieved and happy that Olly likes the choice.

Olly never tells me how to dress. Not overtly. But I've learned what he likes and what he doesn't.

We got together so quickly. Sometimes I think about how Olly doesn't really know who I am, and that if he did he'd leave me. I'm still insecure about it, so I try and be everything I think he wants me to be.

We're at Olly's flat in Earl's Court – three storeys up and with its own roof terrace. It's a big place, especially for this part of London, and is what you'd call a 'bachelor pad'.

There is a mini-fridge full of beer in the living area, a snowboard propped up behind the sofa and a chair made of recycled Coca-Cola cans.

Olly's friends are round often, playing on his old SNES, making jokes about his leg, drinking beer and smoking joints until the small hours.

I prefer the days when his friends aren't round, but it's not my flat so it's not my place to say who comes here.

We're in that weird in-between stage, Olly and I, where I'm not officially living with him, but most of my things are here. I haven't committed to making this my address, but Olly keeps asking me to move in and talking about marriage.

We love each other. Desperately, at times. We can't stand to be apart and when I'm working Olly calls me ten times a day.

Most people think I'm lucky to be in this situation – living in West London, adored by a champion snowboarder.

So why do I feel, sometimes, like I'm losing myself?

Music is playing – Sgt. Pepper's Lonely Hearts Club Band. The proper vinyl version. Olly has a turntable and boxes of records – all given to him by his mother.

'I never know what to wear to your friends' parties,' I admit, rummaging in my makeup bag for my turquoise earrings.

All Olly's female friends are so pretty. Effortlessly so. Hardly any makeup. A lot of them snowboard too, but only one is pro.

'Do you know what?' Olly pulls himself up on the bed, dragging his plastered leg onto the sheepskin rug. 'I'm not really in the mood for this party. I shouldn't drink right now. And getting across London with this leg … So if you're not up for it either, why don't we do something else?'

'Like what?'

'Jump in the camper van, head down to Devon, camp, have a BBQ, hang around on the beach. It's supposed to be amazing weather this weekend.'

'Olly, I don't think camping with your leg is a good idea.'

A flash of annoyance passes over Olly's handsome face. 'It's only a broken leg, Lizzie. I haven't got cancer.'

'Yes, but you should keep the plaster dry and clean. And what about your meds?'

'Bloody hell. What, I can't even go camping now?'

'You shouldn't. Not until your leg heals. I'm only saying this because I care about you.'

'And how long is the healing going to take? Every time I see the specialist, he adds on another month.' Olly thumps the duvet. 'I feel so trapped. I need to get back out on the slopes. I need to. Life is slipping away.'

I sense another argument coming on, so I say, 'I know', and sit on the bed, taking his hand. 'But I'm here. We'll make you well again. Okay? Just give it time.'

Olly's blue eyes turn clear. 'You really are an angel, do you know that? Looking after me. Playing the nurse. Putting up with me and my moods.'

My dad used to call me that. An angel.

I kiss Olly's cheek and slide my hand into his. 'I love you, Olly Kinnock. And you'll heal. Just give yourself time.'

Olly turns to the window then. 'Will I? I'm not sure. I'm forgetting who I used to be. What if I become this moody person forever?'

'You won't.'

'How do you know? How do you know who I really am?'

I suppose we've only known each other a few months. Four seasons, that's what my father used to say. You have to be with someone for four seasons, good and bad, before you really know them. I think he was making a comment about marrying my mother.

'I love you,' I say. 'That's enough for me.'

Suddenly Olly says, 'I love you too, Lizzie Nightingale. Will you marry me?'

Just like that.

I laugh.

'I'm serious,' Olly says, pulling me into his arms. 'I love you. You get me. Even when I'm like this. We're meant to be together.'

'Olly, we've known each other less than three months. We're not even properly living together yet.'

'Oh, so what?' Olly kisses me, and for a moment everything is okay. Maybe we can get married and live happily ever after.

But then I pull back. Things with Olly have been good. But they've been bad too. He's pushed me before – a great, big, open-palmed shove when he was wobbling around drunk, trying a new pair of skis. He said it was an accident. He didn't mean for me to fall. But ...

'Olly—'

'Are you rejecting my proposal, Lizzie Nightingale?'

'It's just … what's the rush?'

'Why wait?'

'Maybe we don't know each other well enough yet,' I say.

'What the fuck are you talking about?'

Anxiety hits my stomach.

I know the signs of his mood swings by now. And I become a child again, desperate to keep the peace.

'Please, Olly, I didn't mean it like that. I love you. Of course we'll get married one day.'

This is what I used to do when my parents fought. Do anything to make it okay, forget myself, humiliate myself. Anything to stop the ugliness growing. And then one day my dad met someone else and left. It was all for nothing. So why do I feel compelled to carry on the same behaviour?

'If you don't want to be with me, just say so,' Olly snaps. 'Because I think you either know or you don't. And if you're not sure, then that means no. Call it a day.'

I clasp his hand, scared of losing him to the other, angry person. 'I didn't mean that. It's just, your leg is still broken.' I try for a laugh. 'I don't want our wedding photos to be spoiled by that big multi-coloured plaster.'

Olly looks at me for a minute, then he laughs too. 'Is that why you said no? Just because of the wedding photos? What is it with women and photos?'

We laugh together then, and everything feels okay.

I've done it.

I've averted disaster.

Just like I used to do with Mum.

I catch a glimpse of my bare back in the mirror. 'Could you do up these buttons?' I ask.

Olly does.

My breasts feel tender, I realise. Sore. We've never been careful, Olly and I. Not really. So often caught in the heat of the moment. Suddenly I have such a strong feeling.

Oh God.

What if I'm pregnant?

Ruth

I was supposed to meet Kaitlyn for tea this afternoon, but I cancelled.

'I visited Elizabeth this morning,' I told her, with a gay little laugh. 'And my daughter needs to make a good impression with the other mothers. She's in desperate need of home-wares. I'm staying in town to do a bit of shopping. Can we reschedule?'

Sometimes, I despair of Elizabeth.

Tatty old furniture, mismatched curtains and nothing on the mantelpiece. Tom's started at an outstanding school and she's a single mother. What will the other parents think?

'Don't wear yourself out,' said Kaitlyn. 'Your daughter needs to stand on her own two feet.'

Kaitlyn is one of the few friends who understands just how unlucky I've been with Elizabeth. Other mothers have children who take them to lunch. Elizabeth doesn't think about me at all.

I'm at Fenwick department store on the High Street. It was recommended by a well-dressed woman in town, and she was right – there are lots of lovely things here.

I take a net basket from a young assistant and click around

the homeware department, imagining how much better I'll feel when Elizabeth has some lovely ornaments on display.

Most likely, I'll get no thanks for it. All Elizabeth ever does is criticise.

'I was in your shadow,' she says. 'You made me feel invisible.'

Perhaps now she realises how difficult it is being a parent.

Elizabeth never excelled at school. Didn't try *hard enough*. In truth, she never applied herself. Tom was top of his class in London, so maybe my grandson will be the one to make me proud.

As I'm examining a china cat with a lace collar, a smiling grey-haired assistant approaches. She has dreadful makeup. Eyebrows far too heavy.

'Oh, that's one of my favourites,' she says. 'It looks just like my cat, Sherbet.'

I slide the cat back on the shelf.

'Shopping for something in particular?' the assistant asks.

I notice her neck, loose with wrinkles.

'Things for my daughter,' I say, with a grand smile. 'She's just moved into a new home.'

'Oh, that's nice,' says the assistant. 'Is she married or single?'

I pull my smile tight. 'Married,' I say. 'Her husband is a champion snowboarder. And she has a little boy. Tom. My grandson. He's a bonny little lad – very well-behaved. A model pupil at school.'

'Not like my grandson then,' laughs the assistant. 'He's a terror, but we love him all the same.'

I smile kindly. 'Maybe it's the school that's the problem. My grandson goes to Steelfield School. They're really on top of discipline there. The headmaster is very ambitious.'

The assistant shudders. 'I've heard about that place. Kids quiet as mice. Teachers so perfect they're like robots.' She glances at me then. 'Sorry to speak out of turn, it's just what I've heard.'

'Oh, I think you can tell a lot from the inspectors' reports,' I counter. 'The official people who assess the schools know what they're talking about.'

'I always think the most important thing is that the kids are happy.'

I wander towards a colourful collection of cookware, but it's far too bright. I'll never understand this modern trend for childish, primary colours. What happened to elegant florals?

The assistant is tailing me. 'How old is your grandson?' she asks.

I catch a glimpse of myself in a hanging frying pan. I look a good fifteen years younger than this assistant, although I'd guess we're around the same age.

'Eleven,' I say. 'He's very bright. The teachers think he'll pass the grammar school exam.'

'Oh, that'll be good,' says the assistant, not really understanding.

'My daughter Elizabeth went to grammar school,' I say. 'She passed her exams and studied at Cambridge University. She's a qualified doctor now.'

'Well done her,' says the assistant. 'Does she work part-time? Now she has her little boy?'

'Oh, she doesn't work,' I say. 'Her husband takes care of everything. She doesn't have to lift a finger. She even has a cleaner.'

'Wish I had one of those,' says the assistant, winking. 'In my house, I'm the cleaner.'

'Elizabeth is a wonderful daughter,' I say. 'We're best friends. She's always inviting me over. Or taking me to lunch.'

'Sounds lovely,' says the assistant, with a kind smile.

'Yes,' I say. 'It's perfect.'

Lizzie

We're early for school today. I'm so determined to be a terrific, organised single parent that I've excelled myself.

Tom's only been here a few weeks. We're still the new family. Still need to prove ourselves.

Mr Cockrun stands outside the gates when we arrive, scrubbing at some graffiti on the school sign. His rubbery cheeks are red with the effort, hand moving frantically.

I make out some faded spray-paint letters written after Mr Cockrun's name: CH and then what looks like a faded E and A and another letter so faint as to be nothing but paint speckles.

As Mr Cockrun scrubs the sign clean he notices three approaching schoolgirls. 'Blazers on properly, please, girls,' he says. 'And let's get the ties nice and straight. If you're neat and tidy the school is neat and tidy.'

He sounds friendly enough, but the effect on the girls is profound. They hurriedly pluck and pull at their clothing, eyes swishing nervously to the headmaster.

Mr Cockrun nods encouragingly. 'Let everyone know how proud we are to be Steelfield pupils.' Then he heads into the school.

I smile at one of the girls. She has red hair, frightened blue eyes and gaps in her teeth. I think she must be ten or eleven.

'He likes you to look presentable,' I say.

The girl gives a funny laugh, glancing after the headmaster. '*We* like to look smart,' she says. 'It's important for the school.'

'Don't you like to be a bit casual sometimes? You're still only children.'

The girl looks deeply uncomfortable. 'No. Mr Cockrun wants everything at school to be perfect.' She glances at her friends, who nod in agreement.

'But no school is perfect,' I say in surprise. 'Even if it *looks* perfect. Surely there must be things you'd like to improve.'

The girl gives a tight shake of her head. 'It's a wonderful place, and we're lucky to be here. *Semper Fortis*. Always strong.'

The girl and her friends scurry off into the playground. I watch them, feeling uneasy.

'Mum,' says Tom. 'I don't want to go today.'

I push aside my anxiety. 'I know, love. But you'll be fine.' I kneel down, pulling him into a hug. 'You're amazing. The best little human being I ever met. I know it's tough starting a new place, but give it a chance, okay?' Then I whisper, 'I know the headmaster is a bit … funny.'

Tom nods. Then he strokes the railings. 'Silver and grey and blue and black.'

Colours again.

Two other mums appear. They're dressed in clean jeans, coats and silk scarfs, figures snapped back in place after children.

One of them says, 'What school *doesn't* have bullying? That's what I told the headmaster. Just because everyone else is too scared to tell doesn't mean it's not happening.'

'And what did he say?' the other mother asks.

'Told me flat out there was nothing going on. That he keeps the Neilson boys in line. "Everything is under control," he said.'

The second mother leans in closer. 'Noah told me social services are involved with them.'

I stiffen at the mention of social services.

'Theo said the older boy was slurring his words in the dinner queue …'

The first mother notices me then. She turns her whole body to block me out, and I see sparrow-like shoulder bones poking through her thin coat.

I feel left out.

I am left out.

For a moment, I question the orange scarf I've chosen to wear – the one I've been knitting in the evenings, listening to music (it feels good to listen to *my* music, not Olly's) while Tom is tucked up in bed upstairs. It *is* a little bright. Maybe even show-offy. Perhaps I should know better than to try to stand out, but I'm ready for change. Something *has* to change.

I can't carry on being the invisible woman.

Tom needs a strong mother.

Behind me, a woman says, 'Scuse me. Are you … Tom's mum?'

The words are an elastic band, stretched to the point of limpness.

I turn to see a skinny woman, thin blonde hair almost see-through. She's attempted a smart outfit – a blouse tucked into tight navy jeans – but it doesn't suit her grey, tired skin or dreamy, slow-moving eyes.

There's a large pram by her hip with a baby girl inside. I know the baby is a girl because everything is pink – snowsuit, blanket and bow.

'Hi,' I say. 'Sorry, I don't think we've met.'

The woman blinks slowly and says, 'I'm … Pauly's mum. Leanne.' She pauses, looking momentarily confused, then regains her concentration. 'Pauly said about Tom. They're … friends?'

'Oh. Right.' My hand finds Tom's shoulder. 'You're Pauly's mum. They're in the same class, but … I didn't know they were friends.'

'You're … separated like me, aren't you?' says Leanne, meeting my eye. 'That's what Pauly … says.'

'Yes.' I wonder what else the kids at school know about us already.

'My boys' dad … left,' says Leanne. She sways a little and adds, 'Good riddance. Did yours leave too?'

'Actually, I left Tom's dad,' I say. 'I tried for a long time to make it work. But you can't change people unless they want to change.' This comment is for the two mums standing nearby. I feel them watching me and don't want to be judged for my failed marriage. It's Olly's shame, not mine.

'We need to look after … each other,' says Leanne with a languid blink. 'Especially at this place. It's not right, is it?' Her eyes are on mine now and her words become more solid. 'Lloyd is scared and he's never scared. And Joey's been having panic attacks. How's Tom doing?'

I bite my lip. 'Not so well, actually.'

'Listen – don't you become one of them. "As long as we get our good grades let's pretend it's all okay." They hide a lot at this place. Sweep it under the carpet to make the school look good. I mean, Lloyd is full of shit but I know when he's lying.'

There's an awkward silence and then Leanne says, 'Can Tom come round … this Saturday?'

Tom looks up, eyes frightened.

I can feel lots of parents watching me now. 'I'm not sure,' I say. 'I never quite know what timings are going to be like at weekends.'

'Oh.' Leanne's eyes register confusion, then annoyance, and her head bobs around again.

'Weekends are busy for us right now. We've just moved house.'

'What about your ... ex, can he ... you know ... help out?'

'No,' I say, hearing a hardness to my voice.

'Adam can pick Tom up, if you like. That's my partner.'

'We might be away this weekend. We have to see my mother.'

Tom looks up then. 'You said it would be just us this week-end.'

I feel myself blushing, caught out. But the last thing I need is Tom involved with a troubled family, and by all accounts the Neilsons are very troubled.

In a bid to ease the irritation in Leanne's eyes, I hold out my hand and say, 'I never told you my name. It's ... Lizzie.'

I've always preferred Lizzie to Elizabeth. It's friendlier. And in this historical town outside London, maybe I can make friends.

At Tom's last school, there was a cliquey vibe. Or maybe there wasn't. Maybe I was just hard to know – the downtrod-den wife, hiding in the shadows.

'Good to meet you,' says Leanne. 'Hopefully we can ... you know ... help each other out.' She wobbles her head towards the gossipy mothers. 'Some people here ... they couldn't care less.'

I smile uncertainly. Then I kneel down and say, 'Are you

ready steady for school, Tommo? Take it easy today.' I kiss him on the head. 'Okay. Off you go.'

'Bye, Mum. Take care today, okay?'

'Okay, love.'

I watch Tom cross the playground. I'm still watching long after he's disappeared into the classroom.

Eventually, the headmaster comes to padlock the gates.

As I turn to go, I nearly trip over my feet.

Oh God.

A green van cruises past in the distance.

It's ... it's ...

No, too small. Olly's camper has a pop-top. That was just a trader's van.

Olly couldn't have found us. There's no *way* he could have found us.

You're being paranoid. Jumping at shadows ...

Lizzie

I'm early for school pick-up today.

It's been a few days since I saw the van, but it's put a picture in my head that I can't shake.

There are no other parents here yet. Standing on the pavement by the black railings, I watch the eerily silent school building, willing the time to pass.

As I wait, the headmaster heads across the playground. He's wearing another smart suit, jet-black today, and his peculiarly boyish face is stretched in a smile.

'Mrs Kinnock,' he says, approaching the gate. 'Hello again. You're here early. Is there something I can help you with?'

I try for a smile. 'I should have said before, Mr Cockrun, but I'm *Miss* Riley now. You must know that Tom's father and I are separated.'

'Yes,' says Mr Cockrun, all earnest and sincere. 'I'm always sad when families separate. Let's hope Tom isn't too badly affected.'

'It was for the best in our case,' I say, surprised by my fierceness. 'By the way, I need to apologise. My mother said she paid you a visit. I never asked her to. She ... doesn't always read social situations very well.'

Mr Cockrun frowns in thought. Then he has a flash of

recollection. 'Ah yes! I remember now. Tall woman. Nicely spoken. Rides horses.'

My mother doesn't ride horses, but she'll say anything to impress people.

'I enjoyed meeting her,' says Mr Cockrun. 'We were in complete agreement when it comes to children's schooling. Wasn't she in education herself at some point?'

'Um … no. She wasn't. I did tell her not to visit again without me. I know schools are busy.'

Mr Cockrun ignores me. '"Act the best and you'll be the best"– that was her motto. A very astute woman.'

I laugh. 'My mother certainly knows how to make things look good.'

'You were very early again this morning.' Mr Cockrun raises a questioning eyebrow. 'I saw you from my office. And now early again for pick-up.'

'I like to be on time.' I lift my chin. 'This is a new start for us. A new life. I want everything to be perfect.'

'Best not to get here too early.' Mr Cockrun notices a dandelion growing in a crack in the tarmac, frowns, pulls it up and pushes it under a shrub in the flowerbed. 'The teachers like a bit of peace and quiet, and so do I.'

'I just—'

'Now, since you're here, let's have a quick word about Tom.' Mr Cockrun turns serious eyes on me. 'His form teacher will want a chat shortly.'

'About what?'

'About the standards here. The behaviour we expect.'

'Yes, I—'

'We were happy to make space for Tom at such short

notice. But if he disrupts other children, we have a problem. A big problem. He's already got a reputation as a bit of a troublemaker.'

Troublemaker. What?

'*My* Tom? But he never gets into trouble.'

'Look, don't take this the wrong way but parents always think that. They never think it's their child.' He gives one of the railings – a rusty-looking one – an experimental tug. When he finds it a little loose, he takes a notepad from his pocket and scribbles something, shaking his head. 'I'd have a word with him if I were you. Sooner rather than later.' Then he strolls away.

I stare at the entrance door as it creaks closed.

Around me, other parents begin arriving. The school bell rings, long and loud. Five seconds of calm.

Then, in one great rush, children spill out into the playground.

I look for Tom and see him trudging among the other children, shadowed by an eerily calm-looking teacher, who is walking with a hand on his shoulder.

The teacher has short, salt-and-pepper hair cut in a jagged, youthful style that actually makes her look older, highlighting her wrinkles and large ears. Her hips, which carry a good twenty pounds of excess weight, strain in an unflattering black trouser suit that would be more at home on a London legal professional.

All in all, it's the look of someone out of place. She doesn't fit in, but she's trying.

Her name is Mrs Dudley, I think. Yes, that's right.

When Tom sees me, he runs and throws his arms around me.

Oh God ... what happened? What happened?

I can feel Tom's chest heave as he sobs into cotton.

'Sweetheart,' I whisper. 'What's the matter?'

Mrs Dudley gives me an empty smile. 'Mrs Kinnock? May I talk to you?'

A hundred faces turn in my direction, and I hear someone suck in their breath.

'I'm Miss Riley,' I say. 'And yes. Of course. Shall I ... should I follow you inside?'

'No.' Mrs Dudley smiles politely, but her expression is firm. 'We don't let parents into the classrooms. For safeguarding reasons.'

'So where should we—'

'Oh, we can have a quick chat here.'

I pull Tom close to my hip. 'Talk about my son in front of everybody? Can't you see he's upset?'

'We'll wait until everyone leaves,' Mrs Dudley says.

I look down at Tom. 'How are you, Tommo? What happened?'

Mrs Dudley flashes me pale grey eyes. 'Give everyone a minute to clear out before we get into it.'

Tom doesn't answer. Just stares ahead, red-eyed and sniffing.

When the crowds have dispersed, I crouch down. 'Tom?' I say.

'I don't know,' he whispers.

'Are you okay, Tom?'

'I got in trouble.' Tom wipes at tears. 'But I don't *remember*.'

'You don't remember? How come?'

'I just don't.'

'Your teacher and I will have a chat.' I kiss his head and

stand up tall. 'We'll get all this sorted out, don't you worry.' I tilt my head at Mrs Dudley. 'So what's going on?'

'Well, I have to tell you, Miss Riley, we had … an *issue* today.'

'What sort of issue?'

'This goes no further, but you do need to be informed.'

'What happened?'

'Two boys were fighting in the playground.'

'*Tom* was fighting?'

'Not me, Mum,' says Tom. 'Pauly and Lloyd. Pauly had to go to hospital.'

'Oh my *God*.'

'Tom wasn't involved in the fight,' Mrs Dudley fills in. 'But a little girl asked him about it and he attacked her.'

'Tom *attacked* someone? A girl? *My* Tom? No – there's been some mistake. Tom would never do anything like that.'

'The girl had to go to the nurse's office. She was very shaken up. Miss Riley, this behaviour is absolutely unacceptable. It *cannot* happen again. The school's reputation means a lot to us. Pupil behaviour is key.'

'I don't believe this happened.' I shake my head.

'I saw it,' says Mrs Dudley. 'The attack came out of nowhere – totally unprovoked. And things like this *cannot* happen here. You have to understand. We won't tolerate it. Not when it puts the school's image on the line.'

She gives a meaningful pause. A pause that says: *We don't like taking on social services children. Keep Tom in line or there'll be trouble.*

Then Mrs Dudley's voice softens and suddenly she sounds just like Mr Cockrun. 'Look. We need parents on the same page. Singing from the same hymn sheet. The appropriate discipline at home. And then we'll say no more about it. Pretend it never happened.'

Pretend it never happened ...

'I've never known Tom to hurt anyone.'

'We'll forgive and forget, Miss Riley. As long as it doesn't happen again.'

I think of my mother, suddenly. And Olly. The perfect image. Make everything look good and to hell with what's really going on.

'Someone has made a mistake.' Upset rises in my chest. 'I mean ... Tom just doesn't *do* things like that. He's not an angry child. I've never even seen him get cross, let alone ... He's very *kind* to other children. He gets stressed but never angry ...'

'Miss Riley—'

'I'm sorry.' I shake my head. 'This is so hard to believe.' My eyes wander to Tom, who still has his arms around me. 'I've *never* known him hit anyone, let alone a younger child.'

'Let's say no more about it.' Mrs Dudley glances at the headmaster's office.

'Tom must have been confused,' I counter. 'He had a seizure. Did the office tell you?'

Mrs Dudley watches me for a moment, then says, 'A seizure? Is he epileptic?'

'We don't think so. No one knows why it happened. But the hospital thinks it was a one-off. An oddity.'

'What sort of seizure did he have?' Mrs Dudley is watching me intently now and pulls a notepad and pen from her suit pocket.

'Well, I ... I don't know. How many sorts of seizures are there?'

'Was he fitting? Or just confused? Dazed?'

'He was … I mean, he had a fit. He was convulsing.'

'Convulsing.' Mrs Dudley nods and scribbles on her pad. 'Anything else?'

'Um … I'm not sure what you mean.'

'Was he confused beforehand? Disorientated?'

'Well, now you come to mention it, yes. Yes he was. What difference does it make? Why on earth are you making notes?'

'The headmaster insists records are kept.'

'I already phoned the school about it. Tom wasn't absent but I thought you all knew he'd been in hospital.'

'"Absent".' Mrs Dudley mock shudders and gives a little laugh, flipping her notepad closed. 'That's a word we don't like here. We like to maintain a good attendance record.'

'Tom was in *hospital*!' I realise I'm shouting the words. 'And why did you want to know those details about his seizure?'

'It's … a seizure is unusual,' says Mrs Dudley. 'We make a note of anything unusual for Alan. He has his reasons. Good reasons. We just have to trust in him. Have faith.'

I stare at her, heart thumping in my chest, a sickly feeling in my stomach. For her to be so callous about Tom's seizure … so clinical … This is the woman I'm leaving my son with all day?

'Tom.' I look down. 'What happened?'

Tom replies without looking up. 'I really don't remember, Mum. Honest. I don't think I did it.'

Mrs Dudley frowns at him, then says: 'Work with us, Miss Riley. *Semper Fortis*. Always strong.'

'Come on, Tom.' My hand tightens on Tom's shoulder.

As we walk away, Mrs Dudley calls: 'And please don't

discuss this incident with anyone else, Miss Riley. Remember the school's reputation.'

Tom and I walk home in silence, his usual chatter absent.

'Tom,' I say, as we near the house. 'Is there anything you want to tell me? Now Mrs Dudley isn't listening?'

'I just don't remember anything,' says Tom, with a very adult shrug. Then he starts to cry, forehead crumpling into frown lines. 'I don't like being in trouble.'

'I know, sweetheart. Are you sure there's nothing else you want to tell me?'

Tom shakes his head. 'Honestly, Mum. Nothing. Except ... maybe someone else did it and they thought it was me. And Mrs Dudley *wasn't there*.'

'Someone else did it? Who?'

'I don't know.'

I heat cans of tomato soup and toast bread for our dinner.

We don't talk like we usually do. No matter how many ways I try to lure Tom into conversation, he only offers one-word answers.

After I've put him to bed, I find myself sitting with my head in my hands again.

Is Tom being bullied? I know sensitive children are vulnerable to that kind of thing. Soft targets.

It will get easier. It *must* get easier. We've been through enough.

Lizzie

'*I've been ditched.*' Olly waves the letter at me, gold embossing dancing under the kitchen spotlights.

He screws up the thick, buff paper and throws it in a perfect arch over the marble breakfast bar. The ball lands in the open kitchen bin – something I imagine Olly, as a competitive sportsman, feels satisfied about.

We're having breakfast in Olly's Earl's Court flat. I still can't really explain how I got here. I don't mean at the flat itself, but I mean in Olly's life. How does someone like me end up living with an Olympic athlete? A trainee nurse who didn't even finish her training?

I suppose the answer is: when an Olympic athlete breaks his femur and can no longer compete.

Perhaps I should think more highly of myself. That I'm worthy of someone like Olly, injury or no injury. But with my upbringing, it's hard. Inside, I often feel like nothing. Invisible.

I grew up in the shadow of my mother – an invisible, empty little thing whose job was to ignore all my own needs and make Ruth Riley look perfect.

Then there was loneliness.

And now I have Olly – a man who makes me feel so loved

I could burst with happiness, yet at other times, casts me back into the shadows.

That's where I am today.

It's times like this I wish I hadn't given up my nurse training to be with Olly. At least if I were a nurse, I'd be something in my own right.

Olly is angry. Erratic. This is a side he hid when we first got together. Yes, he is charming and attentive. But things have changed.

'There's still a chance,' I say. 'If you'd only carry on with your physio exercises. I can help you—'

'I don't want your help!' Olly glares, fists clenched. Then he looks away. 'You don't know what you're doing.'

'It's the physio who doesn't know,' I counter, voice rising. 'He sees you half an hour, once a month. I see you all the time. I see how your body moves. I know about this stuff. It was part of my training—'

'Oh, fuck off.' Olly bangs a fist on the solid wood counter top. 'It's over, isn't it? Everything I worked for. Gone.'

'I'm still here. It doesn't matter to me if you're an Olympic athlete. I love you.'

'No you don't. I see through you, Lizzie Nightingale.'

My hands begin to shake as I stand, clearing the breakfast things.

'Why then?' Olly demands. 'Why do you love me?'

'Because … we're a good fit. When you're not screaming at me. I think you could still be drunk from last night—'

'Oh, fuck off, Lizzie. Stop trying to control me.'

'Why can't you ever just have one drink any more? You don't know when to stop.'

'You're a controlling bitch, that's what you are.'

'Olly. Don't do this.'

'It's true, isn't it?' Olly yells. 'You've never loved me.'

He stands, unsteady, then grabs the plates from my hands and smashes them on the slate kitchen tiles.

I stare at the broken porcelain.

This is what I do when under attack.

Stay still.

I learned, growing up with my mother, not to use teeth or claws against a stronger animal. Camouflage is best. Invisibility has its benefits.

Another plate smashes and I feel a burning on my forehead. Porcelain shards fall on my body, jagged edges clinging to striped fabric. A warm line of blood trickles down the side of my nose and onto my lips. Tears come and, to my relief, Olly's anger subsides.

'Here.' He takes a tea towel and holds it to the blood. 'I love you,' he says. 'You know that John Lennon song? "Jealous Guy"? That's me. I get scared you don't love me. You know that.'

'Of course I love you,' I say, face wet with tears and blood, hands shaking.

'I'll get a bandage,' says Olly.

I nod, pushing Olly's Frosties cereal back into the cupboard.

In the same cupboard is a pile of pregnancy leaflets and magazines from the hospital. I really should read those. But right now, that would make everything too real.

Which is why I've pushed them between the cereals, out of the way.

When I told Olly about the baby, he was ecstatic, dancing

me around the living room, telling me what perfect parents we were going to be. Talking about raising a champion snowboarder. But how quickly that moment passed.

I burst into tears, hands going to my baby bump. This happens almost every day now – Olly getting angry and me crying. An endless, awful cycle. Maybe he's stressed about the baby, the realities of parenthood closing in.

Usually at this point, Olly would comfort me and apologise. But this time he doesn't. Instead, he looks at me with contempt, hobbles to the bedroom and slams the door.

On my stomach, I see my fingers trembling. If things are this bad now, what on earth is going to happen when the baby comes?

Lizzie

Tom and I are having supper on the living-room floor – baked beans, jacket potato and peas.

We don't have a dining table yet, so until I buy one we're having 'fun floor-picnics' at meal times. Tom gets uncomfortable at the breakfast bar.

We've unpacked most of the boxes downstairs now, so there's plenty of space on the floor. The bookshelf has neat rows of books on it and the laundry – although not done – sits in tidy piles ready for the washing machine.

I watch Tom plough his beans and potato into a mashy heap, then fork spoonfuls into his mouth.

He's sorted the peas into a separate 'green' pile and has made the mashed potato turn orange by mixing in the beans.

'Tommo,' I say cautiously. 'Can we talk about what happened at school, then?'

'I don't remember,' says Tom quietly. 'Honest, Mum. I think Mrs Dudley is making it up.'

'She says she saw you.'

'She tells lies sometimes. Probably … another boy did it, but she's scared of his brother. So I got the blame. She *didn't* see. She wasn't there until later.'

'Is this something to do with the Neilsons?' I ask.

'I don't want to say, Mum,' says Tom. 'Please.'

'Tom, this is serious. If your teacher isn't telling the truth—'

'I don't want to talk any more,' says Tom. 'It's giving me tummy ache.'

Tom learned that from his father, I'm sure. Close everything down. Pretend it's not happening and it will go away.

'Tom, it's good to talk about things,' I say. 'I know your father and I didn't set you the best example. But you and I have always been friends. Friends talk to each other.'

'I'm tired,' says Tom. 'I want to go to bed.'

'You've been tired a lot recently. Are you *sure* you're feeling okay? Remember you had a seizure not so long ago.'

'Just sleepy. School is stressy, trying to work out what to do all the time. The rules here are different. All the colours are different. And Mrs Dudley shouts if I ask questions. I want to go to bed.'

'Finish your tea first.'

'I'm not hungry.'

'Just eat a little bit more, Tom. Then you can go up.'

Tom's fork clinks on the plate, scooping up more potato.

'I wish you could tell me what happened with that little girl. Did Pauly *make* you do something?'

Tom eyes widen in alarm. It's the most awake he's looked since he got home. 'Don't say *anything* about Pauly. *I* hit her, okay? *I* did it.' Tom looks at his plate.

'Okay,' I say, trying to stay calm. 'But why would you hit someone?'

'Maybe I just felt angry. Like Dad used to.'

'Are you being bullied, Tom? What you just said about Pauly—'

'Pauly's not doing *anything*. We ... we're friends.'

Sometimes, I see Tom walk out of school with Pauly. It doesn't look friendly. It looks menacing. Like Tom is being forced into conversation.

I can feel the glances of other mothers, hear their judgements ...

Those Neilson boys are trouble. So that new boy must be trouble too.

'No need to make friends too quickly,' I say. 'Not after what we've been through with your father. Reputations can be catching.'

'You don't understand.' Tom puts his fork down. 'I have to be friends with Pauly. If I'm not ... I just have to be, that's all.'

'Maybe I should speak to the headmaster—'

'No! Not *him*. Or Mrs Dudley. They're not on our side. I'm handling it and it's okay. Pauly's all right. His mummy isn't well, that's all. Social services keep saying she's unfit, so it makes him angry.'

Unfit.

They said that about Olly too.

Unfit to parent.

And suddenly, I realise it's *vital* Tom stays away from the Neilsons. This is a new start. I want us to be perfect. No more ugly black marks.

'Do you sit next to Pauly in class?' I ask. I hope this question doesn't sound as transparent as it feels. Because if I find out Tom and Pauly sit together, I'm going to ask the teacher to split them apart.

'No,' says Tom. 'Pauly sits on a table by himself. I sit next to Jacob.'

'Is Jacob nice?' I ask.

'He's all right.'

We eat in silence for a while. Then I say, 'Hey – good job on your potato. Look at that! You've made an orange cave.'

'Dad liked baked potatoes, didn't he?' Tom stares straight ahead.

'Let's not think about Dad,' I say, trying to keep my voice light. 'Baked potatoes are fun. I had them all the time growing up.'

'I had a dream about Dad last night,' says Tom. 'He was chasing me, but I climbed a tree. Then you came and climbed up with me, and we found a treehouse and it was okay.'

I put my knife and fork down. 'Tom … I'm so sorry.' Tears prickle. 'Do you think about him much?'

'Sometimes. When I see something scary.'

'Maybe we should go and see someone again. Like Jane, do you remember her? To help us talk about things.'

'I don't need to talk, Mum. Not any more. It's all fine.'

'Whatever you're feeling, it's okay. You can tell me anything. Even if you miss your father, it's okay. Jane said it's all okay.'

'I don't miss him. I hate him.'

'You can hate and love someone at the same time.'

Tom doesn't answer. Just looks sad. And I feel sad too. So very sad for everything we've lost.

'Did you love Dad?' Tom asks finally.

I hesitate, fork in mid-air.

'Yes. Once upon a time. But now I never want to see him again. Same as you. Okay, Tommo, let's get these things washed up.'

Tom carries his plate into the kitchen and helps me scrape potato and beans into the bin.

'Tell you what,' I say. 'You're looking tired. Better not overdo things. Why don't you go and get showered and ready for bed? Then I'll come up and read you a story. Okay?'

Tom heads upstairs, while I dunk the plates into soapy water and make gentle circles with the sponge.

At the apartment, we had a dishwasher. There's room for one in this kitchen, but the owner told me she didn't want modern things ruining the Victorian design. All the 20th century stuff – the fridge, the washing machine, the tumble drier, the stainless-steel sink – are in the utility room.

I don't mind washing up by hand. It's soothing.

I hear Tom running the shower. He's one of those kids who loves getting clean. When he was younger, we even had a rain dance. It was fun.

I remember Olly doing that dance with him.

The pain comes again and I push those thoughts away.

After a while, the shower trickles to a stop and I hear Tom shuffling around. Washing up finished, I head upstairs to tuck him into bed.

Tom has left a crumpled towel and his school uniform on the bathroom tiles. I should tell him off, but he seems exhausted tonight.

Stooping down to pick up his uniform, I begin checking for stains.

There's a dried piece of rice stuck to his school jumper, a light smudge of chocolate icing – I assume from school. Tom's shirt cuffs are grey and grubby, so I'll have to do a wash tonight – both colours and whites.

'Okay, Tommo,' I say, walking into his bedroom. 'Time for our story.'

But Tom doesn't reply.

He's sitting on the bed, staring into space.

There is something in his hands: a white towelling dressing gown, the one Mum got him for Christmas.

It's stained with something, a huge browny-red circle.

'Oh my God!'

Blood. Lots of blood.

'Tom!' I run to him. 'What *happened*? Did you fall?'

He shakes his head, eyes panicked. 'I don't know how it got there,' he says, voice high-pitched and fearful.

'Okay.' I step back, taking a deep breath. 'Okay. Maybe you had a nosebleed. Could it have been a nosebleed?'

Tom nods. 'Yes. I think so.'

'But there's no blood around your nose.'

'I don't know, Mum.'

'We need to go to the hospital. Just in case. Did something happen at school today?' I check him over, looking for signs of blood elsewhere. There are none.

'You and the little girl today … was it a fight? Something that could have caused a nosebleed later on?'

'No.' Tom accepts the top I hand him. 'We don't need the hospital. It's only a nosebleed. I had one before.'

'A tiny one. Once. Never *this* bad. And you had a seizure …'

'Can I have a hot water bottle for bed? I'm cold.'

Olly used to do that. Distract. Change the subject. Pretend I hadn't said anything. My mother did too.

'Tom, we need to see a doctor,' I say. 'This is *covered* in blood.' I take his face in my hands, tipping his head to the light, looking around his nose and eyes.

'I don't want the hospital,' says Tom. 'I don't *want* the hospital.'

'Listen. Perhaps Accident and Emergency is a bit drastic. But we need a trip to the walk-in clinic, at least.'

'No!'

He's never shouted at me like that before. Protested, yes. But never shouted.

'Tom, we're going.' I open the wardrobe and throw some clothes at him. 'Right now.'

Kate

I should have gone home hours ago, but I'm still at Accident and Emergency with a distraught Pauly Neilson.

He has a head wound and a broken finger, both caused by his older brother, Lloyd, during a fight in the school playground. The teacher says they were fighting over a medicine bottle, which is a cause for concern, but no one can find the bottle.

Usually, Pauly acts like the toughest little eight-year-old. With thick black curls, like his brothers, he carries himself like a champion boxer, all shoulders and fists.

I half expected to see a cigarette behind his ear.

Now Pauly's faux toughness has drained away like dirty bath-water, and I see a shivering little boy, scared and alone.

He'd already been in hospital for hours when I arrived, sobbing with pain and scared the doctors were going to put him in care because his mum couldn't be found.

Tomorrow, I must make an unenforceable ruling – Lloyd and Pauly must never be in the same room together unsupervised.

Then we will have a meeting to discuss Lloyd Neilson and temporary foster care.

'Miss?' Pauly is still wide awake. Of course he is. He's used to staying up late.

I realise I've slumped a little in the chair.

Where is that doctor?

'Yes, Pauly?'

'Them doctors,' Pauly says. 'How do you know they're nice men?'

'Because they're here to take care of you.'

'Our headmaster says that. But he's not a nice man. He just pretends.'

'Most people are nice deep down, Pauly.'

Pauly stares at the hospital curtain. 'Were your teachers nice?'

'Yes.'

'Were they clever, like you?'

I laugh. 'I'm not clever, Pauly. If I were, I wouldn't be working in social services.'

Pauly laughs too. 'Miss, you made a joke. You *are* clever, though. Was your parents clever too?'

'Yes.'

'Is your mum still with your dad?'

'My dad died when I was young. I miss him, actually.'

'Did he get angry?'

'Not much. He shouted at a policeman once for pushing a homeless man. "Leave that man alone." And he got angry with my sister and I when we dug up his potatoes.'

Pauly sits up straighter. 'Was you a bit naughty when you were little then?'

'Well … not often.'

'Oh.' Pauly slumps back, disappointed. 'So you was like … a really good kid? Like, happy and all that.'

'I was lucky.'

Pauly stares with the eyes of a much older person. 'I'm not lucky.'

'I'm going to do everything I can for you, Pauly,' I say. 'Tomorrow, I'll arrange a special meeting for your mother, and I'm going to speak to lots of people – teachers, the headmaster – we're going to work out how we can keep you safe.'

'Mrs Dudley tells lies. And Mr Cockrun. They're both liars. They'll put me in care and then no one will believe me.'

'Teachers don't make those decisions—'

Suddenly the curtain is pulled back, and a tall, tired doctor stands before us, looking sallow under the bright strip-lighting.

'Still awake, Pauly?' the doctor asks.

'Well, if I *was* asleep,' Pauly points out, 'you would have just woken me up.'

The doctor gives a nod, too shattered to challenge the backchat, and asks me, 'Are you the social worker?'

'Yes. I'm Kate Noble.'

'Ah,' says the doctor, as if it all makes sense. Obviously he hadn't placed me as Pauly's mother. 'So, Pauly. Are you going to tell me what happened?'

'I fell,' says Pauly.

'No you didn't, Pauly,' I say. 'You were fighting in the playground—'

Pauly shoots me a warning glance. 'I *fell.*'

'But your teacher said—'

'She wasn't there,' Pauly snaps. 'How would she know? I told you, she lies about everything.'

The doctor checks his watch. 'We'll have the X-ray back soon. Shouldn't be long.'

A wave of tiredness envelopes me. I desperately want to crawl into one of the hospital beds and go to sleep. But of course, all the beds are full.

Stifling a yawn, I remember I have a nine o'clock visit booked in tomorrow. Who? Who is it? Can I shuffle it around?

Tom Kinnock.

Nice and straightforward. Shake hands with the mother, check she's settling in okay, then close up the file.

But I'll have to move that appointment.

Pauly's notes need to be written up first thing.

Lizzie

Most walk-in clinics have a two-hour wait. Three at worst. We've been at this one nearly four hours and our name has only just been called.

Four hours for a five-minute appointment.

'So, what seems to be the problem?' The nurse is cuddly, with feathered, bleached-blonde hair, grey at the roots. There are sandwich crumbs around her mouth. Three empty coffee cups tell me she's working overtime, probably unplanned.

We're not seeing a doctor because there aren't any – the walk-in clinic is run by nurses at night-time.

'I think Tom had a nosebleed,' I tell her. 'There was a *lot* of blood. See?' I show her the dressing gown, which I'd bundled into a bag-for-life.

The nurse frowns, rectangular glasses sliding down her nose. 'It's okay. I don't need to see. You can put that away.'

'He had a seizure not long ago,' I say, re-bagging the dressing gown. 'We're still waiting for the outcome of some reports. If you could just check his medical records—'

'We don't keep medical records here,' says the nurse. 'The whole system needs updating. I can only treat what I see. Has he had a nosebleed in the last four hours?'

'I think so. You really can't see *any* of his medical records? He had a seizure. This may be related.'

'I'm afraid it doesn't work like that.' The nurse leans forward, smiling at Tom. 'Hello, young man. What's your name?'

'Tom,' he answers dutifully.

'So you had a nosebleed, Tom?' she asks. 'Is that right? It must be quite a scary thing to happen at your age. All that blood.'

'A bit,' says Tom, eyes welling with tears.

I put my arms around him, pulling him onto my lap. 'It's okay, Tom. You don't need to get upset. Unless … is there anything else you want to talk about?'

Tom gives a brisk shake of his head.

'Well, I'll just give him a little once-over,' says the nurse, fingers racing around her keyboard, 'and then send you on your way. Tom seems fine in himself, and if he hasn't had a bleed in the last few hours … well, you were right to bring him in, anyway. Better safe than sorry.'

I like the ones who say 'better safe than sorry'.

The nurse holds up a blood-pressure cuff. 'Okay, Tom. So, you've probably seen one of these before.'

'Yes,' says Tom.

'He had his blood pressure taken in hospital,' I say. 'When he had the seizure.'

'I like it done on my left arm,' says Tom robotically.

The nurse nods, not really listening, and lifts Tom's right arm.

She rolls soft cotton up to Tom's elbow, then hesitates.

We both stare.

I hear myself gasp.

Three tiny, bloody holes mark the inside of Tom's forearm, two of them circled with grey bruises.

Each one sits perfectly above a wavy green vein.

The room becomes eerily still.

'Has he had blood taken in the last few days?' the nurse asks, her voice cautious.

'No. Oh my *God*.' I put a hand to my mouth. For a moment, I think I'm going to be sick. But after a few thick swallows, I manage to say, 'Tom. There are marks here. How did you get them?'

'I don't know,' says Tom, eyes wide and frightened.

'Are you his primary carer?' the nurse asks.

'Yes.' I nod my head. '*Tom*. How on earth did you get those marks?'

Tom shakes his head, tears coming. 'I don't *know*.'

I turn to the nurse. 'His school. It's the only place he's away from me … There was an incident today. A fight.'

'Tom,' says the nurse, words falsely bright. 'Can you tell me where you got these little marks?'

She glances at me then, an appraising glance she didn't have time to make when I first came into the office.

I feel exposed, wishing I'd worn something smarter. Put on a bit of makeup.

'I don't know what they are,' says Tom.

'You don't know?' the nurse asks. 'Nobody has put a needle into your arm recently?' She rolls back on her wheelie chair, opens a drawer and holds up a plastic-wrapped syringe. 'Like this one?'

Tom shakes his head.

'Have you had any knocks or bumps recently, Tom?' the nurse asks. 'Played with anything sharp?'

Tom looks between the two of us. 'I haven't done anything. It wasn't me.'

'You're not in trouble, Tom,' I say. 'We just want to know how you got these marks.'

'Would you rather the two of us talked alone?' says the nurse. 'Without Mum? Sometimes that can be easier.'

Ice water pours into my stomach. 'What are you implying?'

'I'm not saying—'

'Yes you are. Believe me, I know what an accusation looks like. I've met with social services enough times to discuss Tom's father.'

'Tom, what can you tell us about these marks?' the nurse asks again, her voice soft. 'They're rather unusual. Surely you can remember something?' She surreptitiously glances at the clock, probably remembering the fifty patients waiting outside and knowing that if she doesn't finish with us soon she'll have to stay past midnight.

'I don't know,' says Tom again.

'Did an adult do this to you?' the nurse asks.

Tom quickly shakes his head.

'Did someone do this to you at school?' I ask.

Tom looks at his lap.

'Listen,' says the nurse, glancing at the clock again. 'I need to make a report about this.'

'Yes. Please do. Can we book in to see another doctor? Tomorrow maybe?'

The nurse changes instantly from kind, cuddly nurse to tired, overworked nurse.

'Not just a medical report,' the nurse says, her voice hard. 'Social services will need to be informed.'

'I suppose … yes, that makes sense.' I feel sick. 'Could you make a note about Tom's school? Ask someone to talk to the headmaster … his teacher. As I said, there was an incident today.'

'His school? I don't think—'

'Where else could it have happened?' I ask. 'It's the only place he's away from me.'

The nurse doesn't say anything. But I can almost read her thoughts.

Impossible.

Lizzie

'*Impossible!*' *my father shouts.* '*Good God, Ruth. Can't you tell the truth, for once in your life? Lizzie didn't even take the exam – how on earth could she have got into grammar school?*'

My mother deftly changes the subject. '*Did you pick up those wine glasses? I need them for the dinner party tomorrow.*'

'*Ruth, this isn't normal.*'

'*Let's sit down and have supper,*' *says Mum, putting on her best 'good housewife' smile. Then her voice goes hard.* '*Don't start an argument, Harold.*'

'*I'm not arguing, Ruth. I'm trying to talk to you.*'

My mother turns then, perfect white teeth gritted. '*I don't want to talk about this. You want to be angry. I don't.*'

With my mother, it's always someone else's fault.

I'm held in a tight, tense bunch on our sofa, watching the debate go back and forth like ping pong.

But Dad will never score his point because Mum cheats. She steals the ball.

'*I'll put supper on the table,*' *says Mum.* '*And when you've quite finished taking your temper out on me, we can sit down and eat.*'

'*Ruth, how did you think this wouldn't come out?*'

Mum whips around. The mask slips, showing fury under

perfect makeup. 'I've told you, Harold, I do not want to talk about this. Do you want us screaming at each other, with the neighbours listening through the walls? I will not get caught up in your ugliness.'

Mum rarely gets visibly angry. After all, it's not ladylike. But we all know that underneath the façade, she's white-hot with fury all the time.

'I won't let you sidestep this time,' says Dad. 'Not when it involves Lizzie.'

Mum plays her winning hand – she starts crying big noisy crocodile tears. These are usually saved for very special occasions, but she's been using them more and more recently.

Dad gives up then, of course. He can't stand seeing Mum cry.

This is what my mother does. Absolutely refuses to admit she's lied. She's been caught out. I don't know how she let the lie get to this point – usually she's clever enough to sidestep before it gets this far. But she'll never admit she's made something up. Ever.

How can you have a relationship with someone who point-blank refuses to see reality?

Some extra guests join our meal that evening. They are called awkwardness, rage and denial. They are regular visitors to our house, joining us whenever we're all together. I'm so used to them that I barely notice the sickly, scared feelings any more. It's like carrying around a heavy bag I can never take off. After a while, you just get used to it.

I start dividing up the food on my plate, scraping the cream sauce off the meat and pushing it towards the mashed potato. We're having a fancy meal because Dad is here. When it's just Mum and me, we eat plain things. Usually bread and butter.

'Eat properly, Elizabeth,' Mum snaps.

Suddenly, Dad says, 'How was your day, Lizzie?' His face is tight and the words are forced and carefully chosen. He can't use the word 'school'. That would allude to Mum's lie.

Ruth Riley has been telling Dad's work colleagues that I won a place at the girls' grammar, when I wasn't even bright enough to sit the exam. It's an obvious lie, even for her, but I suppose she thought that since his colleagues were all based in London they'd never find out. I don't think she thought Dad would find out either.

'It was okay, Dad,' I say. 'We're rehearsing for the school … I mean, for the play. I'm the Angel Gabriel.'

Dad smiles then, a full, genuine smile. 'You're my little angel. You know that, don't you, Lizzie?'

'She isn't special enough to be an angel,' says my mother, irritated that I'm being praised.

Dad looks at me with sad eyes.

Sometimes, I think he is just as trapped as me. Other times, I know he's not brave enough to make a stand and I hate him for it.

People think Dad is the nice one, but really he's worse than Mum. He lets her be the way she is because he's too scared to rock the boat.

Kate

'No, I *like* parties,' I shout, over the uneven whine of electric guitar. 'I just don't like this sort of music.'

'Give it a chance,' says Col, swigging from his plastic pint-glass. 'They spent hours setting this lot up.'

It's true. My ex-housemates, Rebecca and Julie, have excelled themselves this weekend, creating a mini festival in the back garden, complete with plywood stage and thousands of fairy lights.

Friends drink and dance around me. They wear various fancy-dress costumes – a giant banana with star sunglasses, Sid Vicious, Amy Winehouse and, of course, Col, dressed as a woman in floral Laura Ashley and badly applied lipstick.

My phone vibrates in my pocket.

I just *know* it's work.

'I'll be back in a minute, okay?' I tell Col.

'Where are you going?' Col bobs his head, which is the closest he gets to cutting loose on the dance floor. This is a good time for him, having a few drinks and a dance. I don't want to complain about how exhausted I am, or admit that work stuff is running around my head.

'Just … I'll be right back.'

At the front of the house, I find Rebecca having a sneaky cigarette. She's dressed as Princess Leia, with fake wool plaits wound around her ears.

'Don't tell Julie,' Rebecca whispers. 'But her band are giving me a headache.'

'Me too,' I admit. In my jeans pocket, my phone vibrates again.

'They've got better, though,' Rebecca decides. 'Now they've ditched that accordion.'

'This is work,' I say, holding up my phone. 'They've called twice. I should call them back.'

Rebecca blows a long stream of smoke. 'Col's not going to be happy. You're so *stressed*, Kate. They shouldn't be calling you out-of-hours.'

'I said they could. There are people off sick. I have two missed calls. It must be something important.'

'I'm sure everything will be fine.'

'Nothing is ever fine in this job,' I say. 'I feel like I'm failing.' Tears come, and I'm embarrassed.

'Oh, don't be silly. You are a highly competent person. You get up at six a.m. to exercise.'

'Used to. Don't any more. I can barely keep up with this workload, let alone have a hobby.'

'I think you've got to cut a few corners, Kate,' says Rebecca. 'This is the public sector. It's what everyone does.'

'You know me. I can't cut corners.'

Rebecca laughs. 'I know. Not ticking every box gives you anxiety.'

I walk a little way down the street and call the office.

The out-of-hours team pick up immediately. 'Children's Services.'

'Hi, Helen.' I press the phone to my ear. 'What's happening?'

'Kate. Thank God you phoned back. We had a call from Hammersmith and Fulham. Tom Kinnock's father has found the social services out-of-hours site. The duty officer is all shaken up. He's making all sorts of threats, worse than before. She doesn't know what to do and nor do I.'

'Call the police,' I say. 'There's nothing we can do. We can't reveal the mother's location. And Tom doesn't want to see his father. If a child doesn't want to see their parent, no one can force a supervised visit. It all comes down to what Tom wants.'

This is the standard social worker answer, but it's not *my* answer. I would encourage Tom to see his father in a safe environment, try and move things forward. That's the trouble with this job. I'm rule-abiding, but the rules here are often impossible to follow.

'I don't think he's going to like that,' says Helen.

'Of course he won't. But he shouldn't be stalking the out-of-hours team.'

I end the call with knots in my stomach, knowing I haven't solved anything, fixed anything, done anything except make Tom Kinnock's father even more furious.

It sounds like he's already on edge.

Oh God.

I can't leave things like this.

My finger taps redial. 'Helen?'

'Kate. I was just about to call Hammersmith and Fulham.'

'I'll call them. See if I can smooth things out with the father. We can't just drop them in it. What's the number?'

'I'll connect you. Hang on.'

After two rings, I hear Terri from Hammersmith and Fulham out-of-hours team.

'Child Services. Emergency duty team.'

'Hi Terri. It's Kate Noble. I hear Tom Kinnock's father is with you. Can I speak to him?'

'He just left. Big relief. I threatened to call the police in the end. Karen let him in – God knows why, she's been told before. Once he was in the building, he just kicked off, shouting and swearing.'

'Are you okay?' I ask.

'A bit delicate. But I've had worse nights. Are you out and about somewhere?'

'Oh, I'm not missing much. You sure you're okay?'

'Fine. Get back to your evening.'

'I'll call you tomorrow.'

At the party, I head straight for the garden bar and grab a can of cold shandy from the ice bucket.

I hardly ever drink, but this evening feels like a 'hardly ever' sort of time.

'There you are.' I feel Col's warm arm around my shoulder. 'Everything okay? No, it can't be. You're *drinking*.'

'It's just shandy. I had a work call.'

'Ah. Silly me to think you'd finished for the week.'

'I'm sorry. You always knew I was a career girl.'

'Yes. I know.'

Col used to love that about me.

Now, perhaps, he's not so sure.

Lizzie

Monday morning.

Mr Cockrun's office is neat and tidy, with some unusually secure touches.

There is, of course, the two-way glass and bars at the windows and the medicine cabinet locked with a huge padlock. But there is also a Kensington lock holding Mr Cockrun's computer screen to the desk and a PIN entry system on a side door, which I assume to be a stationery cupboard.

A CCTV camera is mounted in one corner. On a long desk under the window is a CCTV screen, flashing with different images of the school – an empty playground, an empty corridor, an empty school field ...

The children are in school right now, but you'd never know it.

There is also desk space for another person with a pen-holder and swivel chair.

The plants are plastic.

He says he wants to keep the children safe, I think. *But what's he really afraid of?*

'I hope you don't mind if we make this quick, Mrs ... *Miss* Riley,' says Mr Cockrun, offering me a chair and smiling his spiky jester smile. 'I know this is important to you so I've made time, but … well, look, how can I help?'

He takes a seat opposite and looks attentive, but I get the distinct impression he doesn't want to help at all.

I hear myself say, 'Yes, thank you for seeing me,' already beaten into gratitude.

Mr Cockrun moves his computer mouse around and squints at his computer screen. 'Where is he? Thomas, Thomas, Thomas … Kinnock.'

'Thomas *Riley*,' I correct. 'He's Thomas Riley now. The name should have been changed.'

Mr Cockrun looks up, nodding and smiling automatically. 'Yes, sure, sure. We'll get that changed. You've cut your hair.'

'My husband liked long hair,' I say, by way of explanation. 'Now we're separated, I have more choices.'

Mr Cockrun's eyes fall back to his computer. 'So what's the issue?'

'I'm extremely concerned,' I say. 'Tom came home from school with marks on his arm last week. They looked like *injection* marks. Blood spots with little bruises around them. He doesn't remember how he got them. Or if he does, he won't tell me. But Tom *always* tells me things. So I think he honestly doesn't remember. School is the only place he's away from me.' I leave a meaningful pause.

Mr Cockrun looks at me then, and for a moment his blue eyes swim with fear. 'Have you discussed this with anyone else?'

'What's that got to do with anything? I'm telling you my son had strange marks on his arms. They looked like *needle* marks.'

Mr Cockrun's expression shifts to mock concern. 'Mmm, yes. But ... perhaps your imagination is running away with you just a tad?'

For a moment I'm wrong-footed and unsure, just like I was with Olly. 'That's what the marks looked like,' I insist. 'The nurse in the drop-in clinic was concerned enough to make a report.'

'Well, I can assure you, Tom didn't get any marks like that here.' The headmaster stands. 'So if that's all—'

'He *must* have got those marks here,' I persist, resisting the urge to stand too. 'Tom is with me every moment of the day. This is the only place he's out of my sight.'

'It simply couldn't have happened here,' says Mr Cockrun. 'I just checked Tom's records. There's nothing. No mention of an injury.'

'Are you saying you watch over each and every child every minute?'

'We keep a very good eye on them.'

'What about his teacher? Maybe she knows something.'

'We're a little short on time, Miss Riley, so if you don't mind—'

'I'd like to speak to Tom's teacher,' I say. 'Can you bring her in here, please?'

'I'm afraid—'

'I won't leave until you do,' I say, my new haircut giving me strength.

The headmaster hesitates. Then he says, 'Fine, wait here. I'll get Mrs Dudley.'

He darts out of the office and returns with the greyish-haired woman I met before. Today she's just as awkwardly dressed in a pencil-skirt suit that makes a giant pear of her sizeable behind, feet large in mismatching brogues and a fashionable hoop necklace that would look better with jeans and a T-shirt.

'Mr Cockrun says you have some concerns.' Although Mrs Dudley's words seem calm, I sense tension behind them. 'But we cleared everything up the last time we spoke.'

'This isn't about the playground incident,' I say. 'Tom came home with marks on his arm. Very odd-looking pin-prick type marks.'

Mrs Dudley and Mr Cockrun exchange a meaningful look.

'It's impossible marks like that could have happened at school, isn't it?' says Mr Cockrun.

Mrs Dudley forces a concerned frown. 'Yes, impossible. Absolutely impossible.'

Mr Cockrun shakes his head. 'I mean, *injection* marks – the implications are very heavy indeed.'

Mrs Dudley's concern is mask-like. 'Have you asked Tom how he got them?'

'He doesn't remember,' I say. 'And I believe him. Tom is used to blocking things out. If you knew his father, you'd understand.'

The sentence hangs in the air, an unswept cobweb.

'Well, I hope we've put your mind at ease,' says Mrs Dudley. 'Something like that couldn't have happened here.'

'Indeed,' says Mr Cockrun again, his voice firmer now. 'We have extremely high levels of safeguarding. You only have to look at the building to know we keep the pupils protected.'

'Mr Cockrun works very hard on safeguarding,' says Mrs Dudley. 'He's turned this school around. Four years ago we were failing. Now we're exceptional. So let's not start accusing the school of … well …' She glances at Mr Cockrun. 'Silliness. It won't do anyone any good.'

'Quite,' says Mr Cockrun.

'Some of the parents were talking about bullying,' I say.

'*Every* child here is successfully managed,' Mr Cockrun interrupts. 'No matter where they come from.'

'Yes, yes,' Mrs Dudley quickly agrees. 'We've eradicated bullying in the school.'

'Tom *must* have got those marks at school,' I say, hands on hips.

'It's simply not possible,' says Mr Cockrun. 'Look, I don't see what we can do to reassure you further.'

'There's nothing more we can say.' Mrs Dudley glances at Mr Cockrun for approval. 'My advice is that you talk to your son again.'

I glare at them.

Mr Cockrun puts his hands together and tilts his head. 'Listen. Sometimes, when children start a new school, parents feel anxious. It's a big change. You're probably still adjusting yourself. I'll bet in a few days you'll think of an explanation for these little marks. Or Tom will tell you himself.'

'They looked like *injection* marks.'

Mr Cockrun nods understandingly. 'Probably as simple as brambles on the path. Something like that.'

'Brambles would cause a scratch. The marks were nothing like that.'

'Mrs Dudley will keep an extra close eye on Tom in class. Put your mind at ease.'

'Of course, Alan,' says Mrs Dudley. 'You have nothing to

worry about, Miss Riley. Support us and we'll support you. I imagine Tom just needs to settle in.'

'We'd better get on with things now, Miss Riley,' says Mr Cockrun, sitting and placing a hand on his computer mouse. 'Mrs Dudley will show you out.'

'But—'

'If you still have concerns in a month or so, we'll talk again.' He doesn't look up.

Suddenly it feels like before. With social services … and no one believing me.

I'm not going to let that happen again.

You're not taking this seriously. You all *need to take this seriously …*

'No,' I say. 'We're not finished. My son got these marks in your care. Yes, okay, there could be an explanation. Something less sinister than an injection needle. But until I *get* that explanation, I will be watching this school closely.'

Mr Cockrun smiles tightly. 'Well, that is your right as a mother. But most of the parents here feel grateful their child has a school place.'

After I'm shown out of the back entrance, I wander down the country path in a daze.

I think of Olly and everything he put us through. How fear can keep you from seeing the truth. And how the counsellor warned us that children with troubled pasts can become victims all over again.

Is someone frightening Tom into silence?

My phone bleeps and I see a text message.

Oh God. Olly's mother, Margaret. She's asking to see Tom.

We haven't met up since the move. It's been months. Too long, really.

Tom loves Olly's mum and so do I.

Margaret is very understanding about what we've been through, because she went through something similar with Olly's father. She was on our side in court. She knows Olly needs help. And she and Tom are best friends when they get together, laughing and gossiping.

I'd better arrange a visit.

Lizzie

The intercom buzzes. It's Olly's mother – coming for her weekly visit.

When I met Olly, I assumed he was from a typical snow-boarding rich-kid family.

But it's not true. Olly's family are ordinary. His mum lives in East London and works as a cashier on Bethnal Green Road. Her partner is a cab driver.

I've never met Olly's real dad, but I know he was a heavy drinker. Olly thinks he lives in France now, but he doesn't know for sure.

Olly and I used to bond over our messed-up parents. Two kids with hard upbringings. He always made me feel my mother was worse than his father. That I was more messed up. I used to believe him.

I don't any more.

Olly grins at the intercom. 'All right, Mum! I'll come down.'

He heads out of the flat, and a moment later I hear the clatter of Margaret coming upstairs.

'And then they tried to charge me an extra fifty p for one of those little plastic things of butter, so I said ...'

'Come on in, Mum.' Olly's accent changes when his mother

is around, losing its clipped edges. It's another unsettling reminder that sometimes I don't really know who he is.

I wonder where he got his other accent – the more refined one he uses with his snowboarder friends. When he started university? Or with the Olympic squad?

'Hi, Margaret.' I give an awkward wave.

'Hello, love.' Margaret is all smiley blue eyes, happy beneath a straw-yellow dyed fringe. 'How are you feeling? I brought you some ginger biscuits for the morning sickness.'

'She's fine now,' says Olly. 'She hasn't been sick in weeks.'

'Oh, you men don't understand how it comes and goes. She might be fine one minute, in the loo the next. I'll leave the biscuits here. Just in case. So, what have you two been up to this morning?' Margaret looks around the flat. 'A bit of tidying up?'

Olly and I look at each other, this morning's fight stomping around the room like an elephant.

'Yeah, just trying to clean the house up a bit,' says Olly.

It's true – Olly did clean the bathroom earlier. Before collapsing on the sofa in pain. I dithered in the living area, unsure what to clear and where to clear it.

If I put things in the wrong places, Olly shouts.

'He's good, isn't he?' Margaret says, giving me a big wink. 'Wish his dad had been a modern man. The only help I ever got was a telling off if dinner was late. And sometimes a clip around the ear.' She hesitates. 'I'll say this for your stepdad, Olly. At least he's never laid a finger on me.'

Olly and I share an awkward glance.

Olly's father was violent to Margaret. I suppose aggression runs in the family. Margaret left him for a cab driver called

Freddy. Freddy is a rude, sexist pig, but he doesn't hit women, so in Margaret's eyes he's wonderful.

'I brought you boiled eggs for lunch,' Margaret announces, rummaging in her huge shopping bag.

'You're staying for lunch?' I ask, feeling myself smile. I like Margaret being here. Olly is always on best behaviour when his mother visits. 'That's lovely.'

Margaret smiles back. 'How's the nurse's training going, love? Still sticking at it?'

'I gave it up,' I say. 'I was slipping behind so I had to make a choice. Helping Olly recover is more important.'

Olly says tightly, 'You slipping behind is nothing to do with my leg.'

'I didn't mean ... Oh, never mind.' I shake my head.

Margaret looks between the two of us. 'Well, I hope Olly is looking after you,' she says. 'You're doing a lot. Taking care of the house. And being pregnant makes you tired enough.'

'He does look after me,' I say, my eyes finding his. 'Most of the time.'

Olly's gaze softens. 'I just want to get better, Lizzie. That's all.'

'I know you do.'

I manage a smile. But it's a dishonest one. Pretty gift wrap for ugly feelings.

Secretly, I want to tell Margaret how Olly is behind closed doors. That he might be much more like his father than she realises. That aggression runs in the family ...

Would she believe me? Would she stand up to him?

I don't know.

Kate

3.47 p.m.

'Leanne Neilson's boyfriend has just been done for assault,' says Tessa. It's casual, as if she's telling me it's going to rain later.

I look up over rectangular glasses, fingers tightening around my biro. 'Oh no. What? When?'

'It was in the newspapers. Didn't you see?'

'No. I don't read the news. I have enough drama at work.'

Tessa snorts. 'Too right! You'll need to speak to the Child Protection Unit. John Simmons is the one you want.'

'I've already spoken to him. After Lloyd put Pauly in hospital. We're still working out next steps. I'll call him again.'

'How did the Tom Kinnock visit go?'

'I haven't had time to make the visit yet.'

'I suppose he isn't in any immediate danger.'

'Actually, there's been a report from the Radley Road drop-in centre—'

'It shouldn't have even been *transferred* over to us.' Tessa raises her voice to drown me out. 'They should have shut it down at the London end. The father has supervised visits. It's done and dusted. Get it off the books and you'll be down to thirty cases.'

'No, *listen*,' I say. 'There's been new information. From a nurse at the Radford Road drop-in centre. The information came late, just like everything else around here. The drop-in centre is overworked too. Anyway, the nurse found marks on Tom's arm a few days ago – the sort you get from an injection needle. The mother thinks it happened at Steelfield School.'

'Surely not.' Tessa narrows her eyes. 'Are you certain you're not getting the records mixed up? You said yourself they were a mess.'

'I've spoken to the nurse.'

'Well, if you don't tackle the Neilsons today, you'll be on a disciplinary, I'm telling you. It's got statutory obligation written all over it.'

'But Tom Kinnock has suspected *needle marks*,' I say. 'If I have to work late, I'll work late. He needs a section forty-seven—'

'Risk of significant harm?' Tessa snorts. 'Over a few pin pricks? What if he did them himself with a biro? Listen, Kate. You're young. New here. But you need to prioritise. Or you'll burn out, just like Dawn and Kirsty. They worked late every night too, you know.'

'All the children in my caseload are important,' I say. 'I can't choose one over another.'

'You'll learn.' Tessa slots a tablet into her Nespresso machine and waits while hot water steams and bubbles.

She has never once offered me a cup of tea or coffee, despite me making her countless cappuccinos.

'I should talk to Tom's teacher,' I say.

'I wouldn't bother,' says Tessa. 'Parents always blame the school, the doctor, the child minder – anyone they can think of. But look at the facts.'

'I can't totally rule out the school,' I say. 'I've heard odd things about Steelfield from Pauly and Lloyd Neilson. The headmaster doesn't sound quite right.'

'Those Neilson boys are trying to blame the school too. I told you, they all do it.'

'So how could Tom Kinnock have got needle marks?'

'Maybe he's a self-harmer,' Tessa suggests. 'He's come out of a messy divorce, hasn't he? Angry father. Lots of stress. Listen – the Neilsons are your priority. I'm telling you, if that mother overdoses with the boys in the house, there'll be national press coverage. We'll be shaken upside down for it. Disciplinary hearings, left, right and centre. The new government even want prison sentences.'

'I can't ignore this drop-in centre report either. We'll be shaken up and down for that too. I'm damned if I do, damned if I don't.'

'Welcome to the public sector. You can't do it all, Kate. You just can't. Take it from someone who knows. Any minute now, your phone will ring and you'll have to deal with some emergency or other.'

Tessa stalks off towards the doughnuts. She grabs two, taking a big bite of one as she walks away. Tessa is on a diet today, but she seems to think food eaten with her back to people doesn't count.

A sad part of me knows Tessa is right about prioritising. If I keep working like this, I'll end up with chronic fatigue like Kirsty.

I'm about to book the Tom Kinnock visit into the computer diary when the phone rings.

It's Lloyd Neilson, calling from Leanne's mobile. Leanne has locked herself in the bathroom. Lloyd is worried she might have taken another overdose. He's distraught, crying and hysterical.

'Please … help us, Kate. *Please.*'

This is a side of Lloyd most people don't see. He loves his mum, despite the fact she couldn't care less about him. And he loves his brothers too, even though he occasionally beats the living daylights out of them.

I listen to Lloyd, while simultaneously attempting to book the Tom Kinnock appointment into the diary.

Then my screen goes black.

The system has gone down again.

'Bloody buggering hell!' Tessa shouts from her office. 'When are they going to upgrade this software? That's just what we need. A lost day of work.'

I stare at the blank screen, resisting the urge to pick up the computer and throw it out of the window.

Calm down, Kate. You can't damage office equipment. We don't have enough resources as it is.

Lizzie

'Have you travelled far?' Margaret offers a cautious smile, pouring tea from a brown-speckled pot. She's wearing a long, ankle-length floral dress. Bleached-blonde hair flows around her shoulders.

Olly's mother has never left the 1970s, fashion-wise. I suppose it was the decade she felt her best. Before everything went wrong with Olly's father.

It's Saturday and we've agreed to meet in the Hyde Park pavilion – miles from Olly's flat, and miles from my new house, although Margaret doesn't know how many miles.

Neutral ground.

Anonymous.

'Not too far.'

A young waitress in jeans and a black apron clinks another teapot onto the table. 'Fruit tea?' the waitress asks.

'Thank you,' I reply. 'And there was a juice too.'

'Oh. Right.' The waitress puts a hand to her forehead. 'For the little boy. Sorry. I forgot.'

Tom sits on Margaret's lap playing with Duplo bricks, sorting them into colours. Tom's too old for Duplo now, but these are the only toys the café has and he's a good boy, not making a fuss.

Tom talks about colours as he sorts: 'This one is *green*. Another *blue*.'

Margaret gives me a look. She knows what colours mean. 'Are you feeling a bit out of sorts, Tom?' she asks, cuddling him extra tight. 'Must be a bit strange. We haven't seen each other in a while, and now we're meeting up in this new place.'

'I like the café,' says Tom. 'I've missed you, Granny.'

Margaret gives the waitress a joyous smile. 'This is my grandson.'

The waitress feigns interest. 'That's nice.'

'Isn't he lovely?' says Margaret. 'I've really missed him.' She turns to me. 'And I've missed you too, Lizzie. I been worrying so much. It's a lot you're taking on: new house, new life. I've been where you are, love. Making a new start. It's hard. How have you been?'

'Really busy,' I say. 'With the house move and everything – it's been hard to keep on top of things.'

'So, have you moved out of London?' Margaret asks.

'I can't tell you that,' I say. 'I'm sorry. In case you accidentally mention something. I don't want Olly knowing where we live.'

'I'd never tell Olly where you are. You know that, love.'

'I know. Not on purpose. But sometimes things slip out.'

'You cut your hair. That's a big change. It looks lovely.'

'Yes.' My hand goes to my new short haircut. It's been neatened by the hairdresser and I'm growing more pleased with it by the day. It suits my face, actually. I have delicate features, like a ballet dancer. I was drowning in the long hair Olly liked.

'This isn't such a bad place, is it?' Margaret gestures to the café, with its huge windows and wrought iron tables. 'A bit expensive, but you can't have everything.'

'We can't stay long,' I say. 'Sorry. Tom has a doctor's appointment later.'

'Oh?' says Margaret.

'We're still trying to find out why he had the seizure.'

'I thought they said it was a one-off.' Margaret rearranges Tom so she can dig into a huge shopping bag placed by her plimsolls.

'Yes. But he hasn't been right since he had it. He's dazed sometimes. Disorientated. Zonked out. He goes to bed so early and he had a terrible nosebleed.'

'I've got a few bits and pieces in here,' says Margaret. '*Transformers* magazine. A few other things. We've got a lot of catching up to do.'

'Tom,' I say. 'Say thank you.'

Tom blinks blue eyes. 'Thank you so much, Granny. You always get me the best things. You always know.'

Margaret's face crumples. 'Have you missed your old Granny then?'

'Yes,' says Tom. 'You're like a big rainbow. All different colours.'

'Oi, less of the big!' Margaret chuckles. 'How long do I get to see you today? Is there time for a play in the park?'

Tom looks at me, and I give the tiniest shake of my head. 'We have to see the doctor.'

'Sorry, Granny,' says Tom.

'Oh, come on,' Margaret colludes. 'Just a little play.'

'I'm sorry, Margaret,' I say. 'We'll arrange a longer visit soon. We've just been so busy.'

'All right, love. I know it's tough, fitting everything in.' Margaret arranges her presents on the table. 'How's your new school, Tom? Making lots of friends? Have you got yourself a best mate yet?'

'Sort of,' says Tom. 'There's this boy in my class – Pauly Neilson. He's looking out for me.'

'He's a little thug,' I say.

'He's okay,' Tom insists. 'I just have to keep on the right side of him. The kids that don't ... his big brother comes after them.'

'They're trouble, Tom,' I say.

Tom's pale forehead creases. 'They're not really. Well, not much. They're too scared of the headmaster.'

'You should stay away from those boys, Tom. Meet some other kids.'

'Is he a bit cheeky then? This Pauly?' Margaret probes, grinning and showing black spaces around her molars.

Tom takes a big sip of juice. 'Yeah.'

'Like your mum says, just stay out of trouble,' says Margaret, wagging a finger. 'Your dad was a bit naughty at school, you know.'

Tom's juice carton slips from his fingers. It falls onto the table, watery orange squirting from the straw.

'Sorry.' Margaret clutches Tom tight. 'I shouldn't have ... Sorry. So, this new school of yours, Tom, it's an academy or something, isn't it? How does that all work? Do you learn the same things?'

Tom slides off Margaret's lap and comes to sit with me, his hand taking mine. I hold it tight to stop it shaking.

'It's hard to remember,' says Tom, voice quiet. 'I think ... we have to say things over and over again sometimes. Like about honour and promising to follow the rules. And … I don't remember.'

'And you're well, are you, Tom?' Margaret asks.

'Yes,' says Tom.

'He hasn't been totally well,' I say. 'Not since the seizure.'

There's an awkward silence, and I know Margaret wants to tell me something.

'Sweetheart, do you want to find more Duplo bricks?' I ask Tom. 'While Granny and I chat?' Obediently, Tom hops down and begins quietly sweeping Duplo bricks together. 'Come on, Margaret,' I say, trying for a smile. 'Out with it. I always know when you want to talk about Olly.'

'I saw him last week,' says Margaret, eyes apologetic. 'I know he's done wrong, but he misses Tom terribly.'

'That's his problem. He should have thought of that before he did what he did.'

'I know,' says Margaret, kind eyes meeting mine. 'I know that. I'm on your side. But he's getting help.'

'From what I hear, people with anger issues rarely change.' I don't mean to raise my voice, but for goodness sake – she was *there* in court. She heard all the details.

Tom's head snaps in our direction, and I lower my voice to a whisper. 'Tom still has nightmares about Olly. He's terrified of him, and rightly so.'

'I know you've both been through the wringer,' says Margaret. 'I know he did wrong. More than wrong. But for-giveness—'

'As long as I'm still breathing, Olly is coming nowhere near my son,' I say. 'Tom doesn't want to see his father. And it's his right to decide. Social services and the courts assured us of that. There is no way I'm setting up visitation. I'm getting organised. The house is coming to order. I'm doing everything on my own. We're leaving the bad times behind us.'

'Maybe in time you can forgive,' says Margaret.

'Forgive?' I snap. 'You know what happened to Tom under Olly's care. I'll never forgive him. Or myself.'

I break down then, words choking in my throat.

Margaret looks at her white fingers, clenched tight around her tea mug. I know she feels bad about Olly's upbringing. 'I'm sorry I brought it up,' she says. 'It was thoughtless. You're right. You can't forgive and forget. Not after what he did.'

On the way home, we stop at the shopping precinct. There is a little pharmacy here, next to a flower shop.

I'm often picking up bits from the pharmacy, but this time I buy something new – a box of platinum-blonde peroxide.

We've moved house. I've changed my clothes. Cut my hair. Now it's time for something bolder.

It's only a change in hair colour. But it symbolises something bigger.

I am a new person without Olly. Capable. Confident.

This is a fresh start.

Kate

Mascara. Should it be all stiff and gritty like this? Does makeup have a sell-by date? I suppose I haven't used it in a while. Probably not since university, now I come to think about it. Oh well.

And this lipstick … it's bubble-gum pink, given to me by a blonde friend years ago. I don't think it suits me, but I'm not about to go and *buy* a lipstick. I only ever wear it a few times a year – today being one such special occasion.

Happy Birthday, Kate. Twenty-six today.

Monday isn't the ideal day for a birthday but Col and I are making the best of it with a rare night out.

I assess my reflection in the work toilet mirror.

Harsh strip-lighting, coupled with a lack of windows, gives my face a 'cyber ghost' effect, turning my skin ash-white and eyebrows see-through. It's impossible to see where 'plain' ends and 'too much makeup' begins.

Col, of course, is unlikely to notice my makeup. He notices very little about my appearance, except when I'm wearing a particular green jumper he likes – one that's tight around the bosom.

Right. Makeup (badly) done. Now to change in the toilet cubicle.

I can't use the extra-large disabled cubicle, since I'm not disabled. So I opt for the normal-sized one and end up noisily bumping my elbows and knees against walls, trying to climb into my dress.

Yes, I'm wearing a dress.

But it's just a plain shift with no patterns or embellishments.

I don't have any sheer or tan tights, so I'm wearing the same thick, black tights I wear to work, coupled with flat black sandals. Technically, the sandals are summer sandals and should be worn with sheer or no tights. But they are the nearest I have to going-out shoes.

I think I can get away with it. It's nice having a husband with low standards. He'll be delighted just to see me showing my legs.

Right.

Beside me, I hear a cubicle door open and close, and then the sound of a woman huffing and puffing, sitting heavily on the loo.

Tessa.

There is an audible groan, then what sounds like a bucket of pig slops being emptied into the toilet.

I hurriedly strap on my shoes and leave the cubicle, unnerved by this unexpected intimacy with my red-faced manager.

Do I need to wash my hands? I've *entered* a toilet cubicle, although not *used* the toilet. I hate it when there's no clear protocol.

I decide on a quick hand-wash. But before I've managed to use the snazzy new vertical hand drier, Tessa comes crashing out of the cubicle, even redder in the face than usual.

She gives a little start when she sees me. 'I thought you'd gone for the day,' she says, busying herself with hand-washing. 'What on earth are you doing still hanging around? You're going out this evening, aren't you?' She looks me up and down and snorts. 'To a funeral, by the looks of things. I thought you church-goers were supposed to like bright colours. What have you got – a church social or something?'

'It's my birthday, actually,' I say. 'We church-goers have them too.'

'Oh, stop being so touchy,' Tessa replies. 'Can't you take a joke? For goodness sake. I'm starting to feel sorry for that boyfriend of yours.'

'Husband.'

'I hope *he* can take a joke. Now listen – before you shoot off, remember the meeting tomorrow, nine a.m. sharp.'

'What meeting?'

'The strategy meeting. Don't tell me you'd forgotten.'

'I hadn't forgotten. That meeting is on Friday.'

'No. It got moved. Didn't Gary tell you?'

'No. He didn't tell me. Tomorrow morning I'm booked in to visit Tom Kinnock—'

'You can't miss the strategy meeting. The paediatrician can't do any other time and he's vital.'

I stare at myself in the mirror, feeling the stupidity of makeup. *No evening out for you, Kate. Not even on your birthday.*

'I'll have to do the Tom Kinnock visit now then,' I say.

'What?' Tessa demands.

'Tom Kinnock. I'll need to visit him this evening. It's six o'clock. There's still time.'

'What's your boyfriend going to say about that?'

'*Husband*. I imagine he'll be upset, Tessa. But not half as upset as if I end up on a disciplinary for failing in my duty of care.'

Lizzie

A knock at the door. I'm perched on the Chesterfield sofa-arm, laptop on my knee.

Tom dozes beside me. He fell asleep in front of the TV, zonked out after a long Monday at school, so *tired* these days.

'Who is it?' I call out, voice stiff and suspicious.

'Mrs Kinnock?' It's a woman's voice. An official-sounding woman.

I stand on elephant slippers, as I push my laptop onto the bookshelf.

With some trepidation, I open the door.

A girl with curly black hair stands on the doorstep. I'm surprised by how young she looks, given the maturity of her voice. She wears an odd mixture of clothing – a smart, sleeveless shift dress, cheap charm bracelet, thick black tights and summer sandals. There's something about her makeup that reminds me of a little girl playing dress-up.

'Can I help you?' I ask.

'Hello, Miss Riley.' She reaches out to shake my hand. Her voice is clipped and direct. No nonsense. 'My name is Kate Noble. I'm from Child Services. Excuse the unannounced visit, but the phone number we had for you didn't work. I *did* send a letter. Can I come in?'

I return her handshake, my fingers stiff. 'I'm Lizzie.'

'Did you get our letter?'

'I did get something in the post,' I admit, remembering the brown envelope from a few weeks ago, still unopened and shoved next to the bread bin. 'I haven't read it yet. Sorry.'

'Can I come in?' Kate rearranges her leather folder. 'There are a few things I'd like to discuss.'

'I'm guessing about the walk-in clinic? Yes, I'd like to discuss that too.'

Kate meets my eye. 'Can I come inside?'

'Shouldn't you have someone else with you? A family support worker or something?'

'No. Not for a standard visit.'

I step back. 'Okay. Well, come in. Tom's sleeping on the sofa.'

'That's all right.' Kate looks around. 'This is beautiful. Very light. I love the sweeping staircase. And all the plants.'

Realising that the only furniture we have to sit on is the occupied sofa, an island on a parquet-wood sea, Kate says, 'I'll just sit on the floor.'

'I can get you a chair from upstairs?'

'No, honestly. It's fine.' Kate kneels in front of Tom, crossing her sandals awkwardly under herself. 'Okay. Let's start from the beginning. What do you like to be called? Elizabeth? Miss Riley?'

'You can call me Lizzie.' I perch back on the sofa arm.

'The original plan was to do a sign-off visit,' Kate explains, 'just to check how you were coping on your own. And then bring this case to a close. But we had a report I'd like to talk about. The drop-in clinic report. I'm sure you're aware, the nurse noticed some unusual marks on Tom's arm last week.'

'Yes. I know. I've spoken to the school, but no one will tell me anything. Tom hasn't been well since he started at that place. And he's been acting so strangely.'

'Children can act up when they're stressed,' says Kate. 'Starting a new school is scary. Before you know it he'll be a teenager with his shirt hanging out, acting more strangely than you could possibly imagine.'

'This school is scarier than most. Trust me.'

'Do *you* have any idea how he got these marks?'

'None. And believe me, I've considered every possibility. School is the only time he's away from me. I've spoken to his teacher. The headmaster. They've just sort of written the marks off. "Couldn't possibly have happened in our care." The school ... it's a funny place. Ideally, I'd like to move him somewhere else.'

Kate frowns. 'I wouldn't recommend that. I'm sorry to put it this way, but if you moved your son again so soon, it would look like you had something to hide. Troubled families often move a lot. I'm sure you don't want to be tarnished with that brush.'

'No. I absolutely don't.'

'Has Tom seen his father since you moved? He's supposed to have supervised visitation—'

'Tom doesn't want to see his father. That supercedes everything.'

'So there's no relationship?'

'Olly doesn't even know where we live.' I look at my tea mug, brown liquid quivering against porcelain. 'He's dangerous.'

'So there's been no contact since the move? Not even phone calls?'

'Nothing.'

'Does Tom have other carers, in addition to yourself?'

'He sees both his grandmothers. No one else. The only time he's away from me is at school.'

'I'd like a quick look at Tom's arm, if I may,' says Kate.

'Yes, of course.' I put a gentle hand on Tom's shoulder, shaking him awake. 'Tom. Can you wake up for me, love? Just for a minute. I need to pull your sleeve up.'

Tom turns on the sofa, blinking sleepy eyes.

'Is everything okay, Mum?' he asks.

'It's fine, love. This is Kate. She's a social worker.'

'Hello, Tom.'

Gently, I pull back the blanket, warm from his body.

'I'm just going to show Kate these marks on your arm.'

Tom's skin glimmers, pale and clear, as I slide up his Transformers pyjama sleeve.

Kate leans closer, peering through her plain, wire glasses.

There are two teeny, tiny scabs on Tom's arm now, no bigger than grains of sand. One mark has completely healed.

'Was it this arm?' Kate asks, looking to me for affirmation. Then she checks her notes and reminds herself: 'Yes, it was.'

'They're nearly gone now,' I say. 'They were much more pronounced before.'

'I should have got to you sooner,' says Kate, shaking her head. 'And arranged for a paediatrician.'

'The nurse at the clinic—'

'A proper paediatrician should have checked it over.'

'I did take him to our GP,' I say. 'She brushed it off, just like the school did. Too busy. Kate … can I call you that?'

'Of course.'

'The marks on Tom's arms ... he *must* have got them at school. There's no other time he's away from me. I don't let him out of my sight. I don't know if he's being bullied, or ... He's hanging out with some rough kids right now. And the school *does* seem a little ... odd. They won't let parents in during the day and there's a locked medical cabinet in the headmaster's office and CCTV cameras and *bars* on the windows—'

Kate interrupts. 'Do you mind if I ask you a few questions?'

I wipe red, swollen eyes. 'Yes. Yes, go ahead.'

'Is it just you and Tom living here at the moment?'

'Yes.'

'Tom's father ... you're separated?'

'Yes.'

'Are you working at the minute?'

'I will be soon. I'm looking for a job.'

'And how is Tom doing? Is he a good boy? Well-behaved?'

'He's perfect.'

'But unwell sometimes? That must be tiring. Especially now you're on your own.'

Our eyes lock, and I know what she's getting at.

Are you exhausted? Fed up with your sick child? Taking your aggression out on him?

'I love my son,' I tell Kate, my eyes defiant. 'I would never hurt him. I'll never forgive myself for what Olly did. But that's behind us now.'

'And you have no idea what could have caused the marks, Miss Riley?'

I shake my head, trying not to cry. 'I've been obsessing over them. Considered every possibility. They *must* have happened at school.'

Lizzie

'Here you go, gorgeous.' Olly slides back a railway-sleeper bench and gestures for me to sit. I'm eight-months' pregnant now. Olly doesn't know how uncomfortable I'll feel sitting on hard wood, and I'm too polite to tell him.

There are tea-towel napkins and tin cans of cutlery on the table. Very casual. This restaurant is built in a conservatory, with a vegetable garden growing outside. Olly thinks it's my favourite place to eat. But actually, it's his favourite place.

I barely know my own tastes any more.

People from difficult families seek other difficult people, isn't that what they say? I think about that sometimes. My mother. Olly. Out of the frying pan and into the fire.

Little by little, my personality has been sucked into Olly's. He took my mind first, my body second. I didn't realise what was happening until it was far, far too late. When Olly's bad side surfaced, he'd already broken down all my defences.

And now he has me. All of me.

To do with what he will.

I've married my mother.

Taking a seat, I wonder if the other diners have noticed how red my eyes are. Will the waiting staff guess I've been crying?

Olly unfolds a napkin and lays it over my lap, putting a

139

casual hand on my baby bump and giving it a little stroke. He does this with tenderness and caring. Like he really loves me. Loves us. Then he sits opposite and takes my hand.

These are my favourite times with Olly. It's almost worth the arguments to see this side of him. Because like day follows night, praise and adoration follow darkness and rage.

I notice other female diners looking at Olly. He's never been short of female attention – his friends have told me all the stories. But his girlfriends didn't last long, apparently. Until I came along.

Olly squeezes my fingers. I flinch, biting my lip.

Olly says, 'You are so unbelievably beautiful. Do you know that?'

I take my hands back to pick up the menu, printed on thick, grey recycled card.

My ring finger throbs. I'm scared it might be broken. Olly again. Careless. Shutting that car door on my hand. Just a mistake …

'Lizzie?' Olly pushes the menu down, blue eyes meeting mine. 'I'm sorry.'

I wonder how long his good mood will last for this time. He sits back, and I realise my hands are shaking uncontrollably.

A woman at the next table glances over. She whispers something to her dining companion, then looks again.

I slide my hair from behind my ears to cover my frightened face.

'Are you ready to order, gorgeous?' Olly asks me, waving the waiter over.

'Oh … um. Not quite.' I try for a more natural smile, but the edges of my eyes are tight. 'You know what's good here. I'll have whatever you're having.'

Olly turns to the waitress – a young girl in a black apron who's just appeared at the table. 'My beautiful fiancée here will have the sea bass,' he tells her, all puffed up with the control I've given him.

I wonder if Olly knows that often I don't like what he orders.

I suppose a better question is: does he care?

Kate

6.30 a.m.

I hold a Tupperware tub of Kellogg's All-Bran in one hand, an apple in the other. No milk, but I bought two pints yesterday so there should be plenty in the work fridge. Breakfast in the office again.

'Good morning,' I call out, praying Tessa isn't here yet.

'Who's that?' Tessa calls from her corner office.

Oh no.

Tessa's door is open. I see her savaging a giant chocolate croissant, pastry exploding over her keyboard. Several empty cappuccino cups decorate her desk.

'Hi Tessa.' I sit on my thinly padded swivel chair.

'*Who* is it?' Tessa barks, leaning back, affording herself a full view.

I give a little wave.

'Oh, it's you.' Tessa considers this, then takes another bite of croissant, more pastry flakes exploding. 'Here to prepare for the multi-disciplinary meeting? I was worried you'd let me down on that.'

'I'm writing up last night's Tom Kinnock visit.'

'Oh, *Kate*.' Tessa lays on some parental sounding disappointment. 'Failing to plan—'

'Is planning to fail. Yes, I know. That was one of my catchphrases at university. But if I don't write up the Kinnock visit now, I could forget important details. This case has been messed around enough. I want to do it properly.'

An understatement.

The Tom Kinnock documents make me, a compulsively organised person, feel physically sick.

It's like someone has jumbled everything up on purpose.

Ten different social workers have been involved with the Kinnock family. Seven left without doing a proper handover.

Patchy information. Missing reports. No wonder the custody decision took so long.

Suddenly, there's a slap of papers and Tessa looms over me, hands on hips. 'You need to read through all sixty pages in the next half hour, Kate, or there'll be hell to pay. They've *finally* shared Leanne Neilson's medical records. She's been at that doctors' surgery every week, near enough, making up story after story. It's all there. She brought in the older boy, saying he gets backache.'

'I can only do one thing at a time, Tessa,' I say, pushing the report bundles to one side. 'Tom seemed tired during my visit,' I murmur, tapping my keyboard. 'The house was somewhat chaotic, washing-up in the sink …'

I can't type without talking out loud. It's one of my most irritating habits, especially when I'm in a shared office space. Even if I try really hard, sounds come out.

'What's that?' Tessa asks, reading over my shoulder. 'Next steps … visiting Tom Kinnock's school? *This* week? What's the *school* going to tell you? He's only been there five minutes.'

'The usual sort of thing. How Tom is in class. Whether he turns up on time. If he seems withdrawn. But I also want to ask about the marks on Tom's arm.'

'How could he have got them at school?' asks Tessa. 'If they were injection marks.'

'The marks had faded by my visit,' I say. 'We don't know anything for certain.'

If Tessa hears the disappointment in my voice, she doesn't show it. 'So, what? You think someone at school is stabbing Tom Kinnock with needles?'

'I have to consider every possibility. If this was a school prank or a dare or something, we could consider closing the case down. There would be reasonable cause.'

Tessa's eyes light up. 'Yes. Yes, I see what you're saying.'

I feel like I've just offered Tessa a slice of cake. But it's cake with a slightly shitty centre, because I doubt there'll be any conclusive proof Tom got those marks at school.

'I wouldn't be doing my job properly if I didn't meet Tom's teacher,' I say.

'If you want to do a proper job, you're in the wrong profession,' Tessa snorts. 'Oh, by the way.' She glances at my Tupperware tub of All-Bran. 'I used all the milk.'

Lizzie

'Hey, Tommo.' I wave, feeling small and invisible in the crowd of parent pick-ups at the school gates.

Tom is on the far side of the playground. *Who's he talking to?*

Pauly Neilson.

Actually, talking is the wrong word. Pauly looms over Tom, a proprietary hand on his shoulder. Tom is making little frightened rabbit nods, while Pauly talks and gestures.

There was gossip about the Neilson family at the school gates this morning. Apparently, the police were called to the Neilson house again after a domestic between Leanne and her boyfriend.

'Tom!' I call out again. 'Hey, Tom! I'm here, love.'

Tom looks up.

Pauly slaps him hard on the back. Tom nods, giving a meek smile. Then he walks towards me, a tired walk, feet barely lifting off the tarmac.

'Hi, Mum.'

'Everything okay?' I ask. 'What were you and Pauly talking about?'

'Huh?' Tom makes a furtive glance over his shoulder. 'Nothing. Just … nothing.'

'You know you can tell me anything, don't you?'

'I don't need to tell you anything.'

'Mums fix things. If you're having any problems …'

'I'm not.'

I decide to lighten the mood. 'Guess what?'

'What?'

'I went shopping today.' I hold up bags. 'Here are the shoes you wanted, and some fun stuff for dinner.'

'Cool!' Tom grabs one bag and pulls out the Nike shoebox. His face crumples. 'These aren't the ones.' He stuffs the box back in the bag. 'These are like … skater shoes. I want ones like Pauly wears for PE. Orange ones.'

'What about "thank you very much"?' I say.

'Thanks, Mum.'

'I can always swap them,' I say. 'But orange is too bright for school.'

'I want orange ones.'

'No, Tom.' I have no intention of buying him bright orange sports shoes. First, I'm sure the school won't like it. They're very strict on dress code. *Very* strict. And second, I don't want him looking like Pauly Neilson.

'So, what did you get for dinner?' Tom asks.

'Fun picnic stuff. I know it's a little chilly but the sun's still out. I thought we'd go to the park and eat Nutella sandwiches.'

The eldest Neilson brother, Lloyd, shoots past on a green BMX, spraying bark chips as he bikes across the flowerbeds at an insane speed.

His head has been shaved at the sides with zigzag tramlines, and he darts his bike back and forth, eyes wide and manic.

I notice a smudge behind his ear. No, not a smudge – a bruise. *Funny place to have a bruise.*

'Aall riiight, Tom!' he yells, words a little slurred and sort of garbled. It's the same kind of slurry speech his mother had when I met her at the school gates and I wonder if he's on something. 'Toooo ... morrow, ye-ah?'

'Yes, okay.' Tom gives another meek little smile.

'You play with Pauly's older brother?' I ask.

'Not *play*. Sometimes he talks to us. We're like his foot soldiers.'

'Broaden your friendship net a bit. Keep your options open.'

'I don't get to choose,' says Tom. 'You don't, with Lloyd.'

'He had a funny bruise behind his ear,' I say. 'Did you notice it?'

'What?'

'A bruise. Lloyd had a bruise behind his ear. Strange place to have one. How do you think he got it?'

'Lloyd doesn't like talking about that kind of stuff.'

'What stuff?'

'He gets in trouble with Mr Cockrun if he talks.'

'What? Why on earth would he get in trouble?'

'Mr Cockrun is funny. You never know *what* you're gonna get in trouble for.'

'You haven't been in trouble, have you?' I ask. 'With the headmaster?'

Tom kicks a stone. 'Not *trouble*. I've been to his office.'

'Why?'

'He wanted to tell me the school rules. He said we mustn't talk about the school to other people. I have to be a nice boy and then everything will be okay.'

'Mustn't talk?'

'We can *talk* but we have to say nice things. We're a family. You don't say bad things about your family.'

'This doesn't sound right, Tom. I should talk to him again.'

'*No!*'

'But Tom—'

'Mr Cockrun helps us, Mum. He listens to me. Mr Cockrun is *nice*.'

We walk in silence for a bit, me wondering if Mr Cockrun is some sort of hypnotist, and then I say, 'So, how about this picnic? Nutella sandwiches?'

'No thanks.'

'But you *love* Nutella sandwiches.'

'No I don't.' Tom's voice is suddenly manic. Like Lloyd Neilson. 'I never eat them. They're for babies.'

'Oh, come on. They're your favourite!'

'Shut up!'

I take a step back. What has happened to my son?

'Tom,' I say. 'You need to apologise.'

Tom puts his head down and mumbles, 'Sorry.'

I hear myself demand: 'If you hate Nutella sandwiches, how come you ask for them in your lunchbox every other day?'

'I don't.'

'You do. Oh, Tom. I know you're growing up, but those Neilson boys ... Anyway, look – shall I carry your rucksack?'

I go to take his school bag, but Tom whirls away from me. 'No.'

There's a dark tone to his voice.

'What?'

'Just don't touch my bag.' Tom stalks ahead.

In two large strides I catch him, grabbing his school bag, skidding on loose stones.

'Get *off*,' Tom protests. 'Get off me.'

'*Tom!* I'm your *mother*. What's going on? Let me see.'

'No.' Tom tries to pull away.

I'm too quick, though. Ripping open the cord, I dig my hand into the black nylon and rummage around. 'What's in here? What are you trying to hide?'

'*Nothing*.'

My fingers close around something smooth and curved. 'Tom. What's this?' I pull out a plastic bottle. It's one of two brown bottles we got from the hospital after Tom's seizure. Blood-thinning meds. 'This is a medicine bottle. *Your* prescription medicine. Why on earth is it in your school bag? And *why is it empty*?'

Tom watches me in silence.

'What's going on, Tom? Why did you bring this to school?'

More silence.

I'm scared now. 'We're not having any picnic food!' I shout. 'Nothing like that. Not unless you tell me what's going on at that school.' I grab his hand roughly and pull him down the path, repeating my threat over and over.

But he won't answer.

'Is it one of those Neilson boys?' I demand, as we reach our front door. 'Is Pauly putting you up to things? Or Lloyd?'

Silence.

I try a different tactic.

'Lloyd had a bruise near his ear. Or some kind of mark. Did you notice?'

'His stepdad did it, probably. It's nothing.'

'Nothing? He got a mark like that from his stepdad and you think that's nothing?'

Tom seems about to say something, then thinks better of it, snapping his mouth closed.

'What's going on at that school, Tom?' I demand.

Tom becomes sullen again. 'Nothing.'

'*Tell me!*'

'Okay, okay.' Tom doesn't look at me. 'Someone asked me to bring the medicine in.'

'*Who?*'

'Someone. They wanted to look at it, so I brought it in.'

'It's *your* medicine. No one else should have it – that's dangerous. You must never, *ever* take medicine from home again. *Ever*. Promise me. *Promise me*!'

Tom runs straight up to his bedroom.

I follow him, standing over his bed, shouting: 'Why, *why* did you take it? Don't you understand it's dangerous? This is *your* medication. Talk to me, Tom. *Talk* to me.'

But he just pulls his duvet over his head, not saying a word.

I spend the evening going up and down the stairs, pleading with Tom, then eventually bursting into angry tears.

Tom is such a sensitive little boy. Usually when I cry, he gives me a hug.

But today, nothing.

It's like he's been body-snatched, and I feel so, so afraid.

What's happening to my son?

Kate

I'm sitting alone in the Steelfield School music room among broken-stringed violins and tom-tom drums, feeling stress tugging at my ribcage.

The headmaster refused his office for my meeting with Tom's class teacher, so I'm seated on an orange plastic chair in an outbuilding in the middle of the school field.

Tom's teacher *still* hasn't turned up. I check my watch again.

Come on, Mrs Dudley. Hurry up.

I'm wasting time I don't have and Tessa is going to lynch me. Then I hear movement outside.

This must be her.

There is shuffling outside the door. Then nothing.

Is she coming in or not? I don't have time for this.

I pull the door open, finding Mrs Dudley on the other side. She looks shocked, but quickly reconfigures her face into a gentle smile.

'Hello there,' she says, voice unnaturally smooth. 'You must be Caroline.'

'Kate,' I correct. 'Kate Noble. Child Services.' I shake Mrs Dudley's large hand.

'A pleasure to meet you, Kate.'

I stand back to let her into the room. 'Shall we get started?'

'Yes. Of course.' Mrs Dudley closes the door tight, checking that the latch has clicked.

We take plastic seats opposite each other. It's a little awkward, our knees nearly touching, no table to shield our bodies.

'I'm guessing there's no kettle out here,' I say. 'Or I'd suggest a cup of tea.'

'Oh, I don't have time anyway,' says Mrs Dudley, offering another showy smile.

'So, as you know, I wanted to discuss Tom Kinnock today.'

Mrs Dudley nods, smile tightening.

'A nurse at the walk-in centre reported some unusual marks.'

'His mother saw us about that. They're nothing to do with the school. It's all been dealt with.'

'Tom's marks are a big concern for us,' I say. 'The nurse thought they looked like injection marks. What are *your* thoughts on that?'

The smile hasn't left Mrs Dudley's face, and it's beginning to make her look deranged. 'I'm not really qualified to answer anything like that. But this is nothing to do with the school.'

'No one is accusing anyone of anything. But you're with Tom for a large part of the day.'

'This is nothing to do with the school. Alan already explained to Tom's mother.'

'This isn't about criticising the school,' I say, starting to feel exasperated. 'I'm just trying to find out what happened. Can you tell me how Tom is in class?'

'Quiet. Tired sometimes. Perhaps his mother … Someone should talk to her about a proper sleep routine.'

'Nothing else? No other causes for concern?'

Mrs Dudley hesitates. 'Have you ... Has anyone mentioned anything else about Tom?'

'Well, that's what I'm asking you. If there's anything you want to disclose.'

Mrs Dudley stares out of the window, smile dropping. 'I don't think so. No.'

As I scribble notes, Mrs Dudley coughs meaningfully and says, 'I mean, perhaps the headmaster ... There could be an incident he feels is relevant.'

For once her eyes meet mine and I see a human being. Someone who wants to help rather than the robot I've been interviewing for the last five minutes.

'An incident?' I ask.

'There could be something Alan might want to tell you, about Tom. It's not for me to say.' The fake smile returns.

'You can tell me,' I urge. 'This is confidential. I won't feed it back to your headmaster.'

Mrs Dudley jerks like she's been prodded with something sharp. 'He'll want to know what we discussed. He wants to know everything.'

'So I'll tell him we discussed Tom and you told me his marks couldn't have happened at school.'

'I really can't ... It was something that happened in the playground.'

'When?'

Mrs Dudley hesitates. 'Last week.'

Pauly Neilson was admitted to hospital last week. Could the two things be connected?

'Which day?'

'Well, it would have been … last Wednesday.'

The same day Pauly was in hospital.

'Would this have something to do with the Neilson brothers?' I ask.

'The headmaster likes us to support one another, so … I'll leave him to fill in the details. Alan is *very* concerned about privacy. What happens in school stays in school.'

I look up. 'Surely a school's reputation is built on honesty.'

Mrs Dudley gives a nervous laugh.

'Let's get back to the marks on Tom's arm,' I say. 'Is there anything in school that could have caused pin-prick type marks? Anything you can think of at all? A sewing club or … loose nails anywhere? Or … I don't know. School injections?'

'No. As I said before. We made it very clear to Tom's mother. The marks didn't happen here.'

'Any indications that Tom is being bullied?'

Mrs Dudley's face goes white. 'There is no *bullying* here.'

I want to laugh. *Do you realise the three Neilson brothers are on my caseload? Lloyd Neilson put his brother in hospital last week. At your school …* But instead, I opt for: 'But surely *every* school has bullying?'

'No. Not here. We take the RCF approach. Rules, Consistency, Follow-through. The headmaster spends a lot of time studying different discipline models. And his methods are very effective. Our good results speak for themselves.'

The way she says it, I feel like she's a politician singing from the party song sheet. It's all a bit *Stepford Wives*.

'How about friends?' I ask. 'Has Tom made good friends since he started here? Who does he spend time with?'

Mrs Dudley pulls at her blouse lapel. 'One of the Neilson brothers. Pauly. I expect you know about him.'

Well, imagine that. Tom and Pauly are friends. Funny how troubled kids seem to find each other.

'How does Tom usually behave with the other children?' I ask. 'Have there been any other incidents of aggression?'

'No. We're an excellent school, Mrs Noble. No problems like that whatsoever.'

I drop the social politeness. 'Pauly Neilson was in hospital last Wednesday, Mrs Dudley. His brother beat him up in the school playground. I'd call that an incident of aggression, wouldn't you?'

Mrs Dudley flinches. 'The Neilson boys ... they're not the usual type of pupil here. And the fight ... it was a family matter.'

'Even though it happened at school?'

'Yes but ... they're a law unto themselves. The Neilson boys ... we look at them differently. They wouldn't have got a place here ordinarily.'

'The same is true of Tom, isn't it?' I say. 'Social services got Tom his place.'

'Yes.'

'So if he gets hurt at school, do you see it as a school-related incident? Or a family matter?'

'I'm not comfortable talking about this without the head-master present,' says Mrs Dudley, checking her watch. 'I really must get back to my class. I've left the learning support assistant in charge ...'

'Does Tom arrive at school on time?'

Mrs Dudley stands. 'For the most part.'

I stand too. 'How about personal care? Does he ever seem hungry? Badly cared for?'

'Well, he often seems very tired. But plenty of children don't sleep well. It's not unheard of. Look, I need to get back to my class now.'

'There was one last thing, if you don't mind.'

'I'm not sure I'll be able to answer—'

'Just to rule this out. Are injection needles kept at school for any reason?'

Mrs Dudley touches the door handle. 'Everything like that is locked up in the headmaster's office. Only Alan has the key.'

'Perhaps I could have a very quick chat with the headmaster now.'

'He's busy,' says Mrs Dudley quickly. 'He won't be free all afternoon. And he has a lot to do. I'm not sure he'd want to waste time like that. He's already told the mother this is nothing to do with us.'

'I'll phone to make an appointment.'

Mrs Dudley looks a good deal more flustered than when she arrived. 'Fine. I'll accompany you back to reception.'

She leads me back across the field and into the reception area, offering a hurried, 'Jen will sign you out,' before she half walks, half runs down the corridor.

As I wait for the receptionist to get the signing-out book, I study Mrs Dudley's photo on the school notice board. In the photo, she wears a blue sunflower-print dress that suits her pale complexion and figure. Her hair is longer and looser, with flecks of soft brown and grey, and a slight wave that flatters her face. She smiles genuinely.

According to the photo description, Kathleen Dudley started at Steelfield School six years ago.

The job seems to have changed her. I wonder if I'll change at the same rate in social services.

My eyes wander further around the reception area and up to a CCTV camera mounted in the corner.

It's a very quiet school. Too quiet, really. And the bars on the downstairs windows ... Lizzie Riley is right. It *is* a bit odd.

'Excuse me.' The receptionist appears. 'Sign out, please.' She offers me a large, lined book, which is empty. No visitors today. Or this week, as a matter of fact. Well, except me.

The reception girl watches as I write my name in neat capitals. 'And write down your purpose of visit, child, relationship to child and detail anything you brought in and left here.'

'Isn't this a bit over-the-top for a school?' I say mildly. 'All this detail?'

'It's just how we do things.'

I put the biro down. 'But why?'

'It's just how we do things,' she repeats.

I leave the school with a lot of questions buzzing around. Probably more questions than I arrived with.

More than anything, I need to speak to the headmaster.

Lizzie

'So, what happened at school today?' I ask Tom, tiptoeing over clothes, Lego and football cards.

The argument about the medicine bottle is still looming, but I've got no more information out of Tom, no matter how many questions I ask.

I've privately resolved to shelve the discussion for now, but I will search Tom's school bag when he gets home each day. And talk to social services again about the possibility of moving schools.

We've just come through our front door, me carrying a brown envelope containing Tom's class photos.

All the children came out today clutching these envelopes – group photos of the whole class and also individual portrait shots.

Tom looked gaunt and ghostlike when I picked him up, his cheeks shadowy and sucked inwards.

He hasn't been eating much, that's why.

'I'm going up to my room, Mum,' says Tom.

Tom and I used to sit and talk after school.

But not recently. He's always 'too tired'.

I don't know when this became normal. This separation between us. The not talking.

'Can't you at least show me these school photos first?' I ask. 'Shall we look at them after I've put the kettle on?'

I love photos of Tom. Maybe I'm biased, but he's so beautiful with his shining golden hair and blue eyes.

He looks like Olly. But personality-wise, he's more like me. Shy. Polite. Accommodating. Or at least, he used to be.

I put the kettle on and rattle some pink wafers onto a plate. 'Want a biscuit?'

'Not hungry,' Tom replies from the living room.

I hold back a sigh. 'Okay, sweetheart. Well, let's look at these photos then.'

'No thanks.' Tom throws his school bag over the bannisters and trudges up the hessian-covered steps.

'Let me guess,' I say, heart heavy. 'You're feeling tired.'

'Yeah.'

I hear Tom's breath, laboured on the stairs, and then his bedroom door slams closed.

'Tom?' I call up. 'Are you feeling okay?'

'Just tired,' he calls down, voice muffled by wood.

'You're sure? You're not feeling ill?'

'No!'

I stand for a moment, looking up the stairs, remembering Olly and how he used to talk to me sometimes.

'Stay up there if you're going to be grumpy then,' I shout after him, trying a different tactic.

'Fine.'

'I mean it, Tom. Stay in your bedroom. You can come down when you're ready to be polite. Like the old Tom.'

'*Fine.*'

Anxiety whirling in my stomach, I head into the kitchen

and pour hot water into my tea mug, taking a while to dunk the teabag up and down.

Then I sit on the sofa and have a much-needed sip of tea.

After a few minutes of staring into space, I absentmindedly slide Tom's school photos from the brown envelope. I put the class photo to one side at first, and find the portrait shots of Tom.

My little boy stares at the camera, blue eyes hazy and out of focus, tie askew.

He looks … in another world. Not quite there.

We need another doctor's visit, I decide. Maybe tonight if they'll fit us in. The doctor always says the same thing. He's getting fed up with me now. *Tom seems right in himself. No temperature. Blood pressure fine.* But Tom *isn't* right in himself. Hasn't been since his first day at this new school.

I pick up the class photo.

Tom's whole class stares back at me, three rows of them arranged on gym benches in the school hall. I've never seen school children look so serious. They are immaculate and identical, hair clipped neatly on the boys and tied back on the girls, school uniforms perfectly worn. None of the children smile. In fact, most look nervous, holding their bodies rigid, eyes wide.

A silk school banner pinned behind them announces:
Steelfield School: Semper Fortis

They're good quality, these photos. Thick and glossy in hard, cardboard frames. They've placed the taller children at the back, so of course Tom is in the front row with a lot of girls and two other shorter boys. Tom looks too young for his class – smaller than the others in his year.

But that's not what worries me.

What worries me is the fear in Tom's eyes. The tension in his body. How terrified he looks.

Pauly Neilson stands behind him, a grimacing mixture of milk and adult teeth. I know Pauly is just a kid, probably with a whole host of problems. But that doesn't make him any less menacing.

Pauly's tanned arms, poking from grey-white summer shirt sleeves, are out of place in the sea of blazers. They spoil the neat lines of the photo and make the class look unruly, as if the photographer can't control him.

Then I notice something. Two tiny circular specks on Pauly's right forearm. It's hard to tell the colour – red, black, grey – because Pauly is just one lot of colourful pixels among thirty other children. But ...

They look like injection marks.

No. The school will say I'm being paranoid.

I am *being paranoid.*

I put a hand to my forehead, feeling a headache coming on.

I should take some paracetamol. Chase the headache off before it takes hold.

Heading to the kitchen, I pull down the cardboard box of medical stuff. It's an old Pampers box with the leaves cut off and ragged cardboard lining the top.

Resting inside, on a mountain of bandages, plasters and antiseptic bottles, is a flimsy plastic box – the sort you get Chinese restaurant food in. The egg-fried rice has long since been eaten, the box cleaned to a salty, opaque finish by Olly's dishwasher, and now it's used to hold paracetamol, cough syrup and anything we're given on prescription.

This includes the blood-thinning meds from the hospital – one bottle of which I found empty in Tom's school bag.

I'm suddenly aware that Tom must have climbed up here to take those meds. Probably using a chair, clambering like a monkey over the kitchen counter. I feel sick at that thought. What could make him so desperate to steal medicine?

The box feels lighter than it should, and I'm frowning when I peel back the plastic lid.

There should be … Where is the new bottle of blood-thinning meds? Am I going mad? I'm sure I picked them up from the pharmacy yesterday … didn't I?

'Tom?' I call up the stairs. '*Tom*. Come down here, please.'

Tramp, tramp, tramp.

Grumpy footsteps pound the stairs.

'There's medicine missing,' I tell him, as he reaches the bottom step.

'I didn't—'

'Don't lie to me Tom!'

He freezes.

'Tell me the truth right now,' I demand. 'Or there'll be trouble. Big trouble.'

Tom won't look at me.

'Why? *Why* did you take it?'

'I didn't take it.' Tom turns on the staircase. 'I'm tired. I'm going to lie down.'

'*Tom.*'

'I just need to sleep.'

I want to grab him. Shout until he tells me everything.

But of course, I can't.

I feel powerless, watching him trudge up the stairs to bed.

But I'm not powerless. Not any more. I don't have to just sit back and take this. Not like I did with Olly.

I grab my phone, searching my contacts for Steelfield School.

I want to speak with Tom's teacher, Mrs Dudley. I need answers.

Today.

Kate

Tessa is annoyed with me. She hasn't said so explicitly, but every time she passes my desk, she huffs like an angry rhino.

I can imagine her inner monologue: *I told her not to do that school visit. She's far too behind on her paperwork. We're already overwhelmed …*

'What are you doing now, Kate?' Tessa is behind me suddenly, frothy cappuccino in hand. 'Not wasting time messing around on the Internet, surely?'

'Looking up incidents of self-harm in children,' I say. 'Just getting an idea of frequency and presentation.'

'You think Tom Kinnock's been poking himself with needles?'

'I'm considering every possibility.'

'Oh, you'll never get that Tom Kinnock file straight now. There'll always be a black mark over it with the paediatrician's report missing. Tom Kinnock needs to be tucked away in a back drawer somewhere and you need to get the Neilsons in order.'

'The boy had possible *injection marks*, Tessa,' I say. 'I'm not tucking him away anywhere.'

That silences Tessa for a moment, which is a rarity. Then her

164

face turns smug and she waves a finger. 'But that's never been proven by a doctor, has it? It could be sewing-needle marks for all you know.'

'It's more than just the marks. Tom's been late to school a few times. And he's tired. He's fallen asleep in class before.'

'I bet the father's still on the scene,' Tessa barks. 'Causing chaos. Probably the boy is kept up at night by his parents rowing. I've seen it a hundred times. The mother goes back for more abuse. It's not our fault or obligation. Let the mother clear up her own mess.'

'Lizzie says she hasn't seen Tom's father since they moved.'

Tessa puffs her chest out, triumphant. 'She's lying. Not our problem. If the mother is too stupid to do what's good for her …'

'I suppose it's *possible* she could be seeing the father,' I admit. 'But when I talked to her, her objective seemed to be hiding from Olly Kinnock. Making sure he didn't find out where she and Tom lived.'

'She could still be lying.'

'And why *injection* needle marks? There's never been any history of drug abuse. There's something else too – Tom had a seizure recently. I found out from the medical records.'

'That's serious. How was the home visit?'

'The house was a bit chaotic, but no other alarm bells. Although the mother seemed anxious.'

'Most people are when social services knock at the door unannounced. How long did you have with her? An hour?'

'Half an hour. She didn't seem like a child abuser.'

'Child abusers rarely *seem* like child abusers. Maybe she's tired. Fed up. Taking her frustrations out on the little boy.'

'Logically, she's the only person who could be hurting him. Unless something's happening at school.'

'What about the bullying angle?' asks Tessa. 'Tom goes to school with the Neilsons, doesn't he? If he's anywhere near Lloyd Neilson, he probably gets stabbed with sharp objects regularly.'

'I need to track down the father,' I say. 'And schedule another home visit.'

'You'll do no such thing,' Tessa barks. 'With a caseload like yours—'

I hold up a placating hand, which makes Tessa's face flush with fury. 'This is my decision, Tessa.'

'If you mess up deadlines for my department, Kate, there will be hell to pay.'

'It's my department too, Tessa,' I say. 'And it's more important that I *do* my job than fill out a load of forms.'

'What's got into you?' Tessa asks. 'You used to be a proper rules-body.'

'I've decided I'd rather help children than tick boxes.'

Tessa lets out a loud snort. 'This place is about keeping your head down and covering your backside. Doing a decent job is a long way down the list.'

'Not for me it isn't.' I rub tired eyes. 'I'm making a cup of tea, do you want—'

'Nespresso cappuccino!' Tessa trills. She marches back to her office, shouting over her shoulder, 'Just pop it on my desk!'

I head to the office kitchen, trying to work out how on earth I'm going to track down Tom's father and do another home visit when my calendar is booked up for the next month.

Lizzie

The smart, navy coat? Or is that too formal? Makeup always looks heavy on my delicate features, but if I wear no makeup at all … is that not smart enough, verging on disrespectful?

Tom's teacher agreed to meet me at 6 p.m. for a 'talk'.

Okay. Navy coat it is. Jeans – well, it will have to be, my smart skirt is in the wash. And a plain jumper.

I grab my patchwork bag from the door hook and wave at the babysitter – a beautiful, willowy teenager called Chloe, who lives two doors down and is studying for her A levels.

I don't like leaving Tom, but needs must.

'I'll be back soon,' I say, heading out of the door.

'Okay, no worries.' Chloe is cross-legged on the sofa, reading a psychology course book. She's a clever girl and studies all hours. Not like a normal teenager. I'm sure she'll get top grades.

I hurry onto the street and, realising it's too wet to use the country lane, half walk, half jog the slightly longer road route.

When I finally reach the school, I'm only just on time. My heart pounds. There's something eerie about the playground, silent in semi-darkness. For once the gates and main door are open, and I walk straight into the reception area.

It's spotlessly clean, without any of the usual children's

drawings that decorate school walls. Almost as if kids are an inconvenience to the headmaster's orderly vision.

I hover there, not sure what to do with myself. Then Mrs Dudley appears from the school office. She's wearing an odd combination of smart trouser suit with very shiny black Mary Janes.

'Ah. There you are, Miss Riley. We'll have to chat here in reception – everything is locked up now.'

'Don't you have keys?'

She smiles as if this is a silly question, and shakes her head.

'What about the school office?' I ask.

'We don't allow parents in there.'

We take seats in the reception area – woolly chairs clearly meant for passing visitors, not parent meetings.

'I'd like to discuss Tom,' says Mrs Dudley.

'Mrs Dudley.' My voice is firm. '*I* called this meeting. And I have something specific to talk about. Tom's medicine has been going missing. I found an empty bottle in his school bag, and—'

'Medicine?' says Mrs Dudley, sitting up very straight. 'Are you saying Tom's been taking medicine from school?'

'No. Of course not.' *What an odd question.* 'Tom took medicine from our box at home. I think he has been bringing it in for someone. He's being intimidated.'

'It sounds like you've taken two and two and made twenty, Miss Riley.'

'I found an empty bottle in his school bag. It was full before.'

Mrs Dudley becomes very stern, benign smile vanishing. 'Miss Riley, I think we're all getting a little tired of these accusations. I don't know what's happening at home, but I can assure you this school is a very good establishment with well-behaved children. No one is being intimidated. If Tom is taking things from home and putting them in his school bag, I'd suggest you take a long, hard look at how you're parenting him.'

I bristle. 'I'm a good parent, Mrs Dudley.'

'Well. I'm glad to hear it. Now, if you've finished—'

'There's something else, too,' I say. 'We got the school photos back yesterday. Tom was by Pauly Neilson. I noticed some marks on Pauly's forearm. Similar to the marks Tom had.'

'Miss Riley—'

'The *marks* I talked to you about. The ones that looked like injection marks.'

'We've already cleared that up. No one has even seen these marks.' Mrs Dudley crosses her arms.

'The drop-in nurse—'

'And I'm amazed you could see anything so detailed in a school photo of thirty-one children.'

I shake my head. 'It wasn't overly clear, but—'

'Then we mustn't jump to far-fetched conclusions. Miss Riley, Tom is lucky to have a place here. Very lucky. A hundred other parents would be delighted. All we're hearing from you are wild accusations.'

'I'm not—'

'This sort of discussion … the headmaster wouldn't stand for it and neither will I.'

'My son came home with marks on his body!' I shout. 'Do you expect me not to be worried? And I found an empty medicine bottle in his school bag. Should I say nothing about that too?'

'Please calm down or I'll have to ask you to leave. Your son's school bag is nothing to do with us. And I hear social services are dealing with this supposed *bodily markings* issue.'

I stiffen. 'This isn't to do with social services. This is to do with my son getting marks in *your* care. And *taking medicine into school*.'

'Tom did not get the marks in our care. We've explained to you over and over again.'

'Mrs Dudley, listen to me. Something is happening at school. Tom is … different. He won't talk to me any more. He's taking medicine from home. I think this Pauly Neilson friendship could be something to do with it.'

'Mr Cockrun works very hard to help every child fit in here and achieve our high standards of behaviour. If your son is making friends with children you consider to be unsuitable, perhaps you should ask yourself why.'

I feel like I've been slapped. 'Are you saying there's something wrong with Tom? He's new to this school, Mrs Dudley. Coming into fully formed friendship groups. And he's vulnerable. He's not going to be picky about who he's friends with – of course he's going to pal up with anyone who shows an interest.'

'All I can say is that as a teacher, Tom's friendships have nothing to do with his problems.'

'What problems?'

'Tom is struggling to meet our academic requirements, Miss Riley. His work just isn't up to scratch. Is he getting enough rest at home?'

'What? Tom's brilliant at school. Naturally bright. He picks up everything so quickly …'

'I've asked the special needs teacher to do a few tests. Just to see if he's processing things in the normal way. She feels he might have some emotional problems.'

I suck in a breath. 'He has emotions to deal with. Given our background. But that doesn't mean—'

'And Tom's been getting angry at school too. Struggling to control his temper. Yesterday, he threw his exercise book on the floor.'

'Tom? *My* Tom?'

'We don't tolerate bad behaviour here. How do you deal with anger at home? Do you have good disciplinary structures in place?'

'Tom doesn't get angry at home. Well, very rarely. He's a good boy. Usually well-behaved. But when he isn't, I certainly tell him off. His father used to get angry ...'

Memories of Olly flash and burn.

Mrs Dudley watches me for a moment, and I can see the cogs turning.

She's wondering if I'm lying. I imagine quite a few parents swear blind their home life is perfect, when in fact there are lots of issues.

I feel tears on my cheeks.

Mrs Dudley watches me without a hint of human understanding. 'We'd really like Tom to spend time with the special needs teacher. Let's see if we can get to the bottom of this behaviour.'

I sit up straight. 'Mrs Dudley, I'm going out of my mind, trying to understand how Tom got those marks on his arms. And he's not himself. I know something's going on at school. Drugs or something ...' I let the sentence drift away.

It sounds ridiculous and we both know it.

'There are no drugs here,' Mrs Dudley says, her voice low. 'Now, your social worker visited yesterday.' She eyes me meaningfully. 'What would she think if I told her you were causing trouble like this?'

I stare, my breathing growing shallow.

'Steelfield School has an outstanding reputation,' Mrs Dudley continues. 'We expect parents to help us maintain that reputation. *Act strong, be strong.*'

Act ...

'So what are the Neilson boys still doing here?' I ask. 'If you want the school to look so perfect?'

Mrs Dudley glares. 'I can assure you that *every* child in this school knows how to behave.'

I swallow tightly.

'Miss Riley? Do we understand each other?'

I give a quick nod.

And once again, I feel that sharp pang. The one that tells me I'm not strong enough to do this alone.

I chase the thought away.

I *am* strong enough. I am a *good* mother. And I *will* get answers.

Lizzie

'It's chaos in here,' Olly shouts, and I stiffen, bracing myself for the onslaught. Olly used to love me. He caught me when I fell. Now, my many weaknesses are abhorrent to him.

This is how it goes: peace for a while. Then a flare-up, followed by heartfelt apologies. One big cycle. Only the cycle is getting tighter.

I keep telling myself he'll change when the baby comes. Only a few weeks now. Or it might come early. They say stress does that.

Sometimes, I think about leaving Olly, but I know I'm not strong enough to have a baby alone. My mother has drummed it into me since my own birth. How weak I am.

So I'm trapped.

We're in Olly's apartment and it is a mess. It's hard to tidy because I never know where Olly wants anything and he keeps buying new things – vinyl records, an electric toothbrush, a Velcro strap for his leg, snowboarding DVDs.

It's worse than usual, the stuff. And for my part, I'm struggling to throw anything of my own away.

The terror I feel at being pregnant has made me verge on hoarding. What if we need those magazines when the baby comes? What if we need those leaflets about double-glazing?

Even things that are clearly rubbish, like the many takeaway pizza boxes littering the flat, give me a sort of hysterical feeling. If I tidy those, what else will I need to organise? The kitchen? The bedroom? My life?

Right now, I'm standing at the island sink, paralysed, not knowing where to start, how to begin to tackle this mess.

'I'm trying,' I tell Olly, my heart beginning to race.

'You're at home all day,' says Olly. 'Doing nothing.'

But I'm not doing nothing. I'm thinking obsessively, worrying about when this baby comes. The anxiety is crippling. So much so, I can barely get out of bed some days. Doesn't he understand how his behaviour affects me?

'I've tried to get a job in a hospital,' I say. 'But it's hard now I'm pregnant. And since I didn't finish my training ...'

Olly limps into the kitchen area. 'Meaning?'

'Nothing.'

'I know it's tough,' says Olly. 'Time for both of us to grow up, right? You're a wife now.'

We're married now, did I mention?

Olly took me to a 1960s diner in Soho, then kneeled in front of my half-eaten Caesar salad and offered me a turquoise diamond ring.

I said yes.

Of course I did.

How could I say no in front of a restaurant of people?

And anyway, Olly is the father of my child. Who else is going to support me when this baby comes? I'm not qualified for anything.

Yes, Olly shouts and rages. And sometimes other things happen. Things I just want to shut away and pretend never happened. Things that cannot be acknowledged, for my own sanity.

After I accepted Olly's proposal, I threw up in the toilet. Hormones, probably.

The wedding ceremony took place the next day, after a short interview at the registry office.

A thunderbolt wedding, Olly called it.

Exciting. Romantic. Just like us.

Except I've never liked thunder and lightning.

None of my friends were there, since the only friends I have are ex-boyfriends and Olly is jealous. My father died when I was sixteen, so I had nobody to walk me down the aisle. But my mother came.

Mum turned up in a cream dress and matching pillar-box hat, smiling like a velociraptor.

'But I'm a terrible stay-at-home wife,' I say.

'You just need practice,' says Olly. 'Try harder at being organised.'

'Olly, I'm so down right now,' I say, gesturing to the messy kitchen. 'This baby wasn't planned. I get anxious. You shouting at me doesn't help.'

'You're going to be a mother,' Olly says. 'You have to work all this out, Lizzie. This self-obsession. Someone else is going to come first soon.'

'I'm self-obsessed?' I laugh, and it sounds like knives. 'I moved into your house. I gave up my nursing course. I'm having our baby—'

'Oh, don't give me that. You didn't give up your nursing course for me. You were failing exams left, right and centre. You were happy to give it up.'

'Nursing gave me a sense of … a sense of something. That I'm more than just a shadow. I feel that way sometimes, Olly. Invisible. Like I'm nothing in my own right. That I'm only real as part of someone else.'

'You're not a shadow.'

'Yes. I am. My mother's little shadow, that's what she used to call me.' Tears well up. 'I don't know how we're going to cope with this baby.'

'Don't say it. Don't you dare say it.' Olly grabs my arms. 'Do you hear me?'

'But I'm scared. I feel trapped.'

Olly looks at me then, his eyes clicking back and forth. 'Just admit it.'

'Admit what?'

'Tell the truth. Admit you don't want this baby. That this is a mistake.'

'I love you. I just …'

'Just what?'

'It's not how I would have planned things, that's all.'

'You don't plan anything. That's the trouble.'

'And your life is so much better?' I say. 'With all your planning and your ambition and your Olympic dream? Life happened and where did planning get you?'

It's a low blow and I know it. But I'm fed up with Olly criticising who I am. Picking away, forcing me to admit all my failings over and over again.

'Shut up!' Olly's fingers tighten. 'Do you hear me? Just shut up! What do you know about anything? You made me worse. If it weren't for you, I'd be able to walk normally. You did everything wrong. You've ruined my life.'

I stumble sideways, adopting my usual duck and cower position. But there is no onslaught.

When I look up, I see Olly limping in circles around the living area.

I grip the marble counter, shaking.

Olly will get better. He'll calm down when the baby comes.

If he doesn't … oh God, that doesn't even bear thinking about. A single mother with no money or support. I couldn't bear it. I've always been so certain I'd give my children a better upbringing than the one I had. Stability. Happiness.

Olly will change. He has to change and this has to work out. What else can I hope for?

Lizzie

It's ten at night and I've just put the washing on. I'll have to wait up for the cycle to finish, then hang the washing out so it's dry for tomorrow.

I keep going over my meeting with Mrs Dudley yesterday. Replaying it over and over.

Tom is fast asleep, following a miserable evening. We ate dinner in silence, then he went to bed early without being asked.

I should go to bed too. But instead, I'm on the Internet, posting questions on Mumsnet. I did this a lot when I was with Olly – going onto medical websites and posting question after question about his broken leg.

But this time I want to know about children's friendships. My question is:

My son started a new school this term and is angrier than usual, keeping secrets, not talking. I'm worried. He seems to be getting in with the wrong crowd. Normal??

I've had a few kind replies telling me I have nothing to worry about. But one mother had a similar experience and moved her son to another school: 'He's much happier now. We all are.'

'Don't worry,' writes another mum. 'All perfectly normal … My daughter made all the wrong friends at first, but has some lovely ones now.'

Most of the answers say it's probably just a phase, don't worry, kids change friendship groups all the time, they go through moody times, maybe he's just tired, and so on.

But … I am worried.

Tom is changing.

My eyes wander to the kitchen, where the new heavy-duty security box sits in a kitchen cupboard. It holds our medical supplies now and I keep the key close to my body at all times.

There is a spare key sticky-taped to the bottom of the bin. But I know every wrinkle and crease of the sticky tape, and check every day to make sure it hasn't been tampered with.

Leaning back in my chair, I cup my eyes with my palms.

Okay. Okay. Maybe we can move schools … Maybe that's the solution to all this. Run away and hope all our problems disappear.

Deep down, I know that's not really an option. Kate Noble said social services take a dim view of children being moved around. The last thing I need is another black mark against us.

But maybe if we moved to a school within the area … I do a quick search for schools within fifty miles.

The word 'oversubscribed' comes up over and over. I knew that already – social services pulled a lot of strings to get us into Steelfield School.

My fingers hover over the keyboard, and I decide to stop my obsessive Google searching and check my emails before bed.

There are three 'parent update' messages from the school, and I feel guilty that I haven't opened them yet. I might have missed something important.

I click open the first email, scanning the news:

Jess Parker in Year 1 has lost her school cardigan. The label is marked JP. If anyone finds it, would they please hand it in to the school office.

I continue to scan, rubbing tired eyes. Nothing important, nothing important ... No – nothing about Tom's class. No special days coming up.

And then ... oh my God ...

A man in a van has been seen around the school gates. If you use a van to drop off children, please let the school know.

And suddenly I'm shaking, an hysterical cry rising in my throat. *Olly.*

For a moment, my mind races around the house, throwing our belongings into boxes, getting ready to run again.

I close my eyes. *Don't get paranoid. There are all sorts of vans in the world. Just calm down. We were always getting messages like this in London. They're very common. It's okay. Calm. Calm. He can't have found us. You were too careful.*

I pace around, waiting for my heart rate to slow down.

Then I make myself some raspberry tea, stirring a dark red swirling storm into boiling water.

You were too careful, I tell myself again. *There's no way he could have found us.*

But I know I'll find it hard to sleep tonight. So I will do what I usually do when insomnia strikes – obsessively Google.

I think of the ten packing boxes, still stacked on the landing upstairs.

I should make a start on those. Get the last of the house in order. Or have a quick nap before the washing finishes. All good solutions for anxiety.

But instead, rubbing bloodshot eyes, I begin yet another Google search – this time looking up drugs that cause behavioural changes in children.

Lizzie

'I call her my little shadow,' Mum tells our neighbour. 'She never leaves my side.' We're in the garden, my mother sipping a coffee. I sit on the grass, pretending to study a mathematics textbook. I don't understand much of it, but I've learned to play the good student around my mother. The more publicly the better.

Dad has been even more absent since the grammar school argument. Working late. Hotel-stays in London. The odd unexplained restaurant bill, if my mother's screaming fits are to be believed …

I sense he's detaching from my mother. And me too, since by staying away from her he stays away from me.

The truth is, my father is a coward. He's running away and he doesn't know me well enough to take me with him. If he didn't bury his head in the sand, he'd be able to see that I'm miserable too. Despite the Good Housekeeping image, Ruth Riley is not a good mother.

Our neighbour, Rita, leans over our slatted wood fence.

Privately, my mother criticises Rita for the weeds growing on her driveway and unwashed net curtains.

I look up at my mother, so tall and beautiful – everything perfect on the outside. Black, curled hair, fitted wool skirt suit showing off her handsome figure and bright-red lipstick around straight white teeth.

Mum never leaves the house without a full face of makeup and styled hair. Even to go into our own back garden. After all, what would people say if she wasn't presentable?

Sometimes I wish I could be like her, all lit up. Bright. The sort of woman people notice. But then again, I'm well aware there's something not quite right about my mother. She's not real, like other people. Everything is empty. An act. The perfect, happy life is just a shell.

When no one is looking, her mouth is tight with anger. She is furious that her husband has all but left her. Furious that I didn't turn out to be the perfect, clever daughter. Furious that her life isn't glamorous or special.

Does she know, deep down, that everything is a lie? Her marriage, her relationship with her daughter – just a picture she paints to cover a grey, sad reality?

My mother reaches down and pats my head, the same way someone might pet a dog.

Rita, a cuddly, grey-haired lady with pink-framed glasses, says: 'So how are you doing at school, little one?'

My mother rearranges her feet just enough to block my body from sight. 'She's doing exceptionally well. Just last week, her teacher was telling me she was one of the few in the class who might go to university.'

This is not true. There are three children in our class who are called 'the bright ones' – Christopher Phillips, Hannah Waldock and Jenny Martin. They're the ones who represent the school for competitions and passed the grammar school exams.

I'm not one of the clever ones. I'm just ordinary.

Rita gives me a warm smile and a little wink. We both know that Mum exaggerates.

I wish Rita were my mum. She hugs me sometimes and it feels real.

My own mother feels like nothing.

Kate

I'm in London. It's hot, but I don't have time to get my water bottle from my bag and take a swig.

Number 11F. Where is it? Where is it?

Olly Kinnock's flat is somewhere on this lovely, tree-lined road of red-brick Victorian townhouses and I have approximately five minutes to find it.

Then I need to run back to the train station. *Really* run. Tessa expressly forbade me from going to London today.

I find it impossible to lie, so I will tell her the truth if she asks. But I've done a lot of paperwork on the train so, as long as I catch the 8.40 a.m. back, she will be none the wiser.

Number eleven … there!

I jog up the sandy-coloured steps and press the buzzer for 11F, which is the penthouse. No reply.

I press again, this time more aggressively. After another minute, I press all the neighbours' buzzers and wait.

I expect the intercom to crackle and ask who I am, but instead a giant shadow appears behind the frosted glass.

The front door opens. 'Can I help you?' The man is tall, with a Scottish accent and a tight rugby shirt that shows off

his muscular shoulders. He wears a straw hat and behind him, by an open door, is a stack of moving boxes.

'I'm Kate Noble,' I announce. 'From Child Services. I'm looking for Olly Kinnock.'

'That bastard?' the man says. 'He left a long time ago. Good riddance.'

'I don't suppose you have a forwarding address for him?'

'I heard he moved in with his mother, the cowardly little weasel. She used to visit him here. Margaret, her name is.'

'So you haven't seen him?'

The man shakes his head. 'I don't associate with men like that. Any post for Olly Kinnock goes straight in the bin. I just hope Lizzie is doing okay.' He eyes me hopefully. 'Have you seen her?'

'I'm afraid I can't—'

'You tell her if she ever needs anything, all she has to do is call. Tell her Stuart said hello. And the offer's still there. She can come live with me in the Shetlands. It's a good place for young Tom to grow up. I'll get her ferry tickets. Pay moving costs. Everything.'

He slides open a drawer, takes out a blue Shetland ferry leaflet, scribbles on it, then hands it to me. 'Give this to her. If you see her.'

I take the glossy paper, seeing an illustration of Saint Nicholas, the patron saint of sailors, printed above a ferry timetable.

Saint Nicholas has a golden halo around his white hair and angel wings – which isn't strictly accurate. Saint Nicholas was a human who performed miracles, not an angel as such. But I suppose everyone feels reassured by angel wings.

The offer still stands, Stuart has written, next to his phone number, name and five kisses.

'I'll give it to her.'

'That bastard should have been locked up for what he did,' says Stuart. 'If you *do* find him, tell him to watch his back.'

'I don't suppose you know his mother's address?'

'No, I bloody don't.'

Stuart slams the door in my face.

Lizzie

Why is there a police car at the school gates? My heart pounds – a memory of a very bad day with Olly. The day the frayed thread binding our family together finally snapped.

Suddenly, I'm running.

It's Wednesday afternoon and lots of parents have arrived already, pressed up tight against the railings, curious, confused expressions on their faces.

Heart pounding, I stand on tiptoes, craning to see through gaps in the railings. I see flashes of neon and black and someone – a child – struggling on the floor.

'Who is it?' I demand. 'Who are they holding down?'

'Lloyd Neilson,' a nearby mother whispers. 'It's about time.'

Recognition snaps like a rubber band, and I see Lloyd's thick black hair and strong little body pulling and twisting under two policemen.

'The headmaster can't pretend there's no trouble here now, can he?' the mother continues.

We watch as the police handcuff Lloyd's wrists and pull him to his feet, dragging him across the playground.

Lloyd is yelling, 'Get your fucking hands off me. Fuck off and die, you fucking dickheads!'

The policemen stoically ignore him.

As the struggling group reach the gate, Lloyd plants his feet on the concrete and shouts: 'If you scuff up these Nikes I'll do you for it.'

One of the police, a grey-haired man with a large stomach, loses his temper then. He has a long, red scratch down his cheek, presumably from scuffling with Lloyd. 'That's enough from you, young man. I'll throw your bloody shoes away if you don't start walking. Send them off to forensics for testing and have them torn apart.'

Lloyd's dark eyebrows turn into one furious line. He walks with the police then, shoes punching the tarmac, *tramp, tramp, tramp*.

The headmaster appears, eerily calm but unsmiling for once. He strides past the police and unlocks the school gate.

Lloyd turns, still struggling. 'Fucking *bastard*. I don't tell, *you* don't tell.'

Slowly and deliberately, the headmaster turns back to Lloyd. I can't see Mr Cockrun's expression, but Lloyd's angry, furrowed eyebrows lift in pure terror and he falls immediately silent.

Once the headmaster has marched back into the school building, Lloyd finds some defiance again.

'Fucking Cockface,' he mutters, as he's led through the gates.

I notice Lloyd is blinking slowly, one side of his mouth hanging down. As he passes, his swimming eyes meet mine. 'Tell Tom: nice one,' he says, giving a thumbs-up.

I flinch.

Parents turn, eyeing me up and down.

Suddenly, I want to be a shadow again. I shouldn't be wearing this orange scarf. Being exposed is too hard.

Why did Lloyd say that? Oh God, I need to talk to Tom. What's going on?

Dimly, I hear the school bell ring. There's a longer pause than usual; I imagine the teachers are keeping the kids back for a minute, making sure the police have removed Lloyd from the premises. Then the doors open and children stream out.

It takes a few minutes for Tom to appear. When he does, he's walking with Pauly Neilson.

I wave frantically at him. 'Tom. *Tom*!'

When Tom finally reaches the school gates, I grab his hand.

'Mum?' he says, looking alarmed.

I don't reply, instead pulling Tom away from Pauly, through the crowd and towards the stony lane.

'What's wrong?' Tom asks, grey school shoes tripping over gravel. He sounds frightened.

When we're a little way down the path and alone, with only birdsong and green leaves for company, I say, 'Tom, the police were here today. Lloyd Neilson was arrested. He gave me a thumbs-up and said, "Tell Tom: nice one". Why did he say that?'

'I don't know.'

'The police led him right through the playground.'

'I know. They arrested him.'

'And you have no idea whatsoever why he would have said that?'

Tom shrugs, and I feel like I've taken the wrong boy home. That I'm holding Pauly Neilson's hand.

'Let's start at the beginning. Why did the police take Lloyd Neilson? Did you hear anything? See anything?'

'They said he had tablets on him. They couldn't find them, though.'

'How do you know that?'

'One of the police searched Pauly in case Lloyd had given them to him. But they couldn't find anything.'

'Listen, Tom ... just stay away from those Neilson boys. Stay away from them. Do you hear me? I'm going to find a way to get you out of this school.'

We walk home in silence.

When we reach the house, Tom goes straight upstairs, school bag still on his shoulders, and I'm left alone, numbly picking up leaflets from the doormat and tidying stray toys.

I notice five missed calls from my mother. She's probably trying to arrange another visit, but I don't have emotional space for her right now.

My head is crammed with thoughts and worries.

Why did Lloyd Neilson say that? What did he want to thank Tom for?

A thought prickles.

Tom took his school bag upstairs. He never does that. He always hangs it on the bannisters.

Suddenly I'm running, two steps at a time, onto the landing, throwing open Tom's door and rushing into his bedroom.

Tom stands with his back to me in his reading corner. His school bag is open a few feet away. The front pocket is unzipped too, which is unusual – he never keeps anything in there.

Tom senses me in the doorway and turns.

He is surprised, an animal caught in a trap.

In his hands, he holds a bag of white tablets.

Ruth

The hairdresser snips and combs, as I admire myself in the mirror. For a woman of my age, I look very well. Everyone says so.

I'm furious with Elizabeth. What kind of daughter doesn't answer the phone to her own mother? I've called so many times now and left messages.

'My daughter can be very thoughtless,' I tell the hairdresser. 'It's been an age since she was in touch.' My voice reaches a higher pitch. 'I could be ill or in pain.'

The hairdresser, a young Asian man called Fam, nods sympathetically. 'Maybe she's busy with the little boy, rushing around, didn't see her phone.'

'She has no excuse,' I say. 'Tom's nearly nine years old. What rushing around does she have to do? It's not as if he's a toddler.'

Fam laughs. 'My nephew is nine and is always jumping on the sofas. Can't sit still. Little boys are a lot of work. Just crazy.'

'Your nephew wouldn't misbehave at Steelfield School,' I say. 'The headmaster has a very effective process for keeping problem children in line.'

'Process?'

I hesitate. 'He has a way with the children. That's what I'm saying.'

'Right,' says Fam, fluffing my hair, not really understanding.

'The problems with Elizabeth started when her father left,' I say. 'He never came to visit and she blamed me. And then he died and I think she blamed me for that too.'

'Very sad, very sad,' says Fam, snipping around my neck. 'Shall we go a little shorter this time? You know? As we get older, short can be better.'

'No,' I snap. 'I don't want anything to change.'

'Okay, okay,' says Fam. 'No problem.'

I think, reading his face, he has some issue with what I just said. But I can't be sure.

In recent years, I've become aware that I don't feel things like other people. It can be useful, I suppose. I only wish it still worked on Elizabeth. But these days, she's slipping further and further out of reach.

Kate

The roundabout glistens with cars, locked tight together, little metal boxes full of irritated mums and cooped-up kids. Usually I know better than to attempt this roundabout during the school run, but I'm on my way to the police station.

Lloyd Neilson is being held there, following an arrest at school. Aged eleven, he is now of legal age to be taken into police custody.

The police station is tantalisingly close – just across the verge of grass and wild flowers. I want to get out and run to it. But I can't.

The traffic inches forward and a half-space opens up. I throw my usual caution to the wind and shoot into it. I'm rewarded with a torrent of angry beeps, but today I couldn't care less. Social work is no profession for cautious drivers, I've discovered. Cautiousness takes time.

The traffic creeps around the roundabout.

Come on, come on.

I rarely check my watch at work any more because I'm always late.

There. Shooting forward into another space, I receive more

194

angry beeps. I put up a sorry hand, and hope they understand that I'm on my way to help a frightened eleven-year-old boy who is being treated like an adult by police.

Finally, I can see the red-and-white striped barrier ahead – the one that should lift and let me into the police station car park.

My phone rings. *Tessa Warwick*. It's never a good idea to ignore Tessa. She's like a bull, easily enraged and prone to charge. Reluctantly, I pick up.

'Kate. Where are you?' she demands. 'I've just had a call from Pauly Neilson. He and his brother are home on their own. Lloyd isn't there to reach the cupboards. They need someone to make supper.'

'The baby isn't home too, surely?'

'No. The mother is off with her somewhere. God knows where.'

'Leanne's probably at her mum's house. Ask Gary to give Jeannette Neilson a call. I'm on my way to the police station. Lloyd Neilson has been arrested and needs an appropriate adult.'

'You'll have to send Gary to the Neilson house then,' Tessa decides. 'Assuming you get held up at the police station for the usual four hours plus.'

'Gary is a family support worker,' I say. 'He's not trained to deal with that on his own. What if Leanne's boyfriend turns up?'

'Kate, sometimes you have to make these kinds of decisions. What other choice do you have?'

I want to bang my head on the steering wheel. 'Fine. Okay. I'll ask Gary to stay with the Neilsons.'

'And pray nothing happens while he's there.' Tessa hangs up.

I approach the red and white barrier. 'Hello?' I shout into the intercom, attempting to text Gary at the same time. 'I'm Kate Noble, Lloyd Neilson's social worker and appropriate adult.'

No one replies, but the barrier clicks open.

I notice the little black windows of the basement police cells and wonder if Lloyd is down there, all fake bravado but secretly scared to death.

By the time I've crossed the car park, I've texted Gary and calculated how many hours I'll be working late this evening.

Right now, I'll be lucky to be home before midnight.

Col won't be happy.

Inside the police station, I'm talked through the arrest, then shown down to an interview room where Lloyd Neilson is waiting – a skinny eleven-year-old boy with floppy black hair, who's just been held in a police cell.

His hands are shoved tight in his trouser pockets, one foot balancing over his knee.

'Where's Mum?' Lloyd asks.

'She couldn't come, Lloyd.' I'm too tactful to add: *Because we don't know where she is.*

'Who took Joey home?'

'Pauly did.'

'Are they on their own, then?'

'I'm sending someone over to be with them now.'

'A man or a woman?'

I pause. 'A man.'

Lloyd explodes, banging his fists on the table. He's had bad experiences with men.

'Look, let's just get this police interview over and then we can leave,' I say. 'Can you tell me what happened?'

'Those police assaulted me,' says Lloyd. 'Fucking dickheads. I wish they were all dead. They say I stole from the school medicine cabinet. But I never.'

It's a game we play – me pretending I believe him, him telling me what I need to know.

'So what *did* you do?'

'Nothing. I was just messing around at the back of the field.'

'They wouldn't *arrest* you for that,' I say. 'There must be more to it.'

'The caretaker thought he saw me with something, didn't he? Fucking army sergeant Jones. But he got it wrong.'

'And then what happened?'

'He tried to put his hands on me. So I went for him – self-defence. And then that fat fucker sat on top of me and called the police. When I get back to school, I'll kill him. And that pervert policeman.'

Lloyd was sexually abused by a neighbour when he was seven years old while his mother was absent. I imagine being sat on by the caretaker brought back some bad memories.

'The police say the caretaker saw you with tablets.'

'If I had tablets, where are they? Search the school, if you want. Search the office. You won't find anything. Pervert Jones is lying.'

'Did you hide them somewhere?'

Lloyd raises an eyebrow at me. 'If I did, I'd be stupid to tell you, wouldn't I?'

'The caretaker says your brother was around during the scuffle. They think you gave the tablets to Pauly—'

'They already searched him!' Lloyd shouts. 'Ask him, if you don't believe me. They never found *nothing*. They're lying.'

'Pauly plays with Tom Kinnock, doesn't he?' I say.

Lloyd stiffens. 'Who?'

'Your brother's friend.'

'I don't know *no one* called Tom.'

'Well, there's a Tom in your class, for a start,' I say. 'You told me you beat him up once.'

'I don't know any *younger* Toms, then.'

'I'm surprised. You usually get to know your brother's friends. It's been a source of trouble before, hasn't it?'

'What are you saying?'

'That you've asked Pauly's friends to carry things, hide things. It wouldn't be the first time you'd got a younger friend of Pauly's to look after tablets so you wouldn't be caught with them.'

'Prove it.'

I decide to try another line of questioning. 'Listen, the police are going to ask you this. Did your mum ask you to get medicine for her?'

'*No*.' Lloyd's eyes become shifty, roaming the bare room.

'But it's an obvious link, don't you think? Your mum has a problem with prescription drugs, and you're caught breaking into the medicine cabinet. I'm here to help you, Lloyd. And I can only do that if you tell me the truth.'

'No comment.'

It's going to be a long night.

Lizzie

I sit up late into the evening holding the tablets, watching the packet turn from yellowy silver to grey shadow as the sun sinks in the sky.

What are they? Where did they come from? What should I do? What should I do?

The thoughts go around and around, unanswered, for hours.

Eventually, I lock the tablets in the medicine box and try to sleep, but can't. Thoughts continue to whirl.

I should take the tablets to the police. I will. Tomorrow.

Before I know it, the sun is coming up and it's morning.

I go through the motions, trying to get Tom ready, finding clothes, giving him meds.

'Mum?' Tom asks. 'Mum? Are you okay?'

I try for a smile. 'Just a bit tired, love. Worrying about yesterday. Those tablets …'

'You won't tell anyone, will you?' Tom's eyes are wide.

'I have to, Tom. We need to get to the bottom of this. We always used to talk, didn't we? About everything. We're friends. All the stuff about your dad … when you told me the truth I could fix it. I couldn't fix it until I knew.'

'You can't fix this.'

Fear weaves around my stomach, a spider spinning a web. 'Well, maybe … look, if you could just *talk* to me.'

'I can't. You don't get it, Mum. I just can't.'

We walk to school in silence, me thinking, thinking about what on earth I'm going to do.

We have to move schools.

That goes without question.

But how can we, without social services marking us as cause for concern?

I squeeze Tom extra tight before he runs into the playground. 'Look, be sensible today, okay? Play with the good kids.'

On the way home, I stop on the stony path, looking through the wire fence onto the playing field.

I can see the children through the school windows, moving between the assembly hall to their classrooms. Everything is so *quiet*. Not like a school at all.

It starts to rain and soon I'm soaking wet, short hair sticking to my head.

Is Tom with Pauly Neilson right now?

I step back, meaning to go, but my canvas shoes find a puddle. Cold water seeps around my feet and I hear Olly's voice, for the first time in a while: *What stupid shoes.*

No, says a higher voice. *You're strong and you're getting stronger.*

The big holes in the fence grin at me, mouths in the wire woven closed with mismatched silver chain.

Who made those holes? Who?

In a school so obsessed with security. A school that padlocks the gates. With CCTV cameras. Why are holes appearing?

I *will* find answers.

Lizzie

Why won't he stop crying? Why? Why?

I clutch Tom to my chest, swaying him frantically from side to side.

'I'll take him out in the camper,' says Olly, hobbling towards me.

'You shouldn't drive him around,' I say. 'Not with your leg the way it is.'

'Don't start that rubbish,' Olly snaps. 'I drove us up to Devon and back when you were pregnant. The doctor said it was fine.'

'She said it was fine if you were comfortable braking,' I say, over Tom's escalating screams. 'But when that van pulled out, you were in agony.'

'You can't keep me prisoner here,' Olly growls, lurching forward. 'Unable to walk, unable to drive. This is about control, isn't it? You want to control me. You fucked up my leg. Now you want to fuck up my mind.'

Olly's mood changes dramatically when Tom cries.

'Stop it. Just stop it.' I put Tom in his bouncy chair. 'He'll fall asleep soon. He always does eventually. You'll see.'

'I'm putting him in the camper,' says Olly, lifting the bouncy chair and carrying it towards the door. 'He sleeps when we're driving.'

'No,' I shout, following.

My fists beat on Olly's broad back, and he turns to me, eyes wild. 'Don't you ever do that again? Do you understand me?' He puts the bouncy chair down, then gives me the look. The one that says he wants to slap me hard enough to make my ears ring. 'Do you understand me? After everything you've done. Everything I put up with. I'm only with you because of Tom. I'm only with you because of this baby!'

I'm frightened, and for a moment I freeze.

That verbal lashing felt worse than any of the others. Not because it hurt, but because Olly hasn't been this angry since before Tom was born. The baby calmed him down. But now it seems the old Olly is back.

This was my fault, though. After all, I hit him. What did I expect?

Olly scoops up Tom, chair and all, and storms down the stairs, his uneven walk pounding on wood. Bump, bump … bump, bump.

'Don't take my son,' I scream down the stairwell, my words turning to shrieks. 'Olly. Come back. Please!'

A door downstairs opens, and I hear the murmurs of Stuart – our neighbour and my friend.

And then Olly's voice: 'Get the fuck out of my way. Get out of my way.'

I hear scuffles and run downstairs to find Olly and Stuart grappling in the hallway.

The bouncy chair rests a few feet away and Tom is letting out low, frightened little moans.

Oh God.

Olly throws a vicious punch that knocks Stuart to the floor.

'Olly!' I scream. 'Stop!'

Olly turns then, seeing me on the stairs. 'Go back inside.' He takes Tom from the chair and storms out of the front door.

I run past Stuart who is clutching his jaw, and out onto the street.

Olly is strapping Tom into the back of the camper van. 'Back off!' he shouts, sensing me approach. 'Just back off. I'm warning you.' He clicks the baby-seat straps into place, pulls to make sure they're tight, then slides the camper van door shut.

'You can't take my son!' I shout.

Ignoring me, Olly stalks around the car with his jolting walk, climbing into the driver's seat.

I pull at the camper's locked sliding door, crying, sobbing, beating the metal panel as I watch Tom behind the glass.

Then the camper van starts up with its usual spluttering roar.

'Don't take him,' I shout. 'Don't take him!'

The van pulls out into traffic.

I'm shaking now, cheeks soaked with tears.

I feel a large, warm body beside me. It's Stuart. He puts a heavy, muscular arm around my shoulder and I feel the familiarity of his great bulk.

'Are you okay, love?' Stuart is Scottish and huge. Most men wouldn't want to tackle him in a fight. But Olly is the sort to act first and think later.

I shake my head, unable to speak.

'You should call the police.' Stuart rubs his jaw and it makes a clicking sound.

'I can't do that. It'll just make things worse. He'll be back. And when he comes back, he'll say sorry.'

'So you're happy to have your little baby son driven around by that man?'

'He would never hurt Tom,' I say. 'He gets angry with me. But never Tom.'

'Hey.' Stuart squeezes my shoulder. 'You're a good mother. You don't need that bastard. It can't go on like this. I hear you fighting, morning, noon and night.' He looks at me meaningfully. 'Did he put his hands on you?'

I look at the pavement.

'Jesus Christ.' Stuart looks up to the sky, grimacing. 'I told you leopards don't change their spots. I'll kill him.' I burst into tears, and Stuart's big arms come around me. 'Hey. Don't cry,' he says, stroking my hair. 'Why don't you leave him? Make a fresh start.'

'I can't.'

Stuart slips his hand into mine and holds my fingers tight. 'This is breaking my heart.'

'Who's going to want a woman with a baby?'

'I do.'

'You don't. Not really.'

'I know my own mind. And I know you pretty well, too.' Stuart raises a thick, dark eyebrow, and I blush.

There was a night. A regrettable night.

Olly and I had been fighting. I suppose I was frightened. Trying to make a safe space for myself. Olly's medication was making him especially paranoid and I ended up downstairs, crying in the communal hall.

Stuart found me. I wanted to be found. Comforted by someone. Noticed.

And somehow I ended up in Stuart's flat.

I'm not even sure how it happened, but he took me into the bedroom. We had sex on the bed and then again in the kitchen. Stuart lifted me, totally naked, onto the breakfast bar and we had sex in full view of the street, curtains open.

I think it was thrilling for him, me being on display, so nearly caught out.

'Please don't talk about that,' I whisper to Stuart. 'If Olly finds out, he'll kill me.'

Kate

It's Friday. Tessa and I are meeting to discuss my workload. Because we don't have time for lunch *and* a meeting, Tessa orders in Pizza Express: American hot, garlic dough balls and chocolate fudge cake for her, plain Margherita for me. And a bottle of red wine from the supermarket – something we're not technically allowed in the workplace.

I don't drink – a source of annoyance for Tessa.

'You eat like a sparrow,' she says, pouring red wine into a balloon glass brought specially from home. 'I thought Lent was months ago.'

'I'm having a whole pizza,' I point out.

'A Margherita?' Tessa scoffs. 'That's barely even a snack. And you won't share any of this pud, I'll bet. Or the wine. It's Friday. Live a little.'

I ignore the dig and say, 'We're here to discuss my caseload. Not whether I should drink wine.'

'Oh, have a sense of humour.' Tessa gulps from her glass. 'All right. So tell me – how are you finding things? Not quite what you expected?'

'More overwhelming than I expected.'

'Ha! Yes, I imagine even a first degree couldn't prepare you for life in child protection.'

'I'm still grateful to be here. In a job that makes a difference.'

Tessa clearly doesn't expect this response and shoves two dough balls into her mouth in contemplation. 'But you just said you were feeling overwhelmed.' She chews the words around a mouthful of dough.

'Yes. I am. I have too much work for one person.'

'That's the spirit! Have a good moan. Now then. *Please* tell me you're finally closing down the Kinnock file. Did you find out anything at school? Reasonable cause to believe he's being picked on?'

'Tom's school teacher couldn't give any clarity on the marks,' I say. '"There's no bullying at our school." A bit *Stepford Wives*. I've got an appointment to see the headmaster. Hopefully he can give me a few more answers.'

'That's what they're like, those academies,' says Tessa. 'They have to brush trouble under the carpet or their funding gets cut. From what I hear, Steelfield School has gone from crap to brilliant within the space of a few years. They'll be desperate to keep their outstanding status. Can't have any nasty rumours rocking the boat.'

'Maybe the headmaster is just very ambitious and good at his job.'

Tessa snorts. 'The best headmaster in the world couldn't fix the Neilson boys. So anyway, what you're telling me is you haven't closed this file down yet?'

'The mother is convinced something is happening at school. Tom had strange marks on his arm. I have to keep him on my caseload. Lizzie is clearly a good mother. When we have people like the Neilsons on our books it seems ridiculous to waste our time on this family. But if something is happening at school ...'

'Tom Kinnock was lucky to get a place at Steelfield,' says Tessa. 'A boy who moved from London ... I don't know what strings they pulled to get him in, but for the mother to be complaining ... it sticks in the craw a bit, doesn't it?'

'We can't rule out harm at school just yet,' I say. 'I mean, for a start the Neilson boys go there. One of them could be ... I don't know. But you know the history with those boys. Anything is possible.'

Tessa takes a glug of red wine. 'From what I remember, those boys only ever hurt each other. What about Tom's family members? Any other adults he sees regularly?'

'Grandparents. But not regularly, from what I can gather.'

'Wait this one out, Kate,' says Tessa, pouring more wine into her glass. 'Put it down until more evidence comes to the surface. You're in no-man's land.'

'Wait until Tom gets seriously injured, you mean? I'm here to protect children, Tessa. To keep them out of harm's way.'

Tessa snorts. 'Okay then. I'll send you to the Bermuda Triangle, shall I? If we're in the business of solving mysteries.'

'If anything else happens to Tom, we're going to have to get the courts involved.'

'Now steady on—'

'Tessa, something is going on with that little boy. I need to visit Tom again, and then make a decision.'

'Look, before you jump to any conclusions, make doubly sure the father isn't still on the scene.'

'I intend to ask about that again when I visit.'

'When?'

'This afternoon. After school pick-up.'

'Ah. Stress-o'clock. Are you hoping to catch the mother screaming at him? Messy house? Rats in the kitchen?'

'If I want rats, I'll go to Leanne Neilson's house.'

'Ha ha!' Tessa slaps my back. 'To see that little rat Lloyd Neilson, you mean?'

'No,' I say, rather shocked by this insinuation. 'They have actual rats. Well, mice. The health inspector made a report on it.'

'Jesus.' Tessa shakes her head. 'Still. Could be worse. It could always be worse.'

I'm learning to ignore Tessa's laissez-faire attitude.

Although, sometimes I wonder – did she always have it? Or did it come about after years of working in under-funded, under-resourced social services?

Lizzie

There's a cheery red Fiat outside our house – not a car I recognise. My grip on Tom's hand tightens.

We're on our way back from school. Tom's been talking about the colour of the trees. Green holly and silver birch.

A sign of stress …

The Fiat's engine isn't running, but I see a shadow in the front seat – a woman. Kate. I'm relieved to see her, desperate to talk about my school concerns and the possibility of moving.

As we reach our front garden, the car door opens and she steps out, plain as ever in her trouser suit and black boots.

'Miss Riley?' Kate gives a wave and hurries to catch us.

I turn the key in the front door. 'Hi. How are you? Would you like to come in?'

'Yes, please. If I may.'

'Of course.' I push the door open.

'You dyed your hair,' Kate remarks.

I touch the bright-blonde tufts. 'I fancied a change.'

Mercifully the house isn't too messy. They spring visits on you, social services. I suppose to catch you in your natural habitat, chaotic and ill-prepared. Plenty of houses are a mess when no one is looking, I'm quite sure.

Suddenly, I realise I forgot to buy teabags earlier and feel my heart pound. Will Kate see this as a sign of a disorganised household?

'I'm really sorry, we're out of tea,' I tell her, moving a pile of laundry from the kitchen counter. 'I was at an interview today; I didn't have time to shop.'

'That's fine.' Kate kneels down to Tom. 'How are you, Tom? Good day? What happened at school?'

'I don't remember,' he says.

'He never seems to remember much about this new school.' I put an arm around his shoulders. 'At his old school, he used to remember lots.'

Tom wriggles away, runs upstairs and slams his bedroom door.

'And he's always in his bedroom these days,' I say. 'Maybe he's just growing up. I don't know. But … I'm worried. Take a seat. Sorry about that blanket. Just move it to one side. I'll put the kettle on. I've only got instant coffee. Sorry.'

Kate moves the crumpled blanket from the sofa and sits down.

I wonder if the neighbours know why Kate is here and if they do, what they think of me.

The kettle boils and clicks. I make two cups of instant coffee and carry them into the lounge, apologising again for the lack of tea.

'It's fine,' says Kate. And then, clearly on a tight schedule, gets straight to the point. 'Miss Riley, has Tom seen his father since my last visit?'

'No,' I say. 'I told you, I don't let him see his father.'

My fingers grip my mug – a rainbow-coloured one I chose to bring cheer into the living room.

'From a social services point of view,' says Kate, 'it's important children have the widest circle of loving adults available to them.'

'I think any parent with such serious issues revokes their right to be a parent.'

'That's not how the system sees it,' says Kate. 'A parent is still a parent, even if they've exhibited aggressive behaviour. Of course, they have to be managed. Supervised visits and so on. You're quite certain Tom hasn't seen his father since you moved?'

'Of course I'm sure.' I clear my throat. 'He doesn't want to see him. They asked him about that in court. Look, this is about more than just his visitation, isn't it? I'm not stupid. Has Olly been in touch with you? Told you how evil I am for withholding his son?'

'Not directly.'

'Kate, Olly is dangerous.' I hesitate, thoughts tumbling over themselves. 'A very good manipulator. I'm even scared he might … God, this is going to sound ridiculous.'

'What?' Kate sits up tall.

I take a sip of coffee, wondering how best to phrase things. 'I keep noticing holes in the school fence. Along the country path. What if Olly … I mean, I know it sounds crazy …'

'Tell me what you're thinking,' says Kate.

I feel hot coffee scald my leg and realise my hand is shaking. My eyes drift to the angry red splash mark on my bare knee. 'What if Olly is getting into Tom's school? Tom hasn't been himself since we moved here. He's withdrawn. Moody, sometimes. Aggressive, even. It's like he's hiding something. And Olly is clever. I was careful, but … that doesn't mean he hasn't found us.'

'Do you really think that's likely?' says Kate. 'I'm sure the school would notice someone sneaking in.'

I have a vision suddenly – a tall, scruffily dressed but handsome man, jogging across the school field. It only takes him a moment, and then he's inside the school, sneaking down the corridors.

The teacher's back is turned.

'Tom. Tom – come and talk to me a sec.'

I shake the vision away, feeling sick.

'The school is such a strange place,' I insist. 'It's like they're hiding something. The bars on the windows, two-way glass, a padlock on the school gate – what normal school has security like that?'

'Yes, I did notice,' says Kate.

'It's weird. And amid all that, there are holes. Big holes cut in the wire. Why? I don't want to sound paranoid …' I let the sentence trail away, aware I definitely *do* sound paranoid.

'I can look into that,' says Kate. 'Do you have any idea where your ex-husband is living now?'

'None.'

'I heard he's staying with his mother.'

'Is he? No. She would have told me.'

'I don't suppose you happen to have contact details for her?'

'Margaret lives in East London.' I stand up. 'My phone is somewhere in this mess. Let me find it for you.'

After five minutes of searching, I finally find my phone on the bookcase, resting on a selection of literary novels and cookbooks.

'I have her address,' I say, scrolling through my contacts. 'I'm guessing she's still at the same place.'

'Thanks,' says Kate, taking the details. 'I'll pay her a visit. And I'm going to visit the school tomorrow.'

She looks at me then, and for moment I wonder if she's going to ask something else. Some really awful question.

But she doesn't. Instead, she thanks me and leaves.

When she's gone, I sit on the sofa, head in my hands.

Lizzie

'Who is it?' I call, voice shaking.

A familiar voice comes from the other side of the door. 'It's me. Stuart.'

'I'm a bit upset, Stuart. Now isn't a good time.'

'Let me in,' Stuart calls, voice deep but soft.

I don't answer.

'Lizzie, I heard shouting. I need to make sure you're okay.'

'I'm okay,' I call back.

'If you don't open the door, I'm going to break it down.'

'Okay, okay, I'm coming.' I go to the door, put a hand to it, then slowly turn the Yale lock.

Stuart fills the doorway with his tall, broad frame, and for a moment I wonder what it would be like being his girlfriend instead of Olly's.

Stuart is handsome, like Olly, but with a broken nose that kinks in the middle. He's a little older – nearing forty – and his brown hair recedes slightly at the temples, which I think is why he often wears hats.

'Doll.' Stuart's eyes crinkle with sadness. 'Are you okay?'

I give a stiff nod.

'Did he do this?' Stuart touches the long, linear bruise on my arm.

I nod again, looking away.

'I'll kill him. This has to stop.'

'No. Please, Stuart. He's getting better. Truly.' I don't know if I believe this. All I know is I want to believe it.

'Where's the baby?'

'Olly took him out. They're visiting his mother. Margaret.'

Stuart puts his arms around me. 'You deserve so much better. Don't cry. You're too pretty to cry.'

I give a half-hearted laugh.

'That's better. So what happened? Do you want to talk about it?'

'What's there to talk about?'

'You. Olly. The future. You can't go on like this.'

'He's a good father. He does things to hurt me, but he loves Tom.'

'Are you sure about that? How can you be? I hear some of the things he says. Blaming you for his bad leg. Calling you names. A man like that is capable of anything.' Stuart takes my face in his large hands, and I feel tiny – a little girl beside a giant. He has coarse, brown stubble and lovely white teeth. And really, he's very kind.

Stuart kisses me gently and then with increasing pressure. He pulls my body tight to his. Perhaps I should say no – he'd back off, be a gentleman about it. But I don't. Olly is right. I don't plan. Things just happen to me. And right now, this tenderness feels wonderful.

'Run away with me, Doll,' Stuart whispers. 'How many times do I have to ask?' He lifts me into his arms and carries me out of the flat and downstairs to his own ground-floor apartment.

Anyone could see us. Olly. Anyone.

But they don't.

Stuart kicks his door closed behind us, staring deep into my eyes like I'm the most precious thing he's ever seen.

The next minute, he is lifting my dress over my head, pushing me onto the sofa. Then he pulls off my knickers, positioning himself between my legs, holding me close, moaning and calling my name as he enters me.

We have sex in different positions, ending with me on my knees by the window wearing nothing but a bra, Stuart behind. He is a little rough sometimes, not realising how strong he is. Or maybe he enjoys throwing me around. I don't know. Maybe all men are violent deep down.

When we're finished, Stuart asks me again to leave Olly. He can finish his current contract any time. His family have property in the Shetlands.

But Stuart isn't Olly. Despite his kindness, he doesn't make me feel the way Olly does. When Olly and I have sex it's like two souls coming together. We become one person, which both scares and thrills me. And, of course, Olly and I have a child.

So I crawl back upstairs and pray my husband never finds out about another stupid mistake.

Kate

The roads around Steelfield School are rammed with cars, so I park on the yellow zigzag lines right outside, declaring it a social services emergency.

I should park ten minutes away and run to the appointment, arriving hot and sweaty. But increasingly, I'm learning that sometimes rules need to be broken.

The school gates are locked tight with a giant padlock and the playground is eerily still.

Most playgrounds have some life and colour to them. The odd piece of bright litter skating around on the tarmac, at least. But this school has none of that.

Everything is scrubbed and clean and devoid of personal touches. It looks sterile to the point of unused. Like a school that's only just had the cellophane taken off.

I notice the barred windows again as I ring the intercom buzzer.

A moment later, Mr Cockrun appears from the main door and strides across the playground. He's well-groomed in a sharp suit and has very red lips. I'd guess him to be nearing fifty, although his dress and haircut make him look younger.

'Hello there.' Mr Cockrun's greeting is cheerful and he's smiling. 'You must be Mrs Noble. Welcome to Steelfield School. I would shake your hand, but I need to let you in first. Ha, ha.'

After the long process of removing the padlock, letting me through the gates, then re-clipping the padlock and tugging it vigorously, Mr Cockrun takes my hand and shakes it warmly. 'Very good to meet you.'

'Thanks for agreeing to meet me at such short notice,' I say.

'Yes. Well, you're a VIP,' Mr Cockrun replies. 'Anyone in our hardworking social services deserves the royal treatment. Shall we go for the tour then?'

'Please.'

'Did you notice the new exercise equipment?' Mr Cockrun asks, pointing to some gleaming metal structures sunk into the tarmac. 'Part of our healthy bodies initiative. Promotes good behaviour too, burning off all that energy.'

'I hear you're very on top of behaviour here,' I say.

'Very. The only trouble we have is with social services children. But we have good processes. Ways to keep even the most unruly child in line. Provided we're not handed *too* many of them.'

He leaves the comment dangling, and I can imagine him in the staff room, complaining to the other teachers: *It's disgraceful that they can force these social services scallywags on us. We want well-behaved middle-class children who help us get good results ...*

'As you can see, the grounds are excellently maintained,' Mr Cockrun continues. 'The caretaker is an ex-army man.'

We're crossing the school field now, walking over short grass. On the way, Mr Cockrun stoops to pick up a stray chocolate-bar wrapper.

We reach a patch of woodland near the fence and Mr Cockrun lifts up a branch for me to duck under.

'The fence that Mrs Kinnock told you about is back here,' he says. 'But this is all a storm in a teacup. One parent causing trouble. It's been very securely repaired for the time being. During the Christmas holidays, the whole fence will be replaced. But obviously we can't do that during term time.'

'I don't see any holes,' I say, looking for them.

'That's because they're miniscule,' the headmaster says, following me under the branch. 'Ridiculous to make a fuss about this, in my opinion. Tom Kinnock's mother is biting the hand that feeds her. Making problems over nothing. It's bordering on paranoid. Not to mention ungrateful.'

Behind us, the school bell rings, but there are none of the usual excited noises of children being let out. It's all too orderly. Bordering on sinister.

'Do you see them?' says Mr Cockrun. He points at wire mesh. 'There. All solidly repaired.'

I stoop down, seeing cut wire repaired with coat hangers and an old bike lock. Despite the unprofessional job, the holes are most certainly secure.

'As I say, the holes have been temporarily repaired until the Christmas holidays. I find them unsightly too, but they are no more than that. There is absolutely no security issue. None at all. Quite the opposite – we're one of the most secure schools you could find. Very well safeguarded.'

'With a padlock on the front gates,' I say.

'Well, of course,' says Mr Cockrun. 'I admit the padlock on the front gate is a little … old-fashioned.'

'Yes. Most schools have an intercom system. Remote locking. And unlocking.'

'The school building is very old,' says Mr Cockrun. 'A remote locking system wouldn't work in our case. But a padlock does the job.'

'With a padlock, I suppose you can control who has the key.' I make the suggestion lightly, but watch Mr Cockrun's face.

He gives nothing away.

'We have to keep the children safe. And the staff.'

'From what?' I ask.

'Look, we really care about these children,' says Mr Cockrun, spreading his palms wide. 'It prays on my mind, the wrong people getting in. Miss Riley has come from a very stressful situation. Divorce and so on. New house. I don't mean to be unkind, but she's paranoid.'

'Why has the fence been cut in the first place?' I ask. 'Could someone have been trying to get into the school?'

Mr Cockrun cocks his head, clearly working out the most agreeable way to answer.

'Mr Cockrun,' I say. 'Spare me the politician's spin. Just tell me the truth. I'm not here to audit your school.'

The headmaster hesitates. Then his eyes meet mine. 'No one is trying to get in,' he says. 'Actually, someone is trying to get out.'

Lizzie

'Come on, Tom. We have to go. I promised we'd see your grandmother.' I'm at the school gates, calling across the playground.

Tom's pale face flicks away from Pauly. He crosses the tarmac in a few seconds.

'Grandma?' he asks. 'Or Granny?'

'Your dad's mum.'

'Ye-ess!' Tom does a little air punch.

'We've got to walk quickly,' I say, taking his hand.

'Why?'

'We're catching the London train.'

'I hate going to London.'

'It's okay, Tom. I always plan these trips carefully. I know you're worried about seeing Dad, but it's a very big city. We'll be safe.'

We head down the country path and then across the park towards the train station.

As we pass the swings, Tom says, 'Guess what? Pauly Neilson has the same social worker we have.'

My feet slow, despite the imminence of the train. 'What?'

'Our social worker. Kate. She's Pauly's social worker too. He told me.'

'It doesn't surprise me that Pauly has a social worker,' I say lightly. 'But it should tell you he's someone to stay away from.'

'What's wrong with having a social worker? *We* have a social worker.'

'But we shouldn't,' I say. 'We shouldn't have one, Tom. They only got involved because of your father. They should have closed our file down by now. The school ... If only you'd talk to me. Give me some answers.'

'There's nothing to talk about, Mum.'

When we reach the station, the train is at the platform and we have to run.

'How long will it take before we see Granny?' Tom asks, as we jump onto the train. 'I can't *wait* to see her.'

'Not long. Just this train, then a short walk to the play park.'

It's a specially chosen play park, of course – one that's very public, with lots of escape routes.

I know Margaret loves us. She's proved it time after time. But she still sees Olly. So I always plan our meetings very carefully.

You can never be too careful.

Kate

'Who is trying to get out of the school?' I ask.

'Lloyd Neilson,' says Mr Cockrun. 'Social services force problem children on us, Mrs Noble, and it becomes a constant struggle to remain unblemished. It's a mystery to me why the government pressures us to get good results, then jeopardises everything with these damaged individuals. Why not send them to a failing school?'

'The idea, Mr Cockrun, is that your outstanding school improves the behaviour of troubled children,' I say. 'That in a school full of well-behaved kids, children with issues can follow good examples. Make better friendships.'

'Theories,' says Mr Cockrun dismissively. 'We live in the real world. A real world with boys like Lloyd Neilson. If there's a loose railing, an open gate or a low fence, that boy will be over, under, through and out. That, Mrs Noble, is why there are holes in the school fence.'

'So Lloyd is cutting the fence?'

Mr Cockrun nods. 'And every time Lloyd Neilson is seen larking about in town, we're forced to report an unauthorised absence. It's all a matter of government record and makes it that much harder to keep our outstanding status.'

I notice the headmaster says, 'every time Lloyd Neilson is seen' not 'every time he gets out'. Presumably absence records are only made when they have to be.

'So Lloyd Neilson makes the holes, climbs out and makes a run for it?'

'Yes.'

'How do you know?'

'He was seen. The caretaker watched him going at the wire. By the time we reached him he'd already cut the hole and made a run for it. The caretaker's pliers went missing at the end of last term. We suspect Lloyd has hidden them somewhere in the school.'

'Do other children play back here?'

'All three Neilson boys. That goes without saying. You give those boys a rule and they break it.'

I think of my car parked on zigzag lines. 'Anyone else?' I ask. 'What about Tom Kinnock? Have you ever seen him back here?'

'No.'

I look over the hole again, assessing it for possibilities. 'And no mention of adults lurking by the fence?'

'Absolutely not.'

'You know about the marks on Tom Kinnock's arm, don't you?' I say. 'The pin pricks.'

'Yes, the mother came in to make a fuss about that. I'm sure it was nothing. Boys rough and tumble. Especially boys of a certain type, if you get my meaning.'

'Oh, you mean social *services* boys,' I say. 'Did they ever teach you about self-fulfilling prophecies, Mr Cockrun?'

'I beg your pardon?'

'Self-fulfilling prophecies. Decide a child is naughty and he'll become naughty. Not every child with social services involvement is badly behaved. Some of them are delightful.'

Mr Cockrun laughs coldly. 'I've yet to meet a delightful one.'

'Maybe you just don't see the delightfulness. Can I ask … do you keep injection needles at school?'

Mr Cockrun doesn't answer right away, jingling coins in his pocket.

'Injection needles?' I ask again. 'Do you keep any at school?'

'For diabetic children,' says Mr Cockrun, turning away. 'We keep the needles locked up, all safely managed. Tom Kinnock did not get any weird and wonderful marks at this school, Mrs Noble. And certainly not from an injection needle.'

'Why lock up the needles? Why not just keep them out of reach of the children? This isn't a mental health facility. It's a school.'

'Look, we're going to have to call time on this for today, Mrs Noble. I've provided you with everything you asked for. You wanted to see the school fence and hopefully I've put your mind at ease.'

'Mr Cockrun—'

'I know you understand, Mrs Noble. Public sector employees have to manage our time efficiently. We have so little of it. So if you don't mind, I'll show you out.'

'If you don't have time now, we'll have to meet again,' I insist.

'I really think we've covered everything.'

'No, we haven't.'

Mr Cockrun sighs. 'I have a little time this Friday. After three p.m.'

This Friday I'm booked solidly from 8 a.m. to 5 p.m., but ...

'Yes, okay,' I reply. '3.30 p.m.?'

The headmaster nods, then notices something on the woodland floor. A small brown bottle – like a medicine bottle. Unlike the chocolate-bar wrapper, he doesn't pick it up.

I follow his gaze.

Mr Cockrun's head flicks up then. 'Let me show you out.'

'That looks like a medicine bottle,' I say.

Mr Cockrun laughs. 'It does a bit, doesn't it? Someone must have thrown it over the fence. Let's head out.'

I stoop to pick up the bottle.

Mr Cockrun watches me, and I get a sense of a bear, cornered and dangerous.

On the shiny brown plastic there's a damp white label with computerised letters printed across it. 'It's prescription medicine,' I say. 'Look, there's the chemist's logo.'

'I'd say it was fairly impossible to read,' says Mr Cockrun, squinting. 'As I said, someone must have thrown it over the fence.'

The writing is faint, but I can see the outline of a name. My eyes walk along the faded letters, lips moving as I sound the words:

'Oliver Kinnock.'

This medicine belongs to Tom's father.

Mr Cockrun turns back to the school. 'Let's talk in my office.'

Lizzie

I have bruises on my arms again. Small finger marks with brown centres and yellow edges.

Yet somehow, amid all this chaos, Tom has grown into a little boy who feels and thinks and has his own voice. I don't know quite how it happened. It's like he grew while we were trying to cope with everything. And now Tom's school-aged, trying to make sense of the crazy world we've brought him into.

It's a cool evening and my skin is goose-bumpy, but I refuse to wear a jumper.

The truth is, I want Olly to see the marks.

This is what victims do – beg for mercy.

Olly is on the red leather sofa, drunk and apathetic. He's gone the other way this week, willingly taking his pain meds – too many, sometimes – and mixing them with alcohol. An empty blister pack of codeine is beside him, but there's more in the cupboard. It wouldn't do to run out.

I sit beside him. 'I'm freezing,' I say.

He turns, but doesn't notice the bruises on my arm.

'When I can get back on the slopes, everything will be better,' he says, a tired old mantra I've heard for years now.

We're silent for a moment, neither of us acknowledging the truth.

Olly will never get back on the slopes.

'If you'd just take the meds how you're supposed to take them—'

'Don't start that again, Lizzie. I'm not an addict, okay? The hospital gave me those painkillers to take whenever I want.'

'Not *whenever* you want. Whenever you're in pain.'

'I'm *always* in pain.'

One of my nursing friends, Fatima, thinks Olly's leg injury could be doing something to his brain. 'Look up Fat Embolism Syndrome,' she said. 'It all fits. The paranoia. The agitation. He needs to see a specialist.'

But Olly is so suspicious of the medical profession now – missing appointments left, right and centre. I try so hard to make him go, but these days he just point blank refuses, flying into a rage if I push things.

And he is so furious about the injury. Furious enough to take his anger out on me. Accusing me of all sorts of things.

In his worst moments, Olly says it's all my fault. He blames me for everything – his broken leg, stalled recovery, failed Olympics dream.

Everything.

There's a knock at the door.

'Who is it?' Olly calls out.

Silence.

Then Stuart calls back, 'Only me, mate. Um … just had a question about the lease. But it can wait. Sounds like you're in the middle of something.'

We hear the tramp of footsteps going downstairs.

Stuart is a terrible liar.

I've tried to stay away from him. From the 'us' that happens *whenever I feel low. But it hasn't been easy and I've lapsed. Several times over the last few years.*

'He came up to see you,' says Olly, turning to me. 'Didn't he?'

I stiffen. 'Why would he do that?'

'He came up to see you!'

'Please,' I say. 'Don't shout. Tom's sleeping. He has school tomorrow.'

Olly stands then, towering over me. 'Matt said he saw you coming out of Stuart's flat the other week.' The words are full of menace. Matt is one of Olly's best friends. A believable testimony.

Oh God. I feel sick to my stomach.

'He saw *you!*' Olly shouts. 'What were you doing?'

'It was probably about a parcel or something. Matt … he's just trying to stir things. He's always been jealous of us. You know that.' A terrible excuse, but the best I can think of. I'm trapped on the sofa, nowhere to hide.

'How many times?' Olly demands, eyes blazing.

'Olly, you're being jealous. Irrational. It's the pills. Nothing's happening between me and Stuart,' I say, desperately.

Olly throws an art deco vase on the floor and it smashes.

I cover my head and suddenly I'm on the floor too. I look up and see the apartement door. Then the staircase outside. Everything flashes black, white and red. I hit the stairs with my arm, my hip, my cheek as I tumble down, down, down.

I land in a crying heap on the floor below, feeling like I've been beaten with truncheons.

Olly stands at the top of the stairs, a look of utter contempt on his face. 'Why did you do that?' he asks. 'Why did you throw yourself down the stairs?'

I want Stuart to come and rescue me. But I don't think he heard. Or maybe he went out.

Olly goes back into the flat and I limp slowly back up the stairs, a beaten, broken animal, back to the shadow I stand in, the man who says he loves me.

Back to our son, whom I pray has slept through all this.

I just don't know what else to do. I'm so desperate for a stable home. To give Tom what I never had. But this isn't stable. It's more dysfunctional than my own upbringing.

When I reach the top of the stairs, I see Tom's bedroom door is open and hear he is crying.

I run to him. 'Tom!'

In the bedroom, Olly stands over Tom's bed, chest heaving.

'What are you doing?' I scream. 'Why is Tom crying?'

Olly eyes are both drug-glazed and panicked. 'I—'

'Why is he crying?' I demand. 'What did you do, Olly? God, what did you do?'

I pick up Tom and see his hand fall at an odd angle from his body. 'Oh God. Oh my God.' I turn to Olly, shaking my head. 'What did you do?'

Lizzie

Margaret is on a swing when we arrive at the play park, swaying back and forth, feet scuffing the ground.

She's dressed young for a sixty-something woman, in a long, blue crepe dress that swills around her white sequin-covered plimsolls, but she carries it off. Some people can wear teenage clothing just the right way, no matter what their age.

This forever youthfulness reminds me of Olly.

Margaret is chatting to a grey-haired man who's leaning against the swing post. She is a very friendly person, Margaret. The sort who could strike up a conversation with anyone.

'Tom! My little Tom!' Margaret's face explodes with smiles when she sees us. She comes bounding over. 'How's my grandson? I've missed you.'

The play park is the sort you see all over London: a tangle of wood logs connected to a wobbly bridge; a nest swing of children's limbs; a zip line whooshing back and forth.

I don't feel safe here, but then again, I don't feel safe anywhere.

'All right?' Margaret waves at me.

'Hello, Margaret,' I say, managing a smile. 'How are you?'

'I'm fine, love,' says Margaret. 'All the better for seeing you two.'

Kate

3.30 p.m.

Mr Cockrun's office is a neat, sterile room with a CCTV screen cycling through school-ground and corridor images.

On one wall there's a large picture of children playing, but it is unframed and unloved, faded and scuffed around mounds of Blu Tack at the corners. And generic too – I doubt Mr Cockrun has ever met or taught these children.

There is also an extra desk. I wonder who it's for. And Lizzie was right about the medicine cabinet – there's one mounted to the wall.

As we enter the office, Mr Cockrun swings around, offering a full smile. 'Do have a seat.'

Diagnosing Special Needs
Helping Kids Concentrate
The Pressure Principle
Success in Education

The books are arranged alphabetically, I notice.

'So let's talk about this medicine bottle,' I say.

Mr Cockrun sits opposite. 'Didn't you want to know about the incident with Tom Kinnock first?' he asks.

A politician's answer. Side-stepping the question.

'You can tell me about that first, if you like. What actually happened?'

'Tom got into a scuffle with a girl in the year below. It was all dealt with in-house. Well handled, I felt. Although the mother has no doubt been blowing it out of proportion.' His red lips set into a firm line.

'A younger girl? Why?'

'Children get into scuffles for all sorts of reasons. Especially boys with issues.'

'And Tom was sent to see you?'

Mr Cockrun hesitates. 'Yes. Yes, he did come to my office.'

'How about the girl? Did you talk to her?'

'There was no need. She was fine. I spoke to her parents. Assured them that the whole issue was somewhat exaggerated. Tom's mother was informed. Told to raise her game. We can't have that sort of thing going on here. Good behaviour is paramount.'

I make furious notes. 'Is this the only incident you can think of?'

'Yes.'

'So there have been no other incidents?'

'Absolutely none.'

'Mr Cockrun, Pauly Neilson ended up in hospital on the same day Tom had this scuffle. Is there any connection?'

'Oh, *that*. Yes, that was something quite separate.' He glances at the medicine cabinet – just a tiny, sideways twitch. But I notice.

'Bit of a coincidence, isn't it? The same day.'

'Well, yes, I suppose so. But coincidences happen.'

'So about the medicine bottle—'

'You also wanted to know about the injection needles, didn't you?' Mr Cockrun says. 'Why we keep them locked up.'

'Well … yes. Why do you?'

Mr Cockrun folds his fingers together. 'Lloyd Neilson again.'

I raise an eyebrow. 'He seems to be your answer for everything.'

'That's because he usually *is* the answer for everything.' Mr Cockrun stands and paces back and forth, hands spread like he's giving a speech. 'Look. A few months ago, things started going missing. Personal stuff belonging to the children. Money. And then medical items. Prescriptions would be given to the school office. Painkillers, antibiotics and so forth. And they'd vanish.' He eyes me meaningfully. 'Do you understand where I'm coming from?'

'Yes. You're saying Lloyd was stealing meds.'

'We caught him red-handed. He seems to have a fascination with the stuff.'

'What about injection needles?'

'We keep them locked up so he can't get to them. I hope that answers all your questions. As you can see, we're just a hard-working school trying to meet government requirements while dealing with some very difficult children.'

It makes sense, I suppose. Leanne has a prescription medication addiction. Children often imitate what they see at home. But I feel there's more to this than the headmaster is telling me.

'So has Lloyd ever got hold of injection needles at school?'

'We've only caught him stealing tablets. The diabetics *shall* have their insulin!'

'So the tablets the caretaker caught Lloyd with – were *they* taken from the school medicine cabinet?'

'Unlikely. You can see we keep everything locked up now. But not impossible. You never know with Lloyd.'

'And the medicine bottle at the back of the field?' I ask, leaning closer.

'My guess is Lloyd again,' says Mr Cockrun. 'Look, I know you're going to say I blame Lloyd Neilson for everything. But it's happened before. Lloyd has … persuaded kids to bring medicine in for him.'

'So you think Tom Kinnock brought in medicine for Lloyd? The bottle in the school field had Olly Kinnock's name on it – Tom's father.'

Mr Cockrun blinks. 'I thought the father wasn't on the scene.'

'That's what I thought too.'

'Well.' Mr Cockrun continues to pace. 'Who can say how that bottle got there? Perhaps we'll never know the truth. All I can tell you is we truly care here, Mrs Noble. We're on the ball. No child left behind. You can see from our results that there aren't any problems at this school. We're one of the best in the country.'

I laugh. 'I work in the public sector, Mr Cockrun. I know first-hand how results can be … shall we say affected? Not tell the full story?'

Mr Cockrun walks to the door. 'And on that note let's call it a day, Mrs Noble.'

'Mr Cockrun—'

'We've said everything we need to say and this situation has taken up too much of my energy.' He opens the office door. 'I wish you well, Mrs Noble. I hope you realise we're just doing our best. You and I are probably more alike than you realise.

I can see you're ambitious. Hard-working. Someone who rises to a challenge.'

'Yes. I am.' Although sometimes, the tired, overworked me wishes I'd followed Tessa's advice and buried Tom Kinnock's file in some back drawer.

Lizzie

I've always felt safe in hospitals. I suppose that's why I trained as a nurse – medicine seemed safe. Reassuring. But right now, I don't feel safe at all. Tom is *still* unconscious and I'm terrified.

What if he doesn't wake up?

I feel sick with worry. I can't bear this.

We're in intensive care, a nurse seated next to Tom's bed. I'm relieved that we're getting close attention, but I'm still terrified.

Tom will wake up. He will wake up. Oh God.

The tears come, thick and heavy.

Across the ward, I hear double doors bounce open and the determined click of the doctor's shoes. After a mumbled chat with a nurse, the doctor heads our way.

'Mrs Kinnock?' The doctor is a short, brown-skinned man with a shiny bald head.

I'm too exhausted to complain that he has my name wrong, so I just nod.

The doctor holds out a chubby hand and says, 'I'm Doctor Ramir. And this must be Thomas? Or does he prefer Tom?'

'He likes Tom.'

Doctor Ramir asks the nurse seated by Tom's bed, 'Has there been any movement? Any signs that he's regaining consciousness?'

'No,' says the nurse. 'We're hopeful it won't be too much longer.'

'And how are *you* feeling, Mrs Kinnock?' the doctor asks me.

'Terrified.'

'Of course. Well, try not to worry. I'm sure he'll come round soon.'

'The other doctor talked about the possibility of brain damage—'

'Unlikely.' The doctor's reply is brisk. 'I'm concerned about two things right now. First, what's caused him to suddenly lose consciousness. And second, the bump on Tom's head.'

'Bump on the head?'

'The paramedic found a rather large lump. On Tom's crown.' The doctor puts his fingers to Tom's scalp, frowning. 'Here. You can feel it for yourself.'

I put my hand on Tom's head, feeling a large, egg-sized bump.

Terror flies up my fingertips. *A head injury …*

The doctor watches me.

'It didn't happen when he fell,' I say. 'I caught him.'

'No, this didn't happen today, Mrs Kinnock,' says the doctor. 'A scab has already formed.'

'Oh my God. *What?*'

'When Tom wakes up, I'd like this lump to be checked over by someone who knows about this sort of thing. Just to be on the safe side.'

'Doctor, if Tom has a bump and it didn't happen when he passed out … how on earth did he get it?'

'It's hard for me to draw conclusions,' says the doctor, scribbling on his clipboard. 'The consultant will tell us more.'

'Someone hurt him?' Hot, heavy tears find my cheeks.

'It could be an accident,' says the doctor. 'Tell me, is Tom a good boy at home?'

'Of course,' I say. 'Why would you ask?' And then it hits me. My chest tightens. We learned to ask questions like this during our nurse's training. '*I* didn't hurt him,' I say, eyes wide.

There's a gentle exhale of breath and a tiny murmur. My head whips around to see Tom's eyelids flutter.

Is he waking? He's waking …

Tom squints, trying to shield his eyes from the bright lights. Confusion swims in his sleep-crusted eyes. He is startled. Afraid. But he's awake.

The relief is incredible.

'*Tom.*' I take his hand in mine. 'It's okay. You're in hospital again, love. Oh thank God.'

'Hello, Tom,' says the doctor.

Tom blinks sleepily, gingerly touching the cannula in his hand.

'How are you feeling?' the doctor asks.

'Sick,' says Tom, his voice rough as pebbles. He looks at the cannula.

'You passed out, Tom,' says the doctor. 'It tells us something still isn't quite right. Maybe we can get some answers this time. Now, take things nice and slowly, but can you remember what happened before you fell down?'

'We were in the play park,' Tom croaks, rubbing his eyes. 'I was with Granny.'

'Is that the lady who was here earlier?' the doctor asks.

'Yes,' I reply. 'She followed the ambulance here. But the bright lights gave her a migraine, so she went home to rest.'

'If she saw Tom before, it would be good to talk to her.'

'Yes. Yes, that makes sense. I'm sure she'll be back soon. But please understand. There are some difficulties in our family. How many days will Tom be kept in, do you think?'

'Two, at least,' says the doctor. 'But we'll move him to an open ward at some point. He'll have his own TV and some toys to play with. More space too.'

And less security.

'We need to be transferred,' I say, my voice reaching oddly high notes. 'To the general hospital near our home.'

'Mrs Kinnock—'

'I'm *Miss* Riley. Please. You have to listen. We can't stay here on an open ward. Tom's grandmother is *Olly's* mother. My ex-husband. Olly is … a violent man. There's a restraining order against him. Margaret always means to help, but if she accidentally tells him we're here …'

The doctor glances at the nurse. 'I suppose … let me see what I can do.'

'And this bump on Tom's head,' I say. 'We need to be sure everything is transferred – all the information, everything. Even the tiniest detail.'

Without looking up, Doctor Ramir says, 'Tom. Do you know what could have caused this bump on your head, then? Get into any fights or anything like that?'

Tom doesn't reply. He just looks frightened.

'There's a bump on your head, Tom,' I say gently. 'What happened?'

'I don't know,' said Tom.

'Well, look.' The doctor stands. 'Let's check everything over today. And hopefully in a few days, time we'll have some answers and he can be back at school.'

'No,' I say. 'I don't want my son anywhere near that school right now. Not until we've found out more about this head injury. If it didn't happen when he fell …'

The doctor eyes me seriously. 'I have to tell you, social services will take a very dim view of you keeping Tom off school. They're involved with you already, aren't they?'

I look back at him, anger flooding my bloodstream. 'Are you saying that I can't even keep Tom off school now? I don't have that choice as a parent?'

'Parents have very few choices when it comes to education,' says the doctor, looking down at his clipboard. 'It's a legal requirement.'

I tuck the blanket tighter around Tom, smoothing the fabric under my fingers, trying and failing to calm myself.

The doctor leaves.

And I'm glad about that, because I was a few deep breaths away from screaming: *Don't you understand? Something is happening at that school!*

Kate

'Will you get us fish and chips then?' Lloyd asks. 'Joey. Get *off!*'

Joey is hanging onto Lloyd's leg, giggling helplessly.

I'm in the Neilsons' kitchen and have just found animal droppings in the cereal cupboard, plus a chewed hole in a box of Crunchy Nut Corn Flakes.

Pauly's little face appears in the doorway, looking hopeful. 'Fish and chips?'

'Well, we can't have cereal,' says Lloyd. 'There was vermin. That is unsuitable.'

Vermin. Unsuitable. It's astonishing how Lloyd has picked up the social services language, aged eleven.

'Are you getting us fish and chips, Kate?' Joey asks from Lloyd's leg.

'I can't leave you alone.'

'But Mum does it all the time.'

'Well, she shouldn't.'

'You're shit, Kate,' says Joey simply.

'You have to give us something,' says Lloyd, volume rising. '*Joey*, get off!' He shakes his little brother onto the carpeted kitchen floor.

I've never seen carpet in a kitchen before. I now understand the hygienic power of lino like never before.

'I can't leave three young boys unsupervised.'

'But we're *starving*!' Lloyd bellows.

'You'll have to wait until your mum gets home.'

'And when will *that* be? She won't be back today. I couldn't get any meds for her.'

My head flicks around. 'What?'

Lloyd, clearly realising he's said the wrong thing, heads into the living room and throws himself onto a leather sofa.

I follow him, finding Pauly with his nose inches from the giant flat-screen, watching zombies kill each other.

'I'm glad you brought that up, Lloyd,' I say. 'That's something we need to talk about. The tablets.'

Lloyd feigns innocence. 'What tablets? I was just joking.'

'The tablets the caretaker said you had. *Those* tablets. The tablets the police couldn't find. The ones your headmaster says you've stolen from the school before.'

Lloyd's expression contorts with rage. 'Fucking Cockface. *Lying* fucking Cockface.'

'Lloyd, just tell me the truth.'

'I already told you. I never got those tablets from the medicine cabinet.'

'So you *did* have tablets?'

'I got given them by a kid in Pauly's class.'

'Lloyd!' Pauly yells. 'That's my *best* mate.' He hurls himself at his brother, all elbows and fists.

Lloyd calmly picks Pauly up and throws him onto the sofa.

'Are you saying …' I pause, choosing my words carefully.

'You're saying a child in Pauly's class gives you his medicine? Prescription medicine?'

'Yeah.'

'And do you, by any chance, throw the empty bottles at the back of the school field?'

'Have you been *spying* on me?'

'Social workers know everything,' I say.

Lloyd snorts with laughter. 'No they don't. Half the time, they don't even spell my name right.'

'And that child,' I say, knowing I'm on dangerous ground, professionally speaking. 'Would that child in Pauly's class be Tom Kinnock?'

'She's Tom's social worker too, Lloyd,' whispers Pauly. 'He must have grassed you up.'

Lloyd balls his fists. 'I'll kill him, the little shit.'

'He didn't say a word to me,' I say. 'I worked it out. Why would Tom Kinnock give his medicine to you?'

'Because I *ask* him to.'

'Ask? Do you mean threaten?'

'I *ask*. It's not my fault if kids are scared of me.'

'So, what would happen if he didn't give you this medicine?'

'I'd … well, we'd have to have a talk, wouldn't we?'

I'm wide awake now, despite being extremely tired, and it's hard not to rush out questions. 'Have you ever met Tom Kinnock's father? His name is Olly.'

'No,' says Lloyd.

'You're sure? He's never come into the school or anything like that?'

'Tom wants to see his dad,' says Pauly. 'He told me. But his mum won't let him.'

247

Lloyd's eyes narrow. 'Should you be asking me about other social worker kids? Isn't that un-pro-*fession*-al?'

He's a much brighter boy than the teachers give him credit for.

'Let's talk about you, then,' I say. 'Why would *you* take medicine from this boy, Lloyd?'

'The doctors won't give our mum enough meds,' Joey pipes up. 'So Lloyd gets them for her. And sometimes he takes them too.'

'*Joey.*' Lloyd turns to him, fists clenched, then leaps on his younger brother.

Not one to miss a fight, Pauly jumps into the punches, trying to defend little Joey from Lloyd's hard fists.

As tough as Pauly is, he's no match for Lloyd, who easily throws him across the room, then sits on him and starts punching his face.

'Stop!' I try to grab Lloyd, but he's strong.

I'm not really sure what happens next, but suddenly I'm on the floor and Lloyd is standing over me, fists clenched.

'Fuck off. Just *fuck off.*'

Little Joey jumps on him, arms around his neck, screaming, 'Lloyd, don't. *Don't.* She'll put you in prison.'

I get to my feet. 'Lloyd Neilson, sit down *right now.*'

My jaw stings – I think I caught a punch somewhere along the line.

Lloyd doesn't sit down. Instead, he starts pacing the room like a caged dog.

Pauly watches him, looking worried.

Joey is crying.

In training, I was told to exit any situation that gets physical, for my own safety. I think that's what the boys expect me to do. But I can't leave them. They haven't even had dinner.

'Listen.'

Three faces turn to me.

'What are you still doing here?' Lloyd asks. 'Leave. Go on. Grass me up to whoever.'

'I'm going to get you some fish and chips,' I say. 'And when I come back, I want you all calm. Okay? Lloyd, you need to sit down.'

Pauly nods rapidly.

Joey says, 'Yesss!'

Lloyd glares.

'Okay, Lloyd?' I say, my voice sterner.

'Lloyd,' Joey whispers. 'She's gonna get us fish and chips. Say yes or you'll go to prison.'

Lloyd looks at his shoes. 'All right then.'

'All right, what?'

'All right, sorry.' Lloyd sits on the sofa.

'Lloyd, forget Tom Kinnock for a moment. The headmaster says you've stolen medicine from the school before. I need to know if that's true.'

'Fucking Cockface. I don't tell, he don't tell. He *promised*. Adults are all liars.'

I turn to Joey and Pauly. 'You two – upstairs. Right now.'

The boys exchange worried glances, then two little pairs of feet trot upstairs.

'Lloyd, this is *extremely* important.'

Lloyd chews at the skin around his thumbnail. 'I mean … yeah, I've taken medicine. But Mr Cockrun knows about it. He lets me.'

'That doesn't sound quite right, Lloyd.'

'Forget it then. Don't believe me. Adults are bullshit.' He looks sullen.

'Is there anything else you want to tell me?'

'Nothing. Just forget it. Are you gonna tell the police what I did?'

'I'll have to write it up. But I'm not going to tell the police. You're hungry. You shouldn't have been left without food so long. You're only eleven. But listen – don't ever do that again.'

'Kate?'

'Yes, Lloyd?'

'I'm, like, sorry for what I did. I shouldn't have done it. You're one of the good ones.'

I sigh. 'Thank you, Lloyd. It's very grown up of you to apologise. I'll be back in twenty minutes, okay? Please don't burn the house down. I really, really shouldn't be leaving you, but you need to eat.'

'Twenty minutes is nothing. Mum's left us for the whole weekend before.'

'I know.' I head out of the front door.

When I'm five paces from the house I burst into tears. No one's ever punched me before.

Stop it, Kate. Stop crying. Get a hold of yourself – you're an adult.

Anyway, this is a happy occasion. The Neilson boys are going to get their first proper dinner in months.

Lizzie

'Okay, Tommo?' I squeeze Tom's hand. He's beside me on a hospital stretcher, being wheeled towards the ambulance by a green-suited paramedic. 'We're getting out of here.'

'Are we going home?'

'Not yet. We're going to a hospital near home.'

'Will Granny tell Daddy we're here?' Tom asks, a slight quiver in his voice.

'She wouldn't mean to, but … anyway, best to move. Nothing to worry about.'

We're not in the ambulance yet. Not free from danger. And until we're loaded on and driving away, my chest will be full of bats, beating their wings.

When we reach the ambulance doors, the paramedic says, 'Hello, Tom. Been in the wars, have you?' He's a black-haired man with a lean, toned body.

'A little bit,' says Tom.

'Well, we're going in this nice big ambulance and then we'll have a quick drive. Okay? Shouldn't take too long. Do you like being driven around?'

'Not really,' says Tom. 'I get car sick.'

The paramedic asks me, 'Are you hopping in the back with him?'

'Oh. Yes. Of course.' I climb into the ambulance, strapping myself in beside Tom, and stare out through the blacked-out windows.

Two visitors are approaching the hospital – a younger man and older woman. As I watch, the mechanical ambulance doors whir shut and the tyres start to creep over the tarmac.

The woman's arm is linked through the man's. He seems to be pulling her along, faster than her older legs can manage. The man is tall, with longish blond hair around his ears.

It takes a moment.

Then recognition hits me like a hammer.

The woman is Margaret.

And the man is Olly.

I unclip my seatbelt, rushing to the window by Tom's stretcher.

Leaning over Tom, I sway dangerously, face pressed to the glass as the ambulance swings around a corner.

'Madam!' the paramedic shouts. 'Sit down, *now*.'

I pull back from the window, eyes still riveted to the glass, but now the ambulance has turned I see only buildings and road.

Oh God, oh God, oh God.

Olly looked ill. Gaunt. Still with that handsome bone-structure and tall body, but a shadow of his former self. It's been so long since I've seen him …

I think I'm going to be sick.

Margaret brought Olly here.

Emotions whirl around, and it's hard to know what is most overwhelming.

Panic, confusion, fear.

Betrayal.

She brought him here. I thought she was on our side.

'What were you playing at?' says the paramedic. 'You could have fallen.'

I feel tears coming.

'It's all right.' The paramedic looks embarrassed now. 'I didn't mean to upset you, love. I just didn't want anyone getting hurt.'

'It's not you,' I explain. 'I just saw Tom's father. There's a restraining order against him.'

'Oh lord,' says the paramedic. 'That's a situation. Should I phone the police?'

I shake my head. 'We're going now. He didn't see us.'

'You're safe with us,' says the paramedic, voice warm and reassuring.

'I hope so,' I say.

'Tom should be back at school in a few days,' the paramedic continues, giving us a cheery smile. 'That's what the nurse was saying. Give you a bit of time to yourself, Mum.'

I look out of the window, thinking: *That's the last thing I need.*

I want Tom at home with me. Tucked up on the sofa where I can see him. As far away from that school as possible.

Kate

Col is still awake when I get home. I'm so tired, I trip on the front door mat.

'Hi, love,' I call out, hanging my coat in the hallway.

There's a pause. Then Col appears from the office room wearing his black glasses, a T-shirt and some tartan pyjama bottoms.

His usually neat blond hair is fluffy and his broad face pale with tiredness. I'm guessing he was waiting up for me – probably playing one of those strategy games he likes.

'Where did you get those pyjamas?' I ask. 'You never wear pyjamas.'

'Oxfam,' says Col, yawning and stretching his long arms into the air, touching the low ceiling with his fingertips. 'You're even later than usual.' He hasn't noticed the bruise on my jaw yet and I'm in no hurry to point it out.

'You went into town?' I ask.

'I had the interview. Remember? Kate? What's wrong?'

I'm crying again and I can't answer.

'What happened?' asks Col. 'Was it something at work?'

I nod.

'What is it, love?' He studies my face, eyes widening at the mark on my jaw. 'Good *God*. What *happened*?'

'One of the kids,' I blurt out, letting more tears come. 'I'm so *tired*.'

'Leave this job immediately,' says Col, pulling me into a hug. 'Hand in your notice tomorrow. This is completely unacceptable. Someone *struck* you.'

'Col, I always knew it wouldn't be an easy road. This is a trial. A test.'

'I love you, Kate Noble,' Col replies. 'I love your faith and determination. But this is getting too much. Hop into bed. I'll bring you a glass of water and we'll talk.'

I head into the bedroom, pulling off my black lace-up shoes and lining them neatly in the wardrobe beside my running shoes. I can't sleep properly if things aren't neat – a little OCD quirk of mine.

Even undressing is exhausting.

Col returns with my water, glances at the bruise on my chin and says, 'I'm serious, Kate. You should leave this job. It's a safety issue.'

'I've trained for years,' I say. 'It's my path. This is … a bad day. A bump in the road.'

'Come on, Kate. I haven't seen you in months. And when I do, you're exhausted. This isn't *one* bad day. It's a bad job.'

'That's why people like me need to be doing it.'

'You're going to make yourself ill.' Col walks into the en suite. 'I'll brush my teeth and then we'll talk.'

'I'm too tired to talk.'

'Seriously, Kate,' Col calls, his words garbled by toothpaste.

'How are we ever going to have children if you fall asleep the moment your head hits the pillow?'

'It's not every night.'

'It *is* every night. We're husband and wife now. Not flatmates.'

Col comes back to the bedroom frowning. Wordlessly, he folds his glasses, puts them on his bedside table and climbs into bed.

'Col?'

But Col pulls the duvet over himself, rolling away from me.

'Are you going to sleep?' I ask.

'Yes,' says Col. 'You are too, I imagine.'

He does this sometimes – gets in moods.

'Hey,' I say, giving his shoulder a shake. 'What's going on?'

'You're always tired,' he tells his pillow. 'We only just got married – oh, it doesn't matter.'

I know what he's saying.

We haven't had sex in a long time.

And yes – he's right. I've been too tired.

I lie back on my pillow, knowing I will fall asleep straight away, then wake up at 3 a.m., thinking, thinking.

I'm just closing my eyes when I hear my work phone bleep from the hall. It does that when emails come in – a very irritating setting that I haven't yet worked out how to turn off.

'Leave it,' Col says, his back still turned.

'I need to turn it off, Col. Otherwise it'll bleep for the next hour.'

I grab my phone, return to the bedroom, and think: *Better check my emails quickly.*

Col, reading my mind, says, 'Don't do it, Kate. Go to sleep.'

'If someone's sent something at this time of night, it must be urgent. I just want to make sure I'm not walking into anything major tomorrow.'

'Oh, *Kate*.'

'It'll only take a minute.'

'It *never* takes a minute.'

I know he's right, but I open up my email account anyway, bracing myself for bad news, tension rising in my chest.

And there it is. Right at the top of the pile.

The worst news.

I've been sent a secure, encrypted email from Westminster Hospital.

It's from a paediatric consultant, informing me that Tom Kinnock fell unconscious this week. Not quite a seizure, but something like it.

While Tom was passed out, the doctors found a partially healed head injury and are flagging this up as cause for concern.

The consultant paediatrician believes the injury happened several days before Tom was taken into hospital and is consistent with being hit with a blunt object.

My working days just got longer.

I need to arrange a multi-disciplinary meeting urgently.

And Col's sex life will just have to wait.

Lizzie

Tom stayed in hospital last night.

I slept beside him on a narrow pull-out bed. Actually, I didn't sleep much. It was hot, bright and uncomfortable, and I had a lot on my mind.

I'm home now, getting Tom a few bits and pieces – fruit, tea, snacks, clean clothes. I've packed a bag, showered off the hospital smell (putting too much shampoo in my new short hair as usual – I'm still not used to the length) and now I'm dressing.

While I'm pulling on my jeans, I hear a knock at the door. I freeze, one foot hovering off the ground, jeans halfway up.

There's a long pause.

Then another knock – louder this time.

I creep to the window, peeking through the line of daylight shining between the curtains. If it's my mother, I can't handle her right now. I just can't.

In the front garden, I see the top of a woman's head. Black, curly hair. A leather holdall over her shoulder. Glasses.

Thank God. It's Kate Noble. I need to talk to her.

I pull on my jeans, doing them up as I hurry down the stairs.

Common sense tells me Kate won't wait long. Social workers don't have time to stand on doorsteps.

Sure enough, the letterbox rattles as I reach the bottom step.

I cross the living room at speed, but I'm too late.

Kate is gone, leaving an unstamped brown envelope on the doorstep.

Inside is a letter:

Dear Miss Riley,

I'd like to arrange a strategy meeting as a matter of urgency. Dates and paperwork will follow.

In the meantime, if Tom is absent from school this must be accompanied by a medical note.

Please call or email using the details below.

Sincerely,
Kate Noble

Oh my God. A strategy meeting. Social workers don't organise those for no reason. And that line about needing a medical note – they're trying to stop me keeping Tom off school.

I feel there is a net hanging over our heads.

And it's about to drop.

Kate

'I need that report *now*, Kate.' Tessa stands over me, hands on hips.

'I haven't done it.' I don't even bother looking up. 'I need to set up a strategy meeting for Tom Kinnock. He's had another unexplained injury, which in my opinion means he's at risk of serious harm.'

Tessa considers this. 'Who reported the injury?'

'A consultant paediatrician at Westminster Hospital.'

Tessa raises a thick, dark eyebrow. 'Well, you can't ignore that one, I suppose. Yes, for once I agree with you. Fine. Make Tom Kinnock a priority. What are you doing now? A report for the mother to read?'

'Yes. It'll go to Lizzie Riley by first-class post this afternoon.'

'Get all the facts in there,' says Tessa. 'Don't worry about saving her feelings. Make sure *everything* is outlined.'

'I have done.'

'Not a nice letter to land on your doorstep,' Tessa remarks.

'No. But she's been to this sort of meeting before. In London. She'll know what to expect.'

'Don't waste too much time on this,' Tessa cautions.

'I never waste time. I don't have nearly enough of it.'

'So when is this meeting going to be then? I have a *very* full calendar.'

'The end of this week.'

'Ha! You'll be lucky.'

'As long as I don't get distracted by anything else and the doctor can make it.'

'Not get distracted?' Tessa snorts. 'When does that ever happen? So listen. I need you at ten-thirty—'

'I won't be free. I'm still trying to find Tom Kinnock's father. Ideally, I'd like to talk to him before the meeting.'

'Watch out there, Kate.' Tessa wags a finger. 'There's a restraining order against him, isn't there? He's violent.'

'Watch out yourself, Tessa,' I say. 'It's beginning to sound like you might care what happens to me.'

'No fear of that,' says Tessa casually. 'I learned my lesson years ago. You'll leave in the end. All the good ones do.'

Lizzie

Tom went back to school today. As my little boy crossed the playground, my heart dragged on the back of his heels. This tightrope of pain is familiar. I balanced on the same barbed wire when I left Olly. No choices are good here. Carry on and life is unbearable. Fall and you could break your neck.

Mum came to visit mid-morning, which was awful. But she didn't stay long because she was angry that I had no tea or milk.

I survived the rest of the morning by Googling parents' rights and child protection laws in different countries. What would happen if we moved abroad?

Now I'm eating lunch – fish fingers I bought for Tom, but am using as an emergency meal.

Perched on a sofa arm, I chew slowly without appetite, swallowing crunchy, charred breadcrumbs and thin, white fish.

Beside me sit social services documents, still unread. They arrived today, and will explain how the meeting will work. It will involve Tom's headmaster, a doctor and other 'relevant' people.

I remember how this all works because of Olly. Time smooths rough edges, makes pain more bearable, but it also rubs away memories. Makes the past hazy.

I must never forget how dangerous Olly is.

Balancing the bowl of fish fingers on the sofa arm, I pick up the envelope, turning it in my hands.

Kate Noble is more competent than the other social workers I've met – something for which I suppose I should be grateful. I mean, at least she's *doing* something. Taking an interest in us.

I notice how bitten and short my fingernails are. Maybe Kate has made a note of this. *A sign of stress.*

Sick with fear, I turn the pages, trying to take in details.

Risk of harm … unexplained injuries …

I look at the fish fingers, now unable to finish them. As I put the bowl by the kitchen sink, I have a thought: *Better check the medicine box key is still under the rubbish bin.*

I tip the silver cylinder to one side and kneel to examine the key taped underneath.

The key is there, but …

Has it been moved? I swear there's an extra crease in the Sellotape. It looks different somehow.

And Mum was here earlier …

No. I'm being paranoid. Letting my stress get the better of me.

The key is fine.

No one has moved it.

I think I'm going crazy.

Kate

Keep your head up. Walk tall. I stride past three teenage boys lounging on a bench. They play tinny music from a mobile phone. They're not quite men, but certainly not young boys.

One of them says, 'She ain't wearing a bra.' And the other two snigger.

I turn around. 'Excuse me?'

Three pairs of eyes widen in surprise. Then the tallest boy regains his composure and mimics, '*Excuse me?*'

I put my hands on my hips. 'If you have something to say, come out and say it.'

The boys look uncomfortable then, and the smallest one says, 'He was just saying he fancied you.'

'Oh. I see. Well, just to let you know, I am wearing a bra. It's a 34D seam-free one from Bravissimo and is the most comfortable bra I've ever worn.'

The boys don't know where to look now.

'We just wanted to know what you're doing here,' the tallest one asks.

'I don't have to explain myself to you.'

The tallest one says, 'If you're looking for someone, I can

show you where they live.' He turns to his friends and boasts, 'I know everyone in this block.'

'Okay. Do you know Margaret Kinnock?' I ask.

'Um … nah.'

One boy snorts. 'You know *everyone*.' Then he says, 'She's an older lady, yeah? Like … sort of yellow hair? She's in that one.'

He points to a first-floor flat. I see long, purple and paisley dresses hanging along the balcony.

'Thank you.' I head past a small play park and up concrete stairs onto the first-floor walkway.

Margaret Kinnock's flat looks neater than those around it, with well-tended marigolds and a funny little sign by the door that says: *Beware of the Owner*.

I ring the doorbell and hear a jangly version of 'Greensleeves'.

There is a soft pad of feet and then the door opens. A lady in a green dressing gown with long, dyed-blonde hair answers.

'Yes?' She looks me up and down.

'Margaret Kinnock?' I ask.

'Who wants to know?' Her accent is East London.

'I'm Kate Noble from Child Services. I'm looking for your son, Olly Kinnock.'

'Who is it?' shouts a male voice from somewhere in the flat.

Margaret puts a hand to her chest. 'Olly's not here. That's my partner shouting.'

'Can I come in?' I ask.

Margaret looks flustered, checking behind her. 'We've only just finished breakfast.'

'Who is it?' the male voice demands.

'Just someone from child something,' Margaret shouts. 'Here for Olly.'

A short, elderly man with a shaved head appears, holding a *Daily Express* newspaper. 'What do *you* want?'

'Freddy!' says Margaret. 'Excuse me, Mrs Noble. This is my partner.'

'Husband,' Freddy snaps. 'Say husband. I hate the word partner. That's what gay people say.'

'Husband then,' says Margaret. 'Common law.'

'I asked her what she wanted,' says Freddy, brown eyes glaring. 'Fair enough question, isn't it?'

'I'm looking for Olly Kinnock,' I reply. 'Your … stepson?'

'He ain't here.' The man stalks off.

Margaret turns to me. 'Why don't you come through to the lounge? Let's not talk on the doorstep.'

'Yes. Okay.'

As I follow Margaret through to the perfumed living room full of china cats and teddy bears, my phone rings.

Tessa Warwick, Social Services Manager.

I can almost feel Tessa's rage through the phone display. She's rung four times now and left a text message: *Neilson report – WHERE IS IT?*

Yes, hell has finally frozen over. I missed a deadline.

There was an eighty-page report to do yesterday, plus two home visits, and there's no way a normal person can do that.

Something inside me snapped.

I'm rebelling.

Sod the paperwork – I'm going to do my job properly instead.

'Would you like a cup of tea?' Margaret asks.

'I don't really have time,' I say.

'Have you seen my grandson?' Margaret's eyes crinkle with

worry. 'He was very poorly last time I saw him. But his mum moved him to a different hospital and I haven't heard from her since. She's not taking my calls.'

'I can't discuss that,' I say. 'You'll have to talk to your daughter-in-law. I'm sorry to visit unannounced but I heard Oliver Kinnock was staying here.'

'I haven't seen him in a while. The next time he comes by—'

'Do you have an address for him?'

'He doesn't have one now he's sold the flat. But every so often he turns up.'

'Mr Kinnock doesn't have any address at all?'

'He's living in his camper van. Travelling around.'

'So when did you last see him?'

'Oh, I can't quite remember. He comes and goes.'

'To this flat?'

'Yes.'

Freddy shouts from the kitchen: 'I tell him to sling his hook. The great unwashed, telling me what newspaper to read in my own home.'

'Freddy, *shush*,' says Margaret.

'What about a phone number?' I ask.

'Oh, Olly doesn't have a phone.' Margaret straightens a porcelain cat's lace collar. 'He got a bit down after the court case. He doesn't want to see anyone.'

'No one wants to see him either!' Freddy shouts from the kitchen. 'He needs a haircut and a good scrub-up.'

'There must be *some* way to contact him?'

Margaret gives a hopeless shrug. 'I just see him when I see him. I could let him know you came by?'

I get the feeling Margaret isn't being totally honest.

'Has Mr Kinnock seen Tom since the court case?'

Margaret shakes her head, lips tasting something sour. 'Lizzie won't allow it. She keeps Tom hidden away. I get what I can out of her when we meet up. Little by little. One of these days, I'll find out where she's staying.'

My phone rings again. Tessa, of course.

'I need to get this,' I say. 'Here are my contact details. If you see your son, please pass them on.'

I press a folded notepad page into Margaret's hand, on which I've handwritten my name, job title, telephone number and email. The Comms department still haven't printed me any business cards (probably thinking I'll quit before they need to), so I write out contact pages whenever I'm stuck in traffic.

Margaret considers the white paper slip. 'You'll send Tom my love, won't you? I don't see nearly enough of him.' Her mouth screws tight and wrinkles stretch from her cheeks to her ears. 'Lizzie is too hard on Olly. It isn't right. He needs to see his son.'

I wonder, quietly, if she was there in court. I've read the court documents a number of times now. Police records and medical evidence.

Olly Kinnock was accused of grievous bodily harm towards his wife and son, including breaking Tom's wrist, actual bodily harm and sexual assault. The sexual assault allegedly followed a physical fight between Olly and his neighbour, after which Lizzie claimed that he forced her to perform a sexual act.

Olly denied the charges.

Tom's broken wrist was later deemed a possible accident – even though Tom provided a video testimony citing his father as the cause.

The case was ultimately dismissed due to lack of sufficient evidence. This is how it often goes with domestic violence cases. No witnesses. The human body heals, destroying years of evidence. Fortunately, the courts gave Lizzie sole custody and Olly only supervised access. The restraining order was upheld for Lizzie, so he can't come near her. And he can only see Tom if Tom wants to see him. Which he doesn't.

A decent outcome, when all is said and done. At least we've worked to keep Tom safe.

Margaret probably didn't attend the hearing. It would have been too painful.

If there's one thing I'm learning on this job, it's the power of denial.

Lizzie

Today, social services will decide if I'm hurting my son.

Needless to say, I didn't sleep well last night. I woke up this morning with knots in my stomach. They're still there, pulling and pinching.

'Please,' I tell the bus driver. 'Can't you just let me off here?' We're stuck in a slow-moving slug of traffic. I think there's been an accident up ahead.

I'm wearing a pin striped skirt suit. It's the smartest thing I own. The skin around my nails is now bitten to bleeding point.

'*Please*,' I beg. 'I'm going to a meeting. About my son. I can't be late. *Please*.'

The bus driver's big shoulders sink a little. 'There's an emergency door handle up there.' He looks straight ahead. 'I never said you could pull it. But you can pull it. Just watch out for any motorbikes, all right? Sometimes they come up on the inside.'

'Thanks.' I pull the handle and the bus doors hiss open, freeing me to jump off and run down the street.

I'm out of breath and pink by the time I reach the Town Hall. Kate Noble waits in the foyer, arms crossed, wearing her usual black trouser suit. She looks tired.

'We're a little behind schedule,' she says. 'Usually I'd talk you through things but there's no time. I did ask you to come half an hour early...'

'I'm sorry, I didn't understand—'

'We should go straight in.'

I follow Kate into a beige meeting room. There is an oval table at its centre and three people sit around it.

'Come on in, Lizzie,' says Kate. 'Take a seat.'

I sit on an upholstered chair, noticing Mr Cockrun across the table. He is as immaculate and tailored as ever, fingers laced together, head cocked attentively, totally unfazed by a meeting that could ruin my life.

My brain swims, assessing the two others at the table: a large, red-faced woman and a tall, bearded man, most likely a doctor.

Kate takes a seat and hands me some paperwork from the centre of the table. Dutifully, I look down. ... *cause for concern ... unexplained head injury ... unusual pattern of illness ... possible injection marks.*

My eyes fix on my fingers, which are locked together in one giant, shaking fist.

'I'll start by reading out the report,' says Kate.

Some words wash over me, others stab like knives.

Considered at risk of significant harm ...

'A paediatrician has confirmed that Tom's head injury happened before he fell unconscious, Miss Riley,' says Kate, reading from pages in front of her. 'A few days previously, he believes.'

In the silence that follows, I realise I'm expected to comment. I lift my head, voice weary. 'I have no idea how he hurt his head. I already told the doctors. School is the only time he's away from me. It *must* have happened there.'

Mr Cockrun sits up straight. 'This really is bordering on slander now, Miss Riley.'

Kate holds up a hand. 'We'll hear from you in a moment, Mr Cockrun. Please don't interject again until you're called upon.'

I'm a good mother. You can't take my son away. Please, please don't take him away.

Kate turns to the tall, bearded man. He has grey hair and an unhealthily pale face. 'Perhaps you should take it from here, Michael?'

The ruddy-cheeked woman beside Kate, who clearly wants to be somewhere else, snaps, 'Aren't you going to introduce everyone first, Kate? Before you get into that? Miss Riley doesn't even know who she's speaking to.'

'Sorry.' Kate clears her throat. 'Yes – Miss Riley, this is Dr Michael Philips. He's a consultant paediatrician.'

'It was another doctor who examined Tom,' I say. 'Mr … Mr … it began with a *rom* sound.'

'Doctor Ramir, yes,' says Dr Philips. 'I'm afraid he couldn't be here today.'

I sit up at this. 'You've never met my son.'

'I can relay what other professionals have told me,' says Dr Philips. 'Tom's head injury was partially healed when he was admitted to hospital. Which tells us the injury happened some time before Tom fell unconscious.'

'How?' I demand.

'The injury could have happened in all sorts of ways,' says the doctor. 'But from our experiences of head injuries, the most likely cause was being struck with something. An object.'

'You believe he was struck?' I say, stomach churning.

'It's a strong possibility.'

'What else could have caused it?'

'Do *you* have any ideas, Miss Riley?' Kate asks. 'Any accidents at home?'

'No.' I shake my head. 'I've already *told* the hospital this. It must have happened at school. Tom doesn't go anywhere else without me. And it's *not me* who's doing this.' I'm angry now. 'Don't you understand? I'm worried *sick*. My son is being hurt. No one knows why or how. And instead of helping me find answers, you're putting me in the dock.'

I wonder if the people walking past this building realise what's happening inside.

They're trying to take my child away.

'Usually the parents are the best source of information,' says Kate.

'Do you understand how frightening this is for me?' I reply. 'Tom had a seizure the moment he started this new school.'

I see Mr Cockrun bristle, but he keeps quiet.

'Then Tom came home with injection marks on his arm,' I continue. 'Now a head injury. And he's *changing* at that school. Why can't anyone see how odd it all is? How many schools do you know with bars on the windows? Who don't let anyone in during the school day? Who padlocks gates so no one can get in and out without a key? It's like all the kids are brainwashed. And the teachers. Tom's not himself. I'm petrified.'

Kate clears her throat. 'Now we can hear from you, Mr Cockrun.'

Mr Cockrun fixes me with cold eyes, the fake smile long gone. 'Children are very well safeguarded at Steelfield School. Physical injuries are recorded immediately. All our staff are DBS checked. Miss Riley has been back and forth to the school on multiple occasions accusing us of whatever she can think of. We have told her repeatedly that these injuries are nothing to do with us.'

'You're not in Tom's class,' I say. 'Tom's teacher can't watch him every minute. What about playtime? There are holes in the fence.'

'This is about a family breakdown and nothing to do with us,' says Mr Cockrun. 'Miss Riley won't let Tom see his own father.'

'If you knew about his father—'

'Divorce can bring out the worst in people,' says Mr Cockrun. 'My feeling is that Tom would benefit from more discipline.'

'Are you saying I can't discipline my son?'

'Two parents are better than one.'

'Not if one of them has very serious issues.'

'You're not thinking about Tom,' says Mr Cockrun. 'What's best for him. The boy wants to see his father.'

I suck in my breath. '*What?*'

'Look, he's told me in confidence,' Mr Cockrun continues. 'He misses his dad.'

'His dad is a manipulator and a liar, and it's none of your business.'

'It's our business if Tom has emotional problems and doesn't behave at school.'

Mr Cockrun starts flicking through papers then, and I catch a glimpse of something – handwriting that looks suspiciously like Olly's scrawled, spiky loops.

'Is that … has Olly written to you?' I hear myself shout. 'Does he know Tom's at Steelfield School?' A shaky hand flies to my mouth.

The handwritten document is quickly covered with a typed sheet.

'I'm not sure I know what you're talking about,' says Mr Cockrun.

'Olly.' I turn to Kate for support. 'Has he written to the school? It looked like his writing …'

Mr Cockrun gives a false-sounding laugh. 'Are you talking about this?' He holds up the handwritten letter for half a second, then buries it again under paper. 'These are Karen's notes. The lunchtime assistant.'

I swallow, knowing I've just made myself look paranoid. Unhinged. But it looked so much like Olly's writing … and I don't trust the headmaster.

What if they're letting Olly into the school? Giving him access to Tom?

Divorce is terrible, Mr Kinnock. What you must be going through. Of course we'll let you spend some time with your son during the school day. What the mother doesn't know won't hurt her …

I put a hand to my stomach, trying to breathe the thoughts away.

'Let's talk about next steps,' says Kate, glancing at Mr Cockrun.

'The next steps are you allowing me to remove Tom from this school,' I say, more loudly than I mean to.

'There's nothing to suggest the school is doing anything untoward,' says Kate, her voice gentle. 'We've worked very hard to get Tom's placement there and give him a smooth transition.'

'He's coming home *injured*!' I scream, eyes furious and

275

accusing. 'He's having *seizures*! And what if his father is getting in? What if they're giving him access?'

Nobody says anything.

It can't be the school, Miss Riley. Just admit something's happening at home …

I feel sick to my stomach.

Absolutely frozen with terror, an animal backed into a corner.

'If I moved Tom to a new school…' I turn to Kate. 'What would happen?'

'We would have to step in. Especially in light of recent information. As we've heard, there's nothing to suggest these injuries are happening there.'

'So how else could Tom be getting them?'

Once again, the room falls silent.

'Please.' There are tears in my eyes. 'Why will no one listen? I'm telling you – *something is happening at that school*. Have none of you read our history? Tom's father was abusive. He's getting into the school somehow.'

'That's simply not possible,' says Mr Cockrun.

'There are *holes* in the fence.'

'I've looked into that,' says Kate, her voice still gentle. 'And I'm satisfied with the explanation.'

'It would be impossible for an adult to come into our school and harm a child,' says Mr Cockrun.

'Then *how* is my son being hurt in your care?' It all becomes too much then. I leap to my feet. 'Excuse me,' I stammer. 'I need … Excuse me.' I stride towards the door, fumbling with the door handle.

Someone calls after me.

Then I'm in a bathroom, being violently sick into a toilet. There is soft tapping at the door. 'Lizzie?' It's Kate.

'I'm sorry,' I say, taking deep breaths. 'I'm just terrified.'

Calm, calm.

'We only want the best for Tom,' says Kate, voice gentler than usual.

'Then *help me* find out what is happening at that school.'

Kate

'Well, that went badly.' Tessa checks her phone as we cross the High Street. A car beeps as she walks out in front of it, but she's oblivious.

I wave an apology at the driver, catching Tessa up. 'I feel we're moving forward.'

'The meeting was rushed, Kate. Far too rushed. You should never have tried to move so quickly. It was a dog's dinner from start to finish.'

We near Sangers sandwich shop, known for its doorstep-thick bread stuffed with generous fillings. Public sector workers need carbohydrates.

Usually, I pack my own lunch and save ten pounds and thirty-seven pence a week by doing so. But last night, I discovered Col had bought real butter instead of the spreadable stuff and I had a stress meltdown, thinking about the two minutes' extra effort he'd added to my day.

Col and I had a heated row, ending with him stuffing five pounds into my purse and saying, 'Just buy a bloody sandwich.'

It was good advice.

'I'm being pulled in fifty different directions here, Tessa,'

278

I say. 'If I'd left the meeting until next month and Tom got injured again, what then?'

'So now Tom Kinnock is subject to a care protection plan and you have even more work to do. And *about* this care protection plan: reading between the lines, it's a road *into* care, isn't it? We're looking to take the boy away from the mother at some point?'

'If these injuries continue, we have to be prepared to take a hard line.'

'I agree with your decision,' Tessa barks. 'I just don't agree with the workload you've put on yourself.'

We reach the sandwich shop, and my heart sinks to see there's a huge queue.

'I can't say I feel a hundred per cent comfortable with the situation,' I admit. 'I mean, no one has ever *seen* the mother hurting him. And the school … it's an odd place. The headmaster is clearly hiding *something*. Lloyd said as much. Maybe I should talk to Lloyd about it again.'

'We never *see* parents hurting their children.'

'Shouldn't we have some sort of concrete proof?'

'I think the point is, however it's happening, it's happening while he's in her care. Oh good gracious, look at this queue.'

We both consider the line, which bends around twice and stretches out of the door.

'Maybe we should go to Marks and Spencer,' I say, checking my watch.

'Nonsense. I want a *fresh* sandwich. Excuse me.' Tessa barges straight up to the counter, tapping the glass top. 'We're in a hurry. We have a meeting to go to. Can you serve us next?'

There are outraged cries from other customers, but to my

surprise, the serving girl says, 'Yes, okay, Tessa. But please don't start shouting again.'

'Great.' Tessa pulls out a smug smile. 'I'll have chicken, avocado and bacon, with grated cheese and mayonnaise. *Brown* bread. Lots of butter. And one of those bags of crisps. Not *that* one. The *large* bag. Kate, what do you want?'

'Um ...' I glance at the angry queue. 'Just a plain cheese sandwich please.'

'Is that it?' Tessa demands. 'No wonder you're all skin and bones. You'll waste away if you're not careful.'

The girl starts preparing our sandwiches, and I watch the white clock on the wall. We have seven minutes to buy sandwiches and eat them. Then we have another meeting at the Town Hall.

Tessa notices the clock too. 'Could you hurry it up a bit?' she shouts. 'I told you we have a meeting.'

The serving girl looks flustered. 'I'm going as fast as I can. I *did* serve you first.'

'Too bloody right! How many unpaid hours did you work last week?'

'What?' The serving girl looks alarmed.

'Come on! Unpaid hours. How many did you do?' Tessa demands.

The girl looks helpless. 'Um ... none? I mean, they pay me.'

'Right. Now ask me how many unpaid hours I did.'

'Err ...'

'Ten. And do you know why? Because the government won't stump up enough cash to look after vulnerable children. So, all of us at the coal face, the ones who see the kids with lice and malnutrition and black eyes, we put in the extra time off our own backs. We should have our own bloody VIP queue, the service we do for this country.'

'I could give you a free can of Coke? Since you've ordered two sandwiches,' the girl says uncertainly.

Tessa snorts in derision. 'I don't drink that rubbish. Now if you sold wine, that would be a different story.'

We head towards the door, to murmurs and moans from others in the queue.

'What are you all complaining about?' Tessa shouts. 'Do *you* have to sit in waste-of-time meetings all afternoon, then catch up on the important stuff at seven o'clock at night? Count your lucky stars and enjoy your full-hour lunchbreak.'

I steer her out of the shop before a fight breaks out.

Much as I admire Tessa's spirited defence of our profession, I really would like to get back and eat my sandwich before the next meeting.

It's going to be a busy afternoon. We're providing supervised contact for the Neilson brothers after the meeting. A two-hour playdate with their violent, drug-addicted father held at the local family centre. Sometimes Leanne doesn't bring the boys. Sometimes their dad doesn't show up. It's a lottery.

Be grateful, Kate. This is the job you wanted. Be grateful.

Ruth

'Are you listening to me, Elizabeth?' My heels scrape gravel as I follow my daughter up the path. 'Why didn't you tell me about this meeting before?'

I arrived at Elizabeth's home this afternoon to find her sitting on the front wall, sobbing and trembling. In *public*.

Elizabeth had forgotten I was coming, apparently.

'I need to know these things, Elizabeth,' I insist. I'm following her up the country track now; she's on her way to pick up Tom.

'It had nothing to do with you,' Elizabeth replies.

'Don't be ridiculous – I'm the boy's grandmother. This reflects on the whole family.'

'Is that all you care about, Mother?' Elizabeth turns then, and a bird flaps free from the trees. 'How things look? No, don't answer that. You might say something truthful for once in your life.'

I take a stiff intake of breath, lips tight to quell my outrage. 'After all I've done for you,' I say. 'A lifetime lost bringing up a sullen-faced little girl. I've driven two hours today. To *help* with my grandson. A little boy who's turning out to be just as sullen as you were.'

Elizabeth shields her eyes from the afternoon sun. 'You

didn't want anything to do with us while we were with Olly. Why the sudden interest?'

'You need help, Elizabeth. The school says so too. You're not strong enough to be a mother.'

She starts crying then. 'You're really going to do this?' she says. 'After the morning I just had?'

'Stop it, Elizabeth,' I say. 'People will see you.'

We reach the school gates and stand in silence, waiting for the bell to ring.

Eventually, Tom crosses the playground with another boy – an unkempt black-haired lad with breadline written all over him.

Tom reaches Elizabeth's side and slips his hand into hers. He glances at me, then looks away.

'Hello Tom,' I say.

'Hey Tommo.' Elizabeth stoops to hug him tight. Her eyes are creased and tired.

'Aren't you going to say hello to your grandmother, Tom?' I ask.

'Hello, Grandma.' The words are empty. Dutiful.

On the walk home I tell Tom, 'You need to behave yourself, young man. You're getting your mother in trouble with all these injuries.'

Elizabeth, of course, rushes to his defence. '*Mum*. Leave him alone.'

'Tell those social workers how happy you are,' I continue. 'Or they'll take you away.'

'God, Mum.' Elizabeth shakes her head. '"Shut it all away. Make it look nice. Don't talk about the divorce, Elizabeth, or no one will like you." What about Tom? What if he's *not*

283

happy? Something's happening at that school. I think Olly … Oh, I can't stand it.' She starts crying again.

'Elizabeth.' I shake my head. 'You have to stop making accusations. It's making you look … I don't know. Crazy.'

When we reach Elizabeth's house, Tom shoots upstairs.

The lounge is a mess. I pick up Elizabeth's green cardigan, fold it into a careful square and head upstairs to put it away.

Tom darts aside as I reach the landing and hurries into his bedroom, closing the door.

I hang the cardigan amid the appalling mismatch of casual clothing in Elizabeth's wardrobe – bright woollens, jeans, striped T-shirts.

I stare inside the wardrobe for a good minute, not quite sure what I'm seeing. And then increasingly horrified.

Elizabeth is *such* a mess.

There's nothing to be done in her case. My grandson, however – maybe he's still young enough.

I march into Tom's bedroom. He's looking at the wallpaper, stroking the butterfly wallpaper, eyes glazed over.

'Tell your mother the truth, Thomas,' I say. 'She's worried you're seeing your father. Of course you're not, are you?'

Tom shakes his head tightly.

'This is all just bad behaviour. Social services want to send you to a home for naughty boys,' I tell him. 'Do you understand? They'll give you grey porridge and itchy blankets. You have to tell them what a nice family you have.'

I sense Elizabeth behind me. '*Mother*,' she says. 'I think it's time you left.'

'But—'

'*Right now*.'

'Mum, I don't feel well,' says Tom, clutching his stomach.

'Okay, darling.' Elizabeth sits on the bed and scoops Tom onto her lap. 'It's okay.'

I purse my lips to show how displeased I am, but it has no effect these days. There's no reasoning with Elizabeth when she gets like this.

She's such a disappointment to me.

Lizzie

Come on. Answer the phone. Why is the doctors' surgery so busy?

I'm worried.

Beyond worried, actually.

After Mum left, Tom's hands felt cold. Now his eyes are glazed.

Answer the phone. Please.

This is my fifth call to the doctors' surgery now, but the line just rings and rings.

I'm standing in the living room, my back to the chaos that is our kitchen. The living room is a mess too, of course, but the kitchen is worse.

I've tucked Tom up on the sofa under a teddy-bear-soft blanket with a bowl of Wotsits. Not the most nutritious choice of snack, but today I'm not winning any good-mother awards. I've been too busy considering how I can keep Tom off school tomorrow without social services finding out.

The phone clicks and finally a voice comes on the line. 'London Road Surgery.'

'It's Lizzie Riley,' I say. 'I need an emergency appointment for Tom.'

'Hello, Miss Riley.' The receptionist sounds tired. She's heard from me so often since we moved here.

'I think Tom may be about to have another seizure,' I say. 'He's gone very pale and cold. I'd just like to get him checked over, if that's okay.'

'If you're quick, the doctor has a few spaces after five. Or you could take him straight to Accident and Emergency if you're really worried.'

'We'll come in right now.' I hang up the phone. 'Tom. Let's go. We're off to see the doctor.'

'Why?'

'You look like a ghost. I'm worried you might have another seizure.'

'I don't want to go to the doctors again. I feel fine.'

Olly used to do that. Insist there was nothing wrong with him. That he could heal all by himself.

'Now, Tom.'

'*Fine.*'

Tom takes a last handful of crisps, then pushes off his blanket. He attempts to slide his shoes on his feet while eating crisps at the same time.

'You should have a bit of juice before we leave,' I say. 'All those salty crisps.'

'I don't want to drink anything.'

'Why are you being so difficult? Tom, this isn't *you*. You're a good boy.' I grab the juice from the fridge. 'Drink some – come on. It's good for you. Vitamin C.'

Eventually Tom takes it, glaring as he drinks.

On the walk to the doctors' surgery, Tom kicks his shoes at the paving slabs.

'Tom. Don't do that.'

'Why not?'

Because it's what Pauly Neilson does … 'Just don't.'

'Why are we going to the doctor?'

'I told you. You don't look well. I'm worried.'

'I don't *want* to go to the doctor.' Tom stamps his foot hard on the ground.

'I've had enough of this. Why are you acting this way?'

'I want to see Dad,' says Tom.

'What?' My heart judders.

'I have a right to see my dad. Pauly said so.'

I feel sharp tears. 'Tom. You don't know what you're saying. Dad hurt you. Until he gets help, *proper* help, it's not a good idea.'

Tom shakes his head, looking back at the pavement. 'Forget it then. You're right about *everything*.'

'I'm not right about everything. But I'm doing my best.'

Tom doesn't answer.

When we reach the doctors' surgery, his hand slides out of mine.

Lizzie

'We're here to talk about Tom's broken wrist.'

It's a female social worker this time – her name is Faye and she looks in her late twenties, with white skin and black hair like Snow White. She can't have been in social work long because her forehead doesn't have any lines.

Faye looks between Olly and me, clearly trying to size us up.

It must be hard to get the measure of us – we're a mess of contradictions.

Olly, well-spoken and educated, yet scruffy in loose, surfer dude clothing, blond hair around his ears.

And me – well, who knows what I am? A skinny girl in a summer dress with DM boots. Long, brown hair. A worried little face. A real person in my own right, or just a girl pretending to be something Olly wants?

I'm not sure any more.

Olly loses his temper immediately. 'Look, I don't hurt my son, okay? We're as confused as you are. Why can't you leave us alone? We have enough on our plate.'

I put a hand over his, the placating wife, but Olly snatches his fingers away.

'Don't,' he snaps. 'Don't do that.'

'We're just here to talk today, Mr Kinnock.' Faye smiles. 'All we want is what's best for Tom.'

Faye's questions become more intrusive after that. Was Tom a planned pregnancy? When did Olly and I marry – before or after the birth? Have we ever separated?

'We're just trying to get to the bottom of things,' says Faye. 'Injuries like this … they're very unusual.'

The word hangs in the air.

'Sometimes,' Faye says carefully, 'parents lose control around their children when they don't feel they're coping. Do you feel you're getting enough support?'

'We get lots of support,' I say. 'Olly's mum is around. My mum visits often enough. Olly works from home now, so … he's around all the time too. But … but …'

I don't mean to, but I start to cry.

'Mrs Kinnock,' Faye asks. 'Is there anything you want to talk about?'

I nod. Then silently, I unbutton my shirt cuff and roll up a sleeve, showing the yellow-green bruise on my shoulder and the carpet-burn cut on my elbow.

Olly sits bolt upright, staring at my arm. His eyes still have the languid look of morphine in them as they blink, confused and scared. He's not quite here. Not quite understanding.

Faye stares at the marks. 'Mrs Kinnock? What are you telling me?'

I swallow, taking deep breaths, summoning all my courage. Finally, I manage to get the words out.

'Olly did this. He threw me down the stairs.'

There's an awful, heavy silence.

Then Olly starts shouting and swearing, calling me unhinged, psycho, a lying bitch.

Faye asks him to leave.

He won't at first, but she threatens to call the police and he limps outside.

I see him at the doorway, a black cloud, pacing back and forth, gait unsteady. He pulls an all too familiar blister-pack of codeine from his pocket, pops out a handful of pills – four or five, probably, I can't see – and throws them into his mouth.

In the suddenly silent room, Faye wants to know why I didn't mention these bruises before.

'Because I'm ashamed,' I say. 'Ashamed that I stay with a man who does this to me. That I had a child with him. And that I'm too pathetic to leave. But I never thought he'd hurt Tom. Never.'

'Does your husband hurt your son? Is that what you're telling me?'

'I've never seen it,' I say. 'I'd have left a long time ago if I had. But I'm not sure I know my own mind right now. Olly is very good at … manipulating things. Making me see things that aren't there. And he takes so much medication these days. Then he drinks on top of that … It makes him aggressive. I never thought he'd be capable of this, but …'

'Mrs Kinnock, do you think your husband caused Tom's injury?'

'It's … possible.' Tears come. 'Living with Olly – sometimes it's hard to know what to think. I didn't want to believe it, but what other explanation is there?' I break down again then,

head in my hands. 'I'm sorry,' I stutter. 'If Olly's been hurting Tom and I've let it happen …'

'It's okay.' Faye puts her hands over mine. 'It's okay.'

But it's not okay.

Not okay at all.

Kate

The Neilson brothers are in good spirits, testing the family centre's play equipment to the maximum.

Lloyd has already broken a plastic penguin slide and is now kicking the swings. He is full of energy, having been given a three-litre bottle of Coca Cola by Leanne before he arrived.

Lloyd innocently shared this news with joy and gratitude: 'We were lucky, Kate. We got *big* Coke for lunch. My favourite!'

I suppose when you're used to missing meals, the larger the bottle of coke the better.

'Stop it,' I shout, as Lloyd kicks the heavy swing high in the air. '*Lloyd!*' Joey, half asleep on my lap, gives a start.

'What?' Lloyd turns with feigned innocence.

'Stop doing that.'

'When's Dad getting here?' Lloyd asks.

I glance at the clock. The boys arrived at 5 p.m..

It's now 5.25 p.m. and their father still hasn't arrived. Probably he's forgotten. Or can't be bothered. If a parent doesn't turn up within fifteen minutes we're supposed to cancel the appointment, but we've learned to give James Neilson more leeway. He does sometimes arrive within half an hour.

Sometimes.

'Your dad might not make it this time,' I admit.

Lloyd slams the swing with all his might, hitting Pauly.

'Lloyd!' Pauly shouts. 'Watch it.'

Lloyd pushes the swing again, whacking Pauly in the chest.

Furious, Pauly runs around the swing, trying to grab his brother. He's smaller than Lloyd, but rage gives him superhuman strength.

Lloyd easily sidesteps Pauly, sneering and holding up two fingers.

'*Boys!*' I shout, causing Joey to flinch again.

'I'll tell on you,' yells Pauly.

'You wouldn't *dare*,' Lloyd shouts back.

Now it's Pauly's turn to run. 'I will tell. I will!' He darts around play equipment, shouting, 'Kate! Kate! Mr Cockface lets Lloyd take drugs from school!'

'*Shut up!*' Lloyd bellows, chasing after him.

Pauly comes to hide behind me. I seat Joey on his own chair, then grab Lloyd to stop him killing anyone.

'Stop it. *Stop it! Sit down!*'

'He's *lying*,' Lloyd shouts.

'Just calm down.'

Lloyd looks furiously at his new Nike trainers, which are almost certainly stolen.

'What's Pauly talking about?' I ask. 'Drugs? Does he mean medicine?'

I expect Lloyd to issue red-faced denials, but he doesn't. Instead he sits on a plastic seat and starts crying.

I realise my mouth is hanging open and close it.

'I'm the honest one,' Lloyd shouts, tears falling. 'But no one ever believes *me*.'

'Honest about what?' I ask.

'I already said,' Lloyd wails. 'I already *told* you. About the medicine.'

Joey puts a small hand on Lloyd's knee. 'It's all right, mate.'

I sift through memories. 'You said Mr Cockface ... I mean, Mr Cockrun let you steal medicine from school. And I said that didn't sound very likely. Is that what you mean?'

'You see?' says Lloyd. 'Even *you* don't believe me and you're one of the nice ones.'

'So Mr Cockrun lets you steal medicine?' I ask, not sure where this is going. 'From the medicine cabinet? Is that what you're saying?'

'It wasn't *stealing*. Cockface let me do it. He left his office open and everything unlocked.'

'Why would Mr Cockrun do that?'

'He was setting me up, wasn't he? So now I'm on camera stealing medicine. If Cockface tells, I go to prison. And who'll look after Pauly and Joey then?'

'I can look after Joey,' says Pauly, chest all puffed out. 'I made him scrambled egg yesterday, and—'

'Shut up, Pauly,' says Lloyd, giving him a shove.

'So ... when the police came the other day,' I say, 'had you taken tablets from the school medicine cabinet?'

'*No.*' Lloyd bangs his fist on the cushioned chair. 'Not that time.'

'I'm confused.'

'I got those tablets from another kid. I *told* you. The headmaster never wanted me arrested *that* time. It was the caretaker who phoned the police. Cockface was furious with him.'

'I'm still confused.'

Lloyd's forehead bunches in frustration. 'And they say I'm the thick one. Listen – Cockface left his office open for me so I could take medicine. You with me so far?'

'Yes. But when?'

'Ages ago. This was *way* before the school inspectors came. Cockface set me up. He wanted to get me on camera stealing medicine. So now he has something over me. If I do the wrong thing, he'll give the video to the police and I'll go to prison.'

'You wouldn't go to prison for that, Lloyd.'

'Yes, I would,' Lloyd insists. 'Because it's *drugs*, isn't it? That's what Mum went to prison for. I'd get at least two years.'

'Is that what Mr Cockrun told you?'

Lloyd nods.

'So the headmaster is blackmailing you?' I ask, horrified. 'Is that what you're saying? He has camera footage and he's using it to make you behave?'

'Behave and keep quiet.'

'Keep quiet about what?'

Lloyd shuffles in his seat.

'Lloyd, you can tell me,' I say. 'You won't go to prison. Mr Cockrun isn't telling you the truth. If he's making you keep secrets … well, that's not okay.'

Lloyd sighs. 'All right. Fine. Cockface does things to make the school look good.'

'Like what?'

'When the school inspectors come,' says Lloyd, 'Cockface opens the holes in the fence and lets us out. All the special needs kids. We go to the park. If anyone asks what we're doing there, we say it's a nature project.'

'We run for it,' Joey pipes up. 'Prison break!'

My head is whirling. 'Why?'

'So we don't make the school look bad,' Lloyd explains. 'By being thick and that. Cockface cheats on the exams. Gets us in his office and tells us the answers on exam day. If the inspectors met kids like us at the school, they'd wonder how Cockface's exam results are so good. Because some of us can only just write our own names.'

'How many children does he let out of the school?'

'*Hundreds*,' says Joey.

'Us three and maybe twenty others,' says Lloyd.

'Why have none of these children told?'

'You're not getting it.' Lloyd let's out another very adult sigh. 'Cockface finds out stuff about us. He gets us in his office. All friendly at first. Pretending to listen. But he's finding out our secrets. Working out how he can scare us. Then he sets it up so we have to behave. And keep quiet. Like with me and the medicine cabinet. But he does different things with different kids.'

'Good God.' I put a hand to my mouth.

'God is bollocks, Miss,' says Joey.

'You've got to give Cockface credit,' says Lloyd, with surprising maturity. 'It does work. Everyone says the school is good.'

'A good school cares about the children, not results. Lloyd, thank you for telling me this. I promise, the headmaster will be the one in trouble, not you. My word, this is absolutely shocking.'

I sound like Tessa.

'So what will happen to Cockface?' asks Lloyd.

'I imagine your headmaster will be suspended from school,

pending a full investigation.' I'm mentally reeling at the days of paperwork ahead. 'I *knew* something wasn't right at that place.'

'Cockface in prison!' says Pauly, rubbing his hands together.

'What about the other kids?' I hesitate, knowing I'm crossing a professional line. 'What about Tom Kinnock? Does the headmaster see him in his office too?'

'He does,' says Pauly. 'Tom gets called there sometimes.'

'If Tom is being blackmailed by the headmaster, it would explain a lot,' I say. 'A *lot*.'

But not everything.

Lizzie

The doctors' surgery smells of fresh paint and has newly laid grey floorboards and beech-wood chairs.

I type Tom's date of birth into the computer screen and we take a seat beside the fish tank. Tom kneels by a beads-frame toy and starts clacking beads around. They seem to be a fixture in hospitals and doctors' surgeries, those things. Tom never gets bored with them.

There's a beep and my eyes flick to the LED board.

Tom slides counters along, *click, click, click*.

No. Not our name yet.

Click, click … click.

Another beep. Another name. Still not us.

I turn to Tom. He's stopped moving beads, eyes dreamy.

'Tom?'

He doesn't reply.

I stand.

'Tom. *Tom*.' I shake his arm.

But Tom doesn't react.

He's staring into space.

Then he falls to the floor, rigid and jerking his legs crazily, eyes rolled back in his head.

It's such a shock that at first I just stare, heart pounding.

Oh *God*.

'*Help!*' I hear myself sob. 'Please help us! Call an ambulance. My son is having a seizure!'

Kate

I'm starving. My freshly prepared sandwich was left unopened – there were reports to write, then the mad rush to the family centre and the Neilsons. I didn't bother taking my lunch there – I've learned from experience you need both hands to deal with Lloyd Neilson.

After that, there were frenzied phone calls to the police, OFSTED and the Steelfield School academy group. I didn't leave the Neilsons until I could assure Lloyd that Mr Cockrun wouldn't be allowed back on the school premises.

Not until there's a full investigation.

Leanne came to collect them late, as usual, and moaned about having to wait for my phone calls.

By the time I returned to the office, Tessa had eaten my sandwich. It was for environmental reasons, apparently. She can't stand waste.

Fortunately, I'd packed a few snacks this morning in case I ended up working late. Now finally back at my desk, I have an opportunity to crack open my Tupperware box of cheese, crisps and a Pink Lady apple.

I've been thinking, thinking, thinking about Steelfield

School, Mr Cockrun, the Neilson boys and Tom Kinnock. Something isn't adding up and it's driving me crazy, throbbing like a toothache.

I believe Lloyd. But it doesn't explain what's happening to Tom Kinnock.

As a teenager, I liked Isaac Asimov sci-fi novels. They were logic puzzles, most of those stories. A robot would misbehave in some way and you had to figure out how it had broken its programming and gone against one of the three robot laws.

But this logic puzzle I'm not enjoying. More pieces are in place, but things still don't make sense.

Just as I take a crisp from its rustling plastic bag, the phone rings. Reluctantly, I put my lunch/dinner down and pick up.

'Hello, Kate Noble, Child Services.' My eyes wander to the crisp packet.

'Good evening, Mrs Noble, it's Doctor Khan here. I'm a paediatric consultant at the general hospital.'

'Hello, Doctor Khan.' I lift my crisps, hoping to grab a quick mouthful while he's talking. 'How can I help you?'

'I'm told you're the social worker assigned to Tom Kinnock. Is that right? He's on your caseload?'

'Yes,' I say.

'Tom has been brought into hospital again. Did you know?'

'No.' I put the crisps down. 'What happened?'

'Another seizure.' The doctor clears his throat. 'We thought it worth flagging up, given his history. I know he's had injuries before. And the seizures … they're following rather an unusual pattern.' There's a pause. 'I had a chat with Tom earlier. I got a very distinct sense there was something he wanted to talk about. He mentioned someone called Pauly. And your name.'

'Me?'

'Yes. I think you should come in. There could be something he wants to tell you.'

'I'll be there as soon as I can.' I stuff my crisps back into the Tupperware box.

'Where are you running off to?' Tessa barks. 'Not *another* home visit – there are reports to write.'

'Tom Kinnock is in hospital again,' I say. 'A seizure.'

'*Another* one?'

'Yes. Another one. And he wants to talk to me.'

'Be careful, Kate. You're in danger of wearing yourself out with all this running around. And we can't have you signed off long-term sick – you're too useful.'

It's the kindest thing Tessa's ever said to me. It would have been kinder still if she hadn't eaten my sandwich.

Lizzie

We've been in hospital for hours.

Tom didn't fall unconscious for long, but he's slept a lot ever since. Apparently, this is normal. Seizures take it out of people.

I need to go home. There are things to pick up: night clothes and so on. But I'm putting it off, not wanting to leave Tom for a minute. Sitting around in hospitals, you get a lot of time to think. To imagine.

A man waits outside the ward. He is dressed in jeans and a frayed sweatshirt, scruffy but handsome. The moment I leave, he walks casually into Tom's ward, flashing a nice smile at the nurses.

The receptionist's back is turned.

The man flips blond hair out of his eyes, catches Tom's attention, winks.

'Hey. Tommo. Come on out here for a minute. Your mum's a liar – I never hurt you. Let's get away from her.'

He takes Tom's hand.

They head past the reception desk, out of the hospital, into a camper van and Tom is gone …

I squeeze my eyes tight, willing the images to go away.

Security in hospitals is excellent. Tom couldn't be safer.

I whisper, 'Tom. Tom. I need to pop home again. I have to get a few bits and pieces. I'll be back as soon as I can.'

I hate going home without him. It's like I'm leaving an arm behind. But we need clothes. Healthy snacks. Stuff the hospital won't provide.

I don't remember the journey back, but at home I walk around in a daze.

What do I need? What do I need?

A knock at the door makes me leap out of my skin.

Oh *God*.

The letterbox rattles, and a thin voice calls through: 'Elizabeth? Are you in there?'

My mother.

I freeze, mooting the possibility of hiding in here, hoping she thinks I've gone out.

I've done that before. In fact, I've even slithered across the floor on my stomach in a bid not to be visible from the windows. I know it's childish, but that's how I am around my mother. You have to be in a strong frame of mind to deal with being constantly put down.

Also, the house is still a state. She'll be furious about that.

'*Elizabeth.*' Even muffled by the front door, I hear the irritation in my mother's voice. 'I know you're in there – I can see you moving around.'

I have an image of Mum, powdered face pressed to my letterbox, listening for movement, waiting to catch me out.

Oh God. There's no escaping it …

I cross the living room and open the front door, knowing my forehead is pinched with worry, grey bags under my eyes.

'Hi, Mum.'

My mother stands in a cloud of rose perfume, black hair in tight, styled curls around her head.

'You were hiding from me,' she says. 'Trying to pretend you were out.'

'I've had a terrible day.' I'm a guilty teenager caught with a cigarette. 'Tom's in hospital again. I'm just picking up a few things for him.'

'My goodness, your hair still looks terrible.' My mother tries to enter the house, but I block her path.

'I'm just on my way out, Mum.'

'Please don't tell me you intend to wear that scarf outside the house.'

My hands go to the soft orange wool – Tom's favourite colour. 'Didn't you hear me? About Tom?'

'This place looks disgusting.' Mum wrinkles her nose at the living room behind me. 'Absolutely disgusting.'

I pull myself up tall, and with as much dignity as I can manage say, 'Tom's in hospital again. I'm terrified. Housework hasn't been first on the agenda.'

'Tom is in hospital *again*?' Mum adjusts her Louis Vuitton handbag. 'What's wrong with him this time?'

I break down in tears. 'Another seizure.'

Mum watches me, mouth open. Then she puts an awkward hand on my shoulder. 'There, there. Let's not make a scene. What did the hospital say?'

Finally, it seems to be sinking in for my mother. Something serious is happening with her grandson.

'They're as confused as I am.'

'Well, I would suggest a nice cup of tea. But you don't have any teabags.'

My mind skips around the kitchen, dancing over dirty cups, into the empty cupboards. 'How do you know that?'

'I came by an hour ago. The house was empty. I was going to make myself a cup, but you didn't have a single teabag in the place. Let alone fresh milk.'

'You were here earlier?' I ask.

'The kitchen was filthy.'

'You were *inside* my house?'

'Oh, for goodness sake, Elizabeth. There's no need to raise your voice. Why shouldn't I be inside your house? I'm your mother. *You* gave me a key.'

'I've never given you a key.' My words are low. Almost animalistic.

'The letting agent gave me a set for safekeeping. Don't you remember? It's not unusual for a mother to have a key to her daughter's house.'

I have a hazy memory of Mum accompanying me to the letting agents when I signed a load of forms.

This is how Mum twists things.

She never mentioned getting her own set of keys cut. I certainly didn't give her any.

My whole childhood, Mum planted the seeds of stories, which grew like weeds, choking what was real.

'I don't like you coming into my house without asking.'

'Don't be ridiculous. Why on earth not? I'm your mother.'

'I need to go now, Mum. I need to go back to the hospital.'

'I'll come with you.'

'No.' My voice is firmer than I mean it to be. 'It's just sitting and waiting. It's better you go home and rest. Maybe I'll see you at the weekend.'

'But—'

'I have to get back to Tom. It's way past his bedtime.'

'Well, how about I have a tidy up around here?' Mum suggests. 'Do the kitchen at least. What if social services come around to check?'

I see the sense in this. 'Okay,' I say. 'Yes, fine.'

'Isn't there something else you want to say?' she asks.

'Thank you, Mum.' I kiss her powdered cheek.

On the way out I think: *I'll have to change the locks.*

Kate

I arrive at the children's ward sweaty and stressed from road-work traffic.

Some parents are pulling out folding beds, readying themselves for a night's sleep. Others are helping their children eat, or sitting on beds with them, watching television.

I introduce myself to the duty nurse, telling her I'm from Child Services.

She doesn't bother checking my ID. 'Who are you here to see?'

'Tom Kinnock. He asked to see me.'

'Tom's in bed eleven.'

'Is his mother here?'

'She just popped home. She'll be back soon. Do you want to wait for her?'

'The sooner I talk to Tom the better.'

'He's been drifting in and out of sleep.' The nurse leads me to a blue curtain. It's the only closed curtain on the ward.

A little girl with bright blonde hair lies in the next bed. 'Hello,' the girl says, all smiles and gaps in her milk teeth. 'I'm not very well.'

'Oh dear,' I say. 'That's not fun, is it? But it looks like your teeth are doing brilliantly. Has the tooth fairy visited you in hospital?'

The little girl beams. 'Yes! Daddy said she'd find me and she did. She left one whole pound under my pillow and a chocolate. But the chocolate melted—'

'You should be trying to sleep, Charlotte,' the nurse says. Then she pulls back Tom's curtain and whispers, 'Tom. *Tom.* Your social worker is here.'

'He'll be tired,' the little girl muses, wiggling her remaining front tooth with her finger. 'He's been sleeping since he got here.'

But Tom is awake, propped up on three pillows.

My goodness. He looks so *pale*. Like he hasn't seen daylight in months. This last seizure has really taken it out of him.

The nurse pulls the curtain around us, then leaves.

'Hi Tom.' I give something like a wave. 'Do you remember me? I'm Kate Noble, your social worker. The doctor thought you might like a chat.'

Tom blinks, eyes darting around. 'I wanted it to be you. You're Pauly's social worker too, aren't you? You got him fish and chips.'

I smile. 'I don't make a habit of that. Just a one-off. How are you feeling?'

'Not very well.'

'Do you remember having a seizure?'

Tom shakes his head.

'Where's your mum?'

'She went home to get clothes and stuff.'

'Listen, the doctor says these seizures are a little unusual.

310

They can't quite get to the bottom of them. And then there are the injuries.' I sit on the chair.

Tom fiddles with his blanket.

'You can tell me anything, you know. Even things you can't tell your mum. I'm here to keep you safe.'

Tom nods his head tightly.

'Tell you what.' I pull a notepad from my bag. 'If you don't want to say it out loud, is there anything you'd like to write down? Would that be easier? Who is hurting you, Tom?'

Tom takes the pad. For a moment, I think he's just going to hold it. But then he scribbles something, rips the paper free and folds it immediately, then hands it to me.

'Can I—'

'Don't read it now,' Tom whispers.

'Okay.' I shift awkwardly in the chair. 'Well, can I read it later? In my car?'

Tom nods.

The little girl, Charlotte, calls through the curtain: 'Can't you sleep, Tom? I can't sleep.'

'Just try and think of something happy,' I call back. 'Like riding a pony on the beach. Or walking in the woods.'

'I'll think of My Little Pony,' the girl decides loudly. 'I like Majesty best. Oh! Tom. I think I can hear your mummy. *Lucky*. Your mummy is so nice.'

Charlotte's right – there are female voices. Lizzie, I think, talking to a nurse.

'Mum's coming,' Tom whispers. 'You can't tell her.'

Closing my hand around the paper, I say, 'I'll read it later. Okay? Somewhere private.'

We hear footsteps and then the curtain slides back.

I see Lizzie, her short, platinum hair glowing white under the neon light. She is smiling and has books and toys under one arm.

'Hey, Tommo. Oh, Kate.' Lizzie notices me and jolts in shock.

'I was just saying a quick hello,' I explain. 'Seeing how Tom was feeling.'

'He's tired,' Lizzie says, stroking Tom's hair. 'But he's awake – that's the main thing. Kate, I'm glad you came. I wanted to thank you. For being so fair at the meeting. They were trying to paint a picture. I know that. And I know you were trying to be even-handed. To see both sides.'

'It was hard on you.'

Lizzie gives a humourless laugh. 'I was terrified. I still am. I know how things look. No one believes me ... the school ... no one believes me.'

I feel the paper in my hand.

Lizzie's bottom lip wobbles. 'It's the not knowing, that's the hardest thing. These seizures. *Why* are they happening? Those marks on his arm ...'

'Hopefully the doctors will find out more this time.'

Lizzie puts the toys and books on the bedside table.

'Bedtime, okay, Tommo? Time to sleep.'

'My teeth hurt,' says Tom.

'That's because you were clenching them. They'll feel better tomorrow.'

'Well, I should be going,' I say. 'Bye now.'

'Bye Kate.' Lizzie gives me a warm smile. 'It's good to see you. Come on, Tom – let's get you tucked in.'

The moment I'm through the beige double doors and out of the ward, I phone Tessa.

'Hi,' I say, without giving my usual introduction. 'I won't have time to do those reports tonight. Tom Kinnock just wrote something down.'

'What did he write?'

'I don't know. I haven't read it yet. I'm about to, once I leave the hospital. But I think he might have disclosed who's hurting him.'

Lizzie

I'm at the vending machine, hands shaking, trying to make the buttons work.

Water. I just want a bottle of plain water. A8? Is that the right code?

I know Kate is kind, but I still hate that she visited unannounced. It's like she's trying to catch us out. That awful, shouty, red-faced manager of hers probably made her come to check on us.

Another seizure. Too many coincidences.

That's what her manager is thinking. She said as much in the meeting.

Behind me, I hear the squeak of shoes on the rubber floor. 'Hello, love. How are you bearing up?' It's Clara, one of the younger nurses.

'Not very well.' I start to cry – a pitiful noise that comes from my stomach. '*Another* seizure, Clara. Social services think it's my fault. I'm scared they'll take Tom away from me.'

I find my face pressed against the comforting cotton of Clara's uniformed shoulder, her arms around me.

'You're doing great,' Clara says. 'Really.'

'His social worker came just now,' I say, the words hot with tears.

'They just have to do their checks. That's all.'

'It's more than that,' I say. 'They need answers. And I don't have any for them.'

'Oh, I'm sure everything will get worked out. You're clearly a loving mother. All the nurses know that. We've seen you with Tom.'

I break down into noisy sobs then.

'Everything will be fine,' says Clara. 'They have to tick their boxes. Tom's obviously from a good family.'

A bottle of water clangs into the vending machine dispensing tray, and with it comes a clarity of sorts.

This is Tom's third hospital visit. It'll go down as another unexplained injury. Which means social services will be making moves to take Tom away. Even Kate Noble with her overriding sense of fairness. She has to tick her boxes. Maybe that's why she was here – to set things in motion.

Too many coincidences.

They will put Tom in a children's home and give Olly visitation.

And suddenly, despite the creeping darkness outside, I'm clear as daylight.

I have to take Tom away.

We need to run.

Yet as obvious as this is, it isn't really a solution. I have no money. My mother won't protect me and my father is dead. I've lost touch with all my old friends. I have nowhere to go.

Think, Lizzie. Think. There must be somebody …

And into my head walks Stuart.

Big, tall, strong Stuart.

We still email sometimes. He's finally moved to the Shetlands.

He's living mortgage-free, trading over the Internet and enjoying a simpler life.

I know his address – he sent it when he moved.

The Shetland Islands are isolated. No social services or police in some parts. It's almost deserted where Stuart lives, apparently. And Stuart knows a boat yard owner. We could go even further afield if we needed to.

I didn't email back. Stuart is caught up in the romance of our affair. With the daily grind and a little boy to take care of, I couldn't see things working.

But maybe …

'I need to go home again,' I tell Clara. 'Is that okay? I forgot some things. I'll be back in a few hours.'

I need to pack a bag and buy Shetland Island ferry tickets.

'Visiting hours are over, aren't they?' I ask, trying to keep my voice from shaking. 'You won't be letting anyone else in tonight?'

'No. It's bedtime. But you can just ring the buzzer.'

'Thank you.'

I hurry to the exit.

Kate

I don't read Tom's note straight away – not until I'm well clear of the hospital. But it burns a hole in my bag as I stride down the hospital corridors, across the grassy grounds and towards the car park.

Sitting in my red Fiat, I take out the paper and carefully unfold it.

This note took Tom seconds, his little hand looping up, down and around. The ramifications will last a lifetime.

Who is hurting you, Tom?

There it is, written in childish handwriting.

One terrible, awful word.

Mum

My head throbs. Flashes of training videos and textbook paragraphs loop and knit together.

Parents can hurt their children in so many ways. One of those ways is making them sick on purpose.

I think of Tom, ill and vulnerable in his hospital bed. The

317

strength it must have taken him to write this note. The risk he took to trust me.

The note drops into my lap and I see my hands pressed together in prayer.

Dear God ... I never doubted her ... I never doubted ...

Lizzie.

How could she have fooled us?

We studied abusive parent profiles in training. Learned about the classic signs: drug addiction, neglect, secrecy and chaos.

I pictured abusers as stoned, angry Leanne Neilsons. But Lizzie ... she seemed completely normal. Nice. Doing her very best. Yet the whole time ...

Tessa was right. It's Lizzie. It's all Lizzie. She's the one hurting him.

I put my hands on the steering wheel, but I don't trust myself to drive. Not just yet. For the first time since I opened Tom Kinnock's case notes, everything makes sense.

Medical child abuse. It's not common. Most social workers will never see it. But it happens.

A switch has flicked and the world has turned dark. I see someone posing as an angelic, caring mother and fooling everybody.

With shaking fingers, I take out Tom's note and read it again.

Mum

Then I call Tessa.

'Hello?' she barks. 'Are you going to tell me what on earth is going on? Where have you been?'

'We need an emergency protection order,' I say. 'For Tom Kinnock.'

'An *emergency protection* order? At this stage of the game? We're already looking to move Tom out of her care.'

'Lizzie is hurting Tom,' I say. 'Medical child abuse. She's causing the seizures. It all makes sense. The odd pattern to them. The injection marks. The head injury – she probably knocked him out to inject him with something.'

'Good lord.'

'We need to get Tom out of harm's way.'

'Steady on. He's in hospital at the minute. That gives us a bit of breathing space.'

'Assuming she doesn't take him *out* of hospital.' I'm in my car now.

'Get yourself back to the office. We'll get the papers sorted out and see what can be arranged.'

It's way past office working hours, but for once, I don't feel tired. I have way too much adrenalin.

Lizzie fooled me so perfectly. Blaming the school. Blaming the father. Such a loving mother. And she's been hurting Tom the whole time …

Ruth

When Elizabeth leaves, I get to work on her kitchen. Try and fail to make it look half decent. I give up in the end. It's a job that will take days and anyway, there are no cleaning products. Or teabags.

No clean cups. Not even fresh milk. The food cupboards are empty and piles of dirty laundry are strewn around the place.

Chaos. Absolute chaos.

Eventually, I find the courage to look in Elizabeth's wardrobe again. To find the box that I saw the other day; one she'd pushed into the far depths of the wardrobe to keep it hidden.

I know about hidden things. What they can mean.

Something about that box wasn't right, but I didn't have the courage to find out exactly how wrong it could be.

With Elizabeth, I never know what I'm going to find.

When I open the box, I'm not surprised at all. I knew all along, somehow.

It's the strangest feeling.

The box is stuffed with empty medicine bottles. Olly's medicine, and some of mine. Clearly Elizabeth has been stock-piling.

I stare at the bottles for a long while, willing them not to be there. Occasionally, I'm able to fool myself like that. But not this time. The implications are just too heavy.

I consider throwing them all away. Destroying the evidence. But if I put my fingerprints all over that stuff and they know I've interfered – well, my life won't be worth living.

When I was growing up, there was a little boy who lived on our street – William.

He was always getting ill. In and out of hospital. And then he started having blackouts. Seizures. Eventually, he died.

We learned from the autopsy that he had sodium poisoning. The mother had done it with table salt. They said she had some sort of illness.

Munchausen syndrome by proxy, it was called.

No one suspected a thing – the mother seemed like such a bright, happy woman. Everyone in the street knew her. She even ran a sewing group.

I remember telling Elizabeth the story. She was fascinated. I've always known she wasn't like other children. She could lie and manipulate from a very early age, no doubt imitating my own little flights of fancy.

But Elizabeth was never careful, like me. She always took it too far. And she's so close to being found out with all these hospital visits.

I admit, I was depressed when Elizabeth was young. Frustrated. Not the kindest parent. Intelligent women had fewer choices back then. I know I got things wrong. But for Elizabeth to be hurting Tom on purpose …

It's just beyond normal.

Sometimes in life it's kill or be killed. Elizabeth is holding me at gunpoint.

I knew there was *something* going on with Olly's health. It didn't seem right to me, the amount of tablets Elizabeth was giving him. Or the fact his leg never seemed to get better. And nurses don't train in physiotherapy – why was she giving him leg exercises and pulling his joints around?

But I kept out of it. It was Elizabeth's business. I stuck my head in the sand, didn't get involved.

I pass the downstairs mirror and see myself, eyes creased with worry and sadness.

There's nothing good about getting old. Beauty fades, leaving only truth.

My father used to say the real monsters of the Second World War were the people who did nothing. Who pretended everything was okay. He was a Jewish-Austrian immigrant so he knew a lot about it.

I look in the mirror and try to smile. It's very important to have a nice smile; I learned that by watching others. I have lovely veneers and I take very good care of them.

That little boy William died.

He *died*.

I leave the medicine bottles in the wardrobe and lock the house up tight, sticking a Post-it note on the breakfast bar for Elizabeth:

Did what I could but no cleaning products, going home now, Mum.

I get in my car and search for Olly Kinnock's number on my mobile phone.

K, K, K ...

There he is.

Oliver Kinnock.

I still have his number.

Lizzie

The front door is locked. This means Mum has gone. Thank goodness.

My hands shake so badly I can barely turn the key. The bus stopped at every red light in town, and I'm beyond stressed.

Inside the house, I race upstairs taking two steps at a time. We'll leave all this chaos behind. Go far away.

I grab a scuffed Quiksilver backpack from my bedroom wardrobe and drag it downstairs, throwing things inside. This used to be Olly's bag and it smells of camping – earth and damp.

Clothes, medicine …

Medicine causes the seizures.

Since they found the injection marks on Tom's arm, I've been a lot more careful. I inject in his groin now and knock him out first, rather than wait until he's asleep. Any movement risks bruising and swelling around the injection site.

A few hours after Tom comes around, I put more crushed-up tablets into his orange juice. Coupled with the stuff racing around his blood stream, this causes him to fit if I get the dose right.

The medicine doesn't just cause seizures. It causes mood swings, drowsiness, aggression, a sickly pallor. I'm fascinated by the effects, seeing what each different tablet does and then trying out combinations.

Medicine … More precious than gold. The source of everything: praise, attention, identity.

And control.

The red metal security box sits on top of a pile of cookery books, too high for Tom to reach. I grab it, holding it briefly to my chest.

Inside are over fifty bottles and packets of prescription drugs, all collected from Olly, my mother and hospitals over the years.

I stash the empty bottles in another box in the back of the wardrobe and dispose of them in bulk whenever we visit London, dropping them in different waste bins. It wouldn't do to throw them away with my rubbish. What would people think?

Now that box of medicine is a liability.

I can't take empty medicine bottles with me and risk them being found on my person. And I can't leave them here.

The solution is obvious in the end.

I soak the labels off so they can't be traced. The cleaned bottles are with the bathroom waste now, stuffed under toilet roll tubes and sanitary products.

When I left Olly, I thought I might be noticed just for being a mother. A real person in my own right, even without a brighter, shinier human being to cling onto.

But it didn't happen. So it started all over again, the medication and the control.

Of course, there's no Olly to medicate now. Olly became dangerous. He worked out who I really was. So it has to be Tom.

I've already bought ferry e-tickets on my mobile phone. We leave from Aberdeen and will reach Stuart's new home on the Shetland Islands by tomorrow morning. We'll be safe from the British child protection services there and I'll make a plan.

I can't stay with Stuart long-term – he's too logical. The sort of man who'll see things that don't add up. I need someone more romantic.

Like Olly. He was a hopeless romantic, willing to believe I was perfect. Buying into all my fantasies.

The violence, the abuse – I'm good at making up stories. The trick is to convince yourself they really happened. I write them down. Get every detail perfect. Once you believe it, everyone else does too.

It worked on Tom, too. I told him over and over again. *Remember your wrist? Remember what Daddy did?*

That injury was for Tom's own good. I had to show Olly in a certain light or else I'd never have got sole custody. And without sole custody, what would I have been? There's a big difference between shared custody after divorce and a vulnerable woman escaping abuse. People sympathise with one, but not the other.

Tom didn't see who knocked him to the ground. The broken wrist happened when he was unconscious. I used Olly's ski boots, then put Tom in bed ready for Olly to find him when he came around.

I do such a good job with Tom, planting the stories, just like my own mother used to do.

After I broke his wrist, I ran through the park with him, telling him we were escaping, running away. Making him afraid of his father.

I watched my mother do this sort of thing, manipulate

thoughts until people believed her version of reality. It took Dad years to see beneath her mask. To realise that behind the pretty face was something very ugly and dysfunctional.

I learned from my mother how to be a victim. How to make everything someone else's fault and have people pity you and look after you.

With Tom it was easy to make him feel protective over his poor, vulnerable mummy. He even started having nightmares about what he thought Olly did.

Have I got everything?

Yes. I think so.

Everything except Tom.

I pull the bag onto my back and head out, slamming the front door behind me. It'll have to be a bus to the hospital. I can't afford another taxi.

Hurrying along the street, I think I hear the rattle and wheeze of Olly's old camper van engine. A vehicle, definitely. Coming this way.

It's just a car, I tell myself. *Don't be paranoid.*

But then, as I reach the end of the street, bright lights approach.

Instinct flattens me to a wall and I slide down an alleyway, watching the street.

It's ... *oh God.* A *police car.*

When the car passes, I head out of the alleyway towards the mini-supermarket where there is a bus stop. The no. 65 is just pulling in.

I need to get back to the hospital.

There isn't much time.

Olly

I'm held at a red light, white knuckles clutching the steering wheel. There is a blue sign ahead: *Hospital*.

Come on, come on.

Lizzie's mother just called me. She told me Tom has had another seizure and is being treated at this hospital. I'm nauseated with worry, foot over-revving the accelerator, eyes fixed on the windscreen.

Finally.

The only thing that's got me through these last few months is believing that *someone* will see through Lizzie and help me find Tom.

I never guessed it would be her own mother. Ruth thinks Lizzie has been medicating Tom and giving him seizures. This is both believable and unbearable.

I rev the engine as the light changes, hot tears rolling down my cheeks.

The hospital staff will be rallying round Lizzie, no doubt. Telling her what a wonderful mother she is. It's what she's good at, evoking sympathy. She copies and imitates until the feelings look real. But inside, she's empty.

The police believe I'm a violent, sexually abusive partner.

London social workers think I'm a lunatic. All because of Lizzie's fantastic ability to manipulate.

The only people who'll give me any time are solicitors. They've been mounting an appeal, although they're 'not hopeful'. One of them even told me I was wasting my money.

I put Lizzie on a pedestal, my little elfin-faced nurse, so timid and vulnerable, I thought. In need of my protection.

But Lizzie is none of those things. She's an expert liar, clever and ruthless.

Little and often, drip, drip. Like coffee filling a cup. *You hit me. You're violent.*

Showing me bruises on her body. Tampering with my medication. Throwing herself down the stairs. Altering clocks. Moving things around the house. Distorting my reality.

I didn't stand a chance.

She must have done the same with Tom. *Daddy hurt you. Daddy hurt you.* Until he believed it himself.

God knows what else she's done to him – I can't bear it. Christ, he had a broken wrist. I thought he fell out of bed, but Lizzie must have … It makes me sick to think of it.

I overtake a bus, veering dangerously into the other lane, not caring about the beeps from oncoming traffic.

Getting myself off the medication – that was the first step to clarity. Not so difficult, actually, because Lizzie took all the medicine when she left. I'll probably never know what she gave me or what it did to my brain.

Lizzie was clever. She had me believing I'd done something. I thought I must be blacking out. A Jekyll and Hyde sort of thing. It was terrifying. I think that's why the court case was such a mess. I didn't know what was true and what wasn't.

How would I ever guess Lizzie was giving herself bruises? That someone could be that crazy, while seeming so sweet and vulnerable?

I suspect our neighbour, Stuart, was inadvertently involved with some of Lizzie's bodily markings – the ones Lizzie couldn't do herself. He probably threw her around a bit when they had sex. Gripped her too tightly. Didn't realise his own strength.

She was having an affair with him – one of my friends kept trying to tell me. I didn't believe the friend at the time, even though he'd been a mate of ten years.

Lizzie told me my mate had made a pass at her and she'd rejected him – that's why he was making up stories. Jealousy. I wanted to believe her. I wanted the fairy tale. I loved her *so* much. But none of it was real.

Confusion. Aggression. Paranoia. Depression. Dizziness and disorientation.

That's what Lizzie gave me.

But I'm to blame too.

If I'd told the doctors how I was feeling, they might have done blood tests. Worked out something was whizzing around my body that shouldn't have been there.

Stupid, male pride.

I'm not a religious man, but now I pray every day.

I'm on my way, Tom.

Dad is coming.

Lizzie

The *pharmacy is clean and quiet, a gentle ticking clock measuring the stillness. Outside, sheets of rain slosh against the window.*

'You're soaked,' *says the pharmacy lady.*

I give her a meek smile, squeezing water from my hair and sliding the prescription slip over the counter.

Yes. Poor me. I'm ever so vulnerable but I never complain.

'Who are you in for today?' *she asks, reading the slip.* 'Your husband again?'

'No. It's for me. I'm going on a trip. My brother is getting married in Thailand and I'm maid of honour.'

'You're going out there on your own?'

'Yes.'

'You're brave.'

I grip my bag strap.

The pharmacy lady pushes the prescription slip through the little window. Usually, a white packet is passed back through the window almost immediately. But today the pharmacist himself comes out of the medicine room, a tall man in a white coat. He has serious black glasses on his nose.

'Name?' *he asks.*

'Elizabeth Kinnock.'

'Address?'

'Apartment 11F, Primrose Gardens.'

'You're aware these can have quite a few side effects? Just to double-check, you haven't any history of mental illness in the family, have you? The doctor asked you about that?'

'He did. No. No history.'

The pharmacist hands me the packet. 'Are you off to Africa? Somewhere like that?'

'South-East Asia.'

'It's important to start taking these a week before you travel,' says the pharmacist. 'Otherwise, you won't be sufficiently protected.'

'Thank you.' My hands close around the paper packet.

Before I leave, I order two packs of codeine, a bottle of cough syrup and an antifungal Candida tablet.

I leave the pharmacy with a spring in my step, not minding the rain in the slightest.

When I get home, Olly is still in bed. His leg is especially painful today because I did his physio earlier. I left Tom sleeping in the cot next to him.

'Sweetheart?' I call out.

'Hey, Lizzie,' Olly groans back.

'I've just come from the doctors,' I say, decanting the white Lariam tablets into a plastic cup. 'I told him you were still in pain. He's given you something extra. He thinks it might help.'

'What would I do without you, Lizzie Nightingale?'

I feel myself smiling.

He thinks he's in charge, but I am. It's such a powerful feeling – better than any drug on earth.

I think to myself, I did that. I changed you and you didn't even know.

No more shadows for me. Not when I have this sort of control.

Kate

9.04 p.m.

The police picked me up as soon as I called. They made very good time, actually – just over five minutes.

'We've got the flashy lights, haven't we?' Sergeant Leach explained, when I complimented him on his swiftness. 'We can cross the town in five minutes flat.'

It was actually five minutes and fifty-two seconds, but I don't point this out.

As we pull up outside Tom Kinnock's house, I say, 'So what will happen now? Will you arrest her?'

'We'll get the wheels in motion,' says Sergeant Leach, a muscular man with grey-blond hair and a perfectly fitting, pressed uniform. He and Constable Matthews climb out of the car.

Matthews, a younger woman with brown hair in a loose ponytail, opens the car door for me. 'Nice place,' she says, looking over the large, Victorian corner plot. 'Front garden could do with a going-over, though. She's let it go wild.'

Sergeant Leach goes to the grand front door, nestled between two pillars, and bashes his fist on the wood.

Bang, bang, bang.

333

'Miss Riley?'

A pause.

Bang, bang, bang.

'Could you open the door, Miss Riley?' he calls through the letterbox. 'It's the police. We'd like to talk to you, please.'

My eyes wander over the grassy front garden and closed curtains. For all its grandness, it has the same vibe as Leanne Neilson's place. Unloved. Neglected.

Everything is still.

'Could we have missed her?' I ask. 'She might be on her way back to the hospital.'

'You'd best go round the back,' says Sergeant Leach, pounding on the door again.

Constable Matthews disappears through a back gate.

'Mrs Kinnock,' Sergeant Leach shouts, banging harder. 'Come to the door. If you don't, we have the right to enter your property.'

We wait for a moment.

Then Constable Matthews reappears, a little out of breath. 'I think the house is empty,' she says, resting her hands on her thighs and exhaling. 'I had a little look around. The back door was unlocked. It's a right mess in there.'

Sergeant Leach pulls his hat firmly on his head. 'Kate – stay here.'

'I'd like to come in,' I say. 'I need to see the state of the house.'

'Best not. She could be hiding inside somewhere. We don't know what she's capable of.'

'Constable Matthews thinks the house is empty,' I point out. 'And if Lizzie is in there, there's only one of her.'

'Yes,' says Matthews. 'But she sounds like a psychopath.'

'Only *one* psychopath,' I reason.

I follow them through the tall gate, treading on ready-meal packets and weeds in the back garden.

'It's a state, isn't it?' Matthews says. 'Wait until you see the kitchen. It's filthy. How could this woman have been given custody?'

'She's an excellent liar,' I say, following her through the back door. 'Very good at playing the perfect parent. The virtuous, vulnerable single mother.'

The kitchen is indeed filthy. Unwashed dishes. Flies. Piles of clutter.

Sergeant Leach and Constable Matthews head upstairs, while I look around the chaos.

Then Leach reappears. 'No one's home. But look what I found.'

He holds up a black bag, opening it to show empty medicine bottles rolling between empty hair-dye bottles and cardboard toilet roll tubes.

'It gets better,' says Sergeant Leach. 'Matthews found a prescription medicine label stuck to the bath. She must have soaked the labels off in a hurry.'

'For a mother to be doing that to her child...' Constable Matthews shakes her head. 'Giving him tablets. Making him sick. It beggars belief. She's a monster.'

'That's probably why she got away with it for so long,' says Sergeant Leach. 'Who would believe a mother would hurt her own son?'

Lizzie

On the bus back to hospital, I sit on shaking hands. It lurches through town, then finally up, up the hill towards the hospital.

As soon as the bus doors open, I'm running – across tarmac, past flowerbeds and patients having sneaky cigarettes, into the hospital, upstairs and along lemon-coloured corridors.

As I reach Tom's ward, I'm lucky. A nurse is coming through the double doors. She holds one open for me. 'Hi Lizzie.'

I smile back – my timid smile that tells people I'm small. Vulnerable. That I mean no harm. And then I pass through the door, into the bright lights of Tom's ward.

No one suspects a stressed-looking woman with a shy smile. Mothers are good. Angelic. Beyond fault.

I learned that a long time ago.

But we're nothing without our children.

I reach Tom's bed and sneak behind the curtain. 'Come on, Tommo,' I whisper. 'Let's get you dressed. We're all packed. We're going on the train. Ready steady go, okay?'

Tom pulls himself up. 'I don't want to go. I want to see Daddy.'

'You can't see your father, Tom.' My voice could strip paint. Through the curtain, I hear the rustle of bedclothes and sense bodies and heads turning in our direction. 'You're mine, not his.' I take some deep breaths, forcing myself to stay calm. 'You can't see your father, Tom. He hurt you.'

Outside the curtain, I hear footsteps.

'This will be the doctor.' My heartbeat quickens, and I open the bedside drawer and pass Tom his clothes. 'Get dressed. I've asked them to discharge you tonight.'

'Lizzie?' a voice calls through the curtain. It's Clara, the nurse I like.

Oh God. We need to get out of here.

'Just a minute.' I start to help Tom get dressed.

But the curtain pulls back anyway.

Clara looks flustered. 'Lizzie, the police just arrived. They want to speak to you.'

'What?' A chill runs through me.

'I'll tell them you're here.'

'Could you just give me a few minutes?'

Clara hesitates. 'No. No, Lizzie, I can't do that.' With a whisk of the curtain, she's gone, hurrying across the ward.

Too many coincidences.

'Quickly, Tom.' I push shoes onto his feet.

'What about the doctor?'

'We'll have to see another doctor.' I lift Tom into my arms, folding his skinny body over my shoulder.

This ward has a fire escape – it's one of the first things I noticed.

Escape is always on my mind.

Briskly and unapologetically, I carry Tom straight across the ward, past the nurse's station and through the double doors to the fire escape. I don't know if the nurses see me walk past. I hope not, but I don't turn to look.

As I push the silver door-bar with my hip, I brace for the *peep, peep* of the door alarm.

I hold my breath, but to my relief hear nothing.

Typical NHS cuts – the door alarm doesn't work.

Tom wriggles around in my arms, clinging to my neck, his body jogging up and down as I run down the stairs.

Kate

9.37 p.m.

'They were here.' The young nurse is breathless, holding the curtain back. *'Right here.'*

We all stare at Tom's empty bed.

'She must have taken him,' says Sergeant Leach, putting a hand to his radio. 'I'll go out the front. Constable, search the ward. Check the toilets.'

The police officers peel off in different directions, Sergeant Leach calling into his radio.

I stand, impotent, by Tom's rumpled sheets.

Where could they have gone?

In the next bed, the little girl, Charlotte, pulls herself up. 'Oh, hello. You're the lady who talked about My Little Pony.'

'I'm looking for Tom,' I say. 'Have you seen him?'

'He went with his mummy. That way.' She points to double fire-escape doors.

'Thank you.' I look around for the police, then, not seeing them, run to the doors.

'My mummy is coming tomorrow,' the girl says.

'Oh, lovely!' I call back, pausing at the fire exit, noticing the 'Emergency Use Only' sign.

For a split second, I debate whether this counts as the right sort of emergency. I mean, there isn't a fire. Then I shove open the doors and run down the wrought-iron staircase.

It's dark outside. Bright buses cruise past the hospital entrance.

One flight.

Two.

Lizzie is stronger than she looks if she carried Tom down these stairs.

Or maybe she didn't go this way.

I'm on tarmac now, running towards the bus stop.

A bus is just pulling away, and I ask an old lady with a shopping trolley: 'Excuse me. Have you seen a woman and a little boy?'

'Yes,' says the woman. 'Blond hair, both of them? Yes. They got on the last bus.'

'Do you remember the number?'

She shakes her head. 'It wasn't my one. I want the sixty-one. Do you know when it's coming?'

'No, sorry.' I spot Sergeant Leach at the hospital entrance and wave him over. He jogs towards me.

'This lady saw a woman and small boy catch a bus,' I tell him.

Sergeant Leach takes off his cap, rubbing his damp hair. 'Hello, madam – what can you tell me?'

'Oh yes, officer. Well, there was a woman and a little boy. Both very fair-haired. Are they in trouble, officer?'

Sergeant Leach turns to me. 'You may as well head home, Kate. We'll get a search underway. I'll call when we find them.'

If you find them.

Because Lizzie Kinnock is very good at staying hidden.

I head towards the car park, thoughts racing.

Where could they be going?

My phone rings and I see Tessa's number flash up yet again.

Go away, Tessa.

As I rummage in my bag for my keys, lost in thought, I nearly walk in front of another vehicle – a large green camper van.

Beep! Beep!

Chest tight with shock, I hold up a hand, mouthing, 'Sorry, sorry.'

The driver is a scruffy-looking man. Handsome, in a way. Nice white teeth. His forehead is knotted with stress, which I suppose is typical of anyone visiting a hospital. But he looks familiar.

I remember a black-and-white photocopy, bunged in among some court documents. A passport.

The driver … it's Tom's father.

Oliver Kinnock.

Lizzie

The electronic sign says: *London King's Cross – Delayed, exp 22.15.* Seven minutes late.

Come on, come on.

I've bitten my last fingernail to the skin. My other hand grasps Tom's fingers. 'We're getting a train, Tommo,' I say, in my best, I'm-a-good-mother voice. 'Won't that be exciting?'

Beside us, an elderly couple smile, touched by this lovely relationship between mother and son.

And we *do* have a lovely relationship.

Tom is part of me. My shadow.

A glass shard of panic tells me it's ending. Something *was* happening at school. One of those Neilson boys was pressuring Tom to bring in medicine. *Our* medicine. And worse – Tom is growing up. Learning to think for himself.

Leaving me.

I blame Pauly Neilson. He sowed a seed of doubt – and I can feel it growing. *Mothers aren't always perfect.*

We need to start again. Tom will forget in time.

Come on, train.

Suddenly, the electronic sign flashes and changes. *London King's Cross – Delayed, exp 22.29.*

Oh God.

I put on my bright mum voice again, covering my anxiety. 'Ready, Tom? For the big adventure?'

'I don't want to go.'

I give him the eyes. The eyes that tell him: *Don't even think about it.*

'I love you, Mum,' he says obediently.

Kate

10.15 p.m.

'Excuse me.' I knock on the camper van window with rapid knuckles. The window rolls down, slowly and jerkily.

'You're not going to give me a hard time, are you?' The man has sad blue eyes and deep worry lines cast in grey skin. I'd guess him to be in his early thirties. 'Trust me, it's not the day for it. You walked out in front of me.'

He looks so much like Tom.

'Olly – Oliver Kinnock?'

The man flinches. 'Who wants to know?'

I hold up my card on its woven string. 'Kate Noble. From Child Services.'

Olly pulls the gearstick into reverse. 'Never heard of him.'

'Wait, *please*.' I grab the van by the open window, some stupid instinct telling me I could stop it moving just by holding on. 'If you *are* Mr Kinnock, I'm here to help you. I know the truth. About Lizzie.'

Olly's hand lingers on the gearstick.

'Look – can you show me some ID?' I ask. 'And then I can help you, honestly I can.'

'Fine.' Olly rummages in the glove box, then flashes a driving

344

licence showing a healthier, tanned man with glowing blond hair and bright white teeth.

Oliver James Kinnock.

'Listen,' I say. 'I know about Lizzie. I need to talk to you. But I can't do it here—'

Olly opens the van door and jumps out. 'I'm not wasting any more time. I need to get to Tom.'

'He's not here.'

'Yes he is. Lizzie's mother told me.'

'Lizzie just left with Tom,' I say. 'The police are trying to locate her. They know everything. What she's been doing. The medicine.'

Olly grabs the car door for support. 'When did she take him?'

'Within the last half an hour. But ...' I look around the car park. 'Technically, we should discuss this in private—'

'She's got my son, okay?'

'We think she took him on a bus.'

'Get in,' says Olly.

'I really shouldn't—'

'Oh Jesus. Just get in, would you? Lizzie will be on her way to the train station.'

'How do you know?' I ask.

'Because she's trying to escape and a train is faster than a police car. She's not stupid.'

No. Lizzie is very, very clever.

Lizzie

I see a red light in the distance.

'Tom. *Tom!* This is our train. Here it comes.'

The train pulls agonisingly slowly into the station, sliding to a stop an inch at a time.

Come on. Come on.

I rush to the doors, pressing the electronic entry button over and over again. The doors won't open. Not until the driver releases the lock. I know that. But I keep pressing it anyway.

Open!

With a *ding* the button lights up and I bash it with such severity that the older woman behind me gasps. The train doors glide apart.

'On you get, Tom. There's a good boy.' I load Tom onto the train, watching the car park, scanning the diamond fencing.

Then I see something.

Oh God. Olly's camper van.

I'm always noticing camper vans, but this one is definitely Olly's.

The train doors slide closed.

Very slowly, we ease along greased rails, pulling out of the station, rolling past the car park and into shrubby woodland.

I sit by the window, heart pounding. Then I motion Tom to sit beside me.

There's one more stop in this town and then the train will pull away, fast into the night, through countryside, all the way to London.

'Just sleep on me, okay, Tom?' I smile at the fidgety, bald man opposite, and say: 'This is quite an adventure for him.'

'I'll bet.' The man smiles back.

The train rocks and rolls along the track.

Kate

'They're not here.' Olly stalks up and down the train platform. The ticket office is unmanned and the platform empty. He looks at the overhead timetables. 'Where *are* they?'

'The police will find them. Have faith.'

Olly glances at the small silver cross around my neck. 'I'll say this for religion: it has the audacity to give advice during moments of unbearable pain.'

He sits on a bench, puts his head in his hands and cries – big, noisy man sobs.

Faith *is* a little bit ridiculous. As a sci-fi fan, I know there's no logic to it. But sometimes, you just have to believe.

'It's going to be okay,' I say.

Olly looks up, forehead a bunch of muscles. 'My solicitor said that before the court case. "Everything will be okay." And then I lost my son. She had everyone fooled. She can do it again.'

'The police are experts in this sort of thing.'

Olly gives a humourless laugh. 'So is she. They gave me a restraining order based on her lies. I don't have a lot of faith in the police. Nor would you, if you were me.'

'Well, where do you think she could be going?' I ask. 'You know her better than anyone.'

'The woman I knew was just a shell. An image for other people to look at. I never really knew her. Not the real Lizzie.' He rubs his eyes. 'But I do know this. She'll be looking for somewhere to start over. And ideally some idiot to look after her.'

Something ticks in my brain.

I see a picture of Saint Michael, illustrated with big angel wings, on a Shetlands ferry leaflet.

I never gave the leaflet to Lizzie. I meant to, but I forgot. Maybe stress-related disorganisation has a useful purpose sometimes. I pull out the neatly folded page from an inside pocket of my bag.

'What about your neighbour?' I ask, showing Olly the leaflet. 'The guy downstairs. Could Lizzie be going to see him? He asked me to give a message to her. About going to the Shetlands with him.'

'Shit. *Shit*. If that's where she's going ...' Olly jumps to his feet. 'It's a wilderness out there. Half of those islands don't have phone signal. And she could travel by sea to Germany or ... or anywhere. If she gets on that ferry with Tom, he's lost.'

'She might not be going to the Shetlands,' I say. 'I never gave her this leaflet.'

'Stuart is a perfect target for her right now. Let's go.'

'Where?'

'Aberdeen. The ferry port. Right now.'

My work phone rings.

Bloody Tessa ... at this time of night.

I think of all the times Tessa has told me not to wear myself out, and now she's phoning me at gone 10 p.m. *Ha, ha.* It would be funny, if I weren't so tired.

'Hi Tessa. I'm about to drive to Scotland.'

'*Scotland?*' Tessa's volume rattles the tinny speaker.

'Yes, Tessa,' I say. 'With Olly Kinnock. We think Lizzie might be on her way to the Shetland Islands.'

A verbal tirade follows, but I'm barely listening because I'm running back to the car park with Olly.

'We can't risk waiting until morning, Tessa,' I shout back. 'If Lizzie gets on the Shetland ferry with Tom, the chances of getting him back again … There are too many ways she can hide or escape out there.'

Olly opens the camper van door for me. It occurs to me that he is likely to break the speed limit, given the circumstances. I never usually drive with people who break the speed limit – it's a rule I have.

Never mind the rules. Think about Tom.

I jump into the van.

Lizzie

The elderly man on the train is having a panic attack. He's gone all sweaty and is saying out loud what I think in my head sometimes: 'Oh no, oh no, I can't cope, I can't do this, help, I think I'm dying, help.'

Tom is watching the man, eyes wide, body stiff.

I catch a glimpse of myself in the train window and realise I look frightened, too.

What's happening? Have they stopped the train because we're on it? Are the police after us?

I see a flash of yellow neon on the platform and my heart pounds in my forehead.

Boom, boom, boom.

'Tom, let's use the toilet.' As I hustle Tom along the gangway, the neon people enter the carriage.

Oh God, oh God.

'Hello there.' The voice is booming. Authoritative.

I turn.

Across the carriage, the bald man says, 'It's too much. I can't do it. I need to get off.'

Relief floods through me.

The neon people are transport police, here to help the man on the train. Someone must have pulled the emergency cord.

One of them says, 'Okay, sir. We'll help you out and check you over. Are you going anywhere important this evening?'

'I'm seeing my daughter.' The man gulps. 'But I can't do it. Could someone phone her?'

'Let us help you off and we'll sort it out.'

'Mum,' Tom whispers.

'*Shush*, Tom. Just be quiet.'

I watch, heart racing, as the bald man is led off the train.

An announcer says, 'We're sorry for the delay to your journey. A passenger required medical attention. We will shortly be on our way.'

After a moment, the train doors *whoosh* closed and the carriage jolts. We move along the track again, slowly at first, then faster and faster.

Towards London and the overnight train to Scotland.

Lizzie

Olly is lying on the sofa looking drunk and pliable, watching the Winter Olympics on YouTube.

'Are you okay, sweetheart?' I put my arms around his shoulders and kiss his cheek.

'What?' Olly turns to me, his eyes hazy. 'Oh. Yeah.' He points at the TV screen. 'They're amazing, these guys. The heights they reach.'

'We should sort out your meds,' I say. 'You haven't had any today.'

'Haven't I?' he says, blinking languidly.

'No, love. There's a whole new lot to take now. Remember?'

'You know, maybe I should see the doctor again. It's about time I had another blood test. I can't have you doing my visits forever.'

'Olly.' I put a gentle hand on his shoulder. 'I'm a nurse, remember. I'm telling you, you don't need a blood test. You're just depressed, that's all. Trust me. I've seen it a hundred times. You'll just be wasting the doctor's time. And you know how painful it is to move on your leg now. Let me sort out your meds.'

People take power in all sorts of ways. Being tough. Sexy. Rich.

Without power, we are nothing. Empty.

For years, I was a shadow. Impotent. Part of someone else. I had no control. No life of my own. No profession or identity.

But now I am powerful beyond measure.

A real nurse who cares for the sick.

Sometimes, that means making people sick.

Kate

We've driven all night. The sun is bright and I don't feel tired any more. Just anxious.

We're nearing the ferry port.

Olly is beside me, gripping the steering wheel like a life buoy. Whenever I hear the word 'distraught' from now on, I will think of Olly's face and know that most people misuse the word.

The petrol-gauge needle hovers over the big E for empty.

'We need petrol,' I say.

'We'll make it,' says Olly.

'But—'

'The petrol doesn't just run out when you hit empty,' says Olly. 'They make allowances for people who refuel at the last minute. You can get twenty miles out of the reserve. The ferry leaves in five minutes, Kate.'

'Four minutes.'

Olly plants his foot more firmly on the accelerator and tailgates a big, swaying lorry that has planted itself in the fast lane.

'Come on, come on!' Olly beeps the horn and flashes his lights.

I grip my seat. 'What if we run out of petrol?'

'We won't,' says Olly, as we roar past the swaying tanker. 'The port is three miles away. The fuel tank has only just hit empty. Believe it or not, I have a logical brain on my shoulders.' He glances at me. 'I know Lizzie painted a different picture. Highly competitive. Reckless. A womaniser. I read the court papers.'

I think back to the case notes about Olly. How Lizzie seamlessly conveyed Olly as a competitive alpha male, psychotic when provoked, without ever saying those words.

'I've never even had a one-night stand,' says Olly. 'Elizabeth twisted everything, and I walked right into it. Ignored all the warning signs. I didn't see what she was doing until it was too late. What a gullible idiot.'

'She's a manipulator, Olly,' I say. 'She's probably been fooling people since childhood. Maybe she even believes it herself. Delusion is a big part of all this.'

I hear the faint sound of the Red Hot Chili Peppers, 'Give It Away'.

Olly whips an iPhone from his back pocket. The van swerves on the road as he holds the phone against the steering wheel.

'Mum!' Olly shouts. 'We're nearly there.'

'Put the phone down!' I shout, gripping my seat with renewed vigour. 'It's illegal to hold a phone with the engine on. Not to mention dangerous. They've done studies. Phones affect your reaction times as much as five units of alcohol.'

Mrs Kinnock's worried, wobbly voice comes through the speaker. 'Don't use your phone in the van, Olly. It's as dangerous as drink-driving.'

'Yes it is, Mrs Kinnock,' I call out.

'We're nearly at the port, Mum.'

'Oh God, don't do anything stupid,' his mother gabbles. 'You know how Lizzie works. Don't walk into it and make yourself look like the villain again.'

The van veers again.

'Put the phone away, Mr Kinnock!' I shout.

'Gotta-go-Mum-bye.' Olly drops the phone onto his lap. 'Kate, she's sixty-five years old. If I hadn't picked up, she'd have thought something bad had happened.'

'Would she prefer you died at the roadside?'

We reach a roundabout, but Olly barely slows down, zooming around and off at the ferry port exit. My eyes return to the petrol gauge.

'Ferry port,' says Olly, glancing at a sign. 'Two miles.'

The van starts to splutter.

'We have to make it,' says Olly. 'Say a prayer for us.'

'I don't think even God can sidestep the scientific laws of petrol consumption.'

'Kate, I'm in hell every second of every day. Awful, gut-wrenching, nauseating pain. Indescribable. Screaming in the wind, begging people to believe me, having doors slammed in my face. And I'm one of the good guys. I recycle. God owes me big time.'

'Have faith, Olly.'

I say a silent prayer.

We pass a sign. One mile until the port.

The spluttering is getting louder and every few seconds it sounds like the engine is cutting out.

'It's okay,' Olly insists. 'It's okay. We'll make it.'

But it's not okay. I think we're running out of petrol.

As the engine stops and starts, we pass blue freight lorries lined up in a port-side car park.

'Please, God,' I say. 'Please let us make it.'

Olly drives the van straight across a mini roundabout and now we can see the blue and white ferry at the end of the road.

It is moving, slowly, slowly.

Olly roars the van down the road. He must be doing 50 mph in a 30 mph zone but I don't challenge him.

Men appear from somewhere, shouting and waving as Olly screeches the van to a halt.

We leap out of the car, but I know it's too late. A metre of churning green-brown water lies between the ferry and the boarding platform. The car ramp has been cranked up and the ferry is powering up its engines, blasting through the water.

'You have to stop that ferry!' Olly shouts at the men. 'My son is on-board!'

When he doesn't get a response, Olly begins stripping off, apparently about to jump into the water.

'Don't do anything stupid, mate.' One of the men, short, fat and bald, hurries forward. 'Calm down.'

'My *son*!' Olly shouts, face contorted in pain and anger.

'You'll drown before you catch the boat,' I say. 'And then you'll be no good to anyone.'

Olly sinks to the floor, sobbing and howling, one trainer in his hand.

'Tom might not even be on that ferry,' I say. 'We don't know for certain. Maybe the police found him. Tessa was going to search through the London records. Look at other options.'

Although it's just as likely Tessa gave up and went to bed.

Getting the London records at 11 p.m. ... well, that's tricky, if not impossible.

'The police would have called you, wouldn't they?' says Olly. 'If they'd found him.'

The last tiny bit of hope drains from my body. I've never known failure like this – total, overwhelming failure. I don't want to do this job any more. When we get back to England, I'm handing in my notice. Tessa's warnings were right. You can't care too much in this job or it tears you apart.

I'm burned out and it's time to go.

Lizzie

'Are you okay, Tommo?' I put an arm around my son, holding him close.

We're on the ferry, watching the water spill and chug around us.

This is the sort of ferry I remember going on as a child. Stressful, awkward holidays to the Hebrides with Mum and Dad. It has a café selling Scottish toffee and shortbread and bad cups of tea, with a good view.

Neither Tom nor I slept on the overnight train. Tom lay on the seat with his eyes closed, but I could tell by his breathing that he was pretending.

When we arrived at the ferry port, I made a big fuss about buying Tom a croissant. It's so easy to be the loving mother when I have an audience.

Tom didn't eat the croissant and I ended up throwing it in the bin. 'Never mind, darling. You're probably travel-sick.'

Then I dragged Tom on foot over the passenger bridge and onto the ferry.

Now we're on the deck watching the water.

'I'm cold,' says Tom, teeth chattering.

Water swells and churns as the ferry sways and there's a fine mist in the air. It's made Tom's face damp, I think. Or maybe he's crying.

'It'll be a fresh start, okay?' I say. 'We'll be safer now. Maybe we can go without medication for a bit. Things might be different.'

Tom doesn't reply – just stares.

'I won't let them take you away from me, Tom,' I say. 'I would kill myself first. Don't you understand that? You're my whole world.'

'I want to stay,' says Tom.

'Hush now, Tom. It's for the best. You can't stay here – who would take care of you?'

'Dad.'

'He hurt you, Tom. You're mine, not his. I won't ever let you leave me. Not ever.'

Tom goes silent then, sensing in his childlike way that I'm wandering into a place there's no way out of.

I look up, meaning to appreciate the clear sky, the gleaming white boat, our lucky escape. But instead, I see two police officers in yellow high-vis jackets.

I put on a forced, bright voice and look down at Tom. 'Ready for an adventure, sweetheart?'

Smile. Don't look so frightened.

But I am frightened. The ferry hasn't left yet – passengers are still getting on.

I didn't take the Aberdeen ferry in the end. The port is too well-known. Someone might have guessed where we were going. Instead, Tom and I have boarded the Scrabster ferry. It's more of a round-about route, but less traceable.

'Mrs Kinnock?' One of the police officers steps forward.

My grip on Tom's hand tightens.

The police officers have the ring of Laurel and Hardy about

them – one tall and skinny, the other short and fat. The short, fat one is female, her bright jacket pulled tight over a large bust.

'Mrs *Kinnock*.' A bright yellow high-visibility jacket blocks my path.

I'm a rat caught in a trap. 'I'm not Mrs Kinnock.' I look between the officers. One of them – the woman – has her fists clenched.

'We've come to talk to you, Mrs Kinnock,' the male police officer announces. 'You have to get off the boat. Would you come with us, please?'

'I'm *not* Mrs Kinnock.'

'We know it's you,' says the policeman. 'Tessa Warwick from Child Services traced your ticket purchase through the ferry company. If you could just come with us.'

I grasp Tom's shoulder. 'The police need to talk to us for a minute, okay? Nothing to worry about. And then we'll be on our way to the Shetlands. Fresh air. Beautiful scenery. Sheep. All of that.'

'You won't be going anywhere, Mrs Kinnock,' says the policeman. 'We're here to arrest you and take Tom into protective custody.'

I grab Tom, holding him to my body. 'You won't take him. This is my *son*. He's part of me. I love him more than *life*.'

It's a good show, and I feel the onlookers responding with pity, wondering what the police are doing to this poor, kind mother.

The short, fat policewoman steps forward, angry tears in her eyes. 'I've given birth to three kids, Mrs Kinnock. Three of them. I love all of them more than life. But I've never given any of them medicine to make them sick.'

The man puts a hand on Tom's shoulder. 'It's okay, Tom. It's all okay. You'll see your dad soon.'

I look between the officers, wondering if I can outrun them.

No. Not with Tom. And what am I without Tom? Nobody. Invisible.

'I've done nothing wrong,' I insist.

'Come with us, please,' the male officer says. 'Alison, you take Tom.'

The policewoman kneels down to Tom. 'We're taking you somewhere safe. All right, Tom? And then we'll get you reunited with your dad.'

Tom's face lights up, and I want to claw the smile back.

My feet become unsteady and I feel the hard metal gangway against my hip. 'You can't take him away from me,' I say. 'He's my son. *My* son. He belongs to me!'

'Mrs Kinnock, we have an emergency protection order,' says the policeman.

Now I'm shouting: 'You won't take him away from me. *You won't take him away from me!*'

The short police officer's hand goes to the handcuffs on her belt. 'If you could just come with us.'

There are high-pitched, animalistic screams.

Mine.

Somewhere, amid the noise, there's a struggle. My head is pushed down, more forcibly than necessary, and I watch brown water churn under the criss-crossed metal gangway.

Olly

When the call came through, I couldn't believe it.

'It's the police,' said Kate. 'They have Tom. Lizzie took him to a different ferry port. Scrabster. My manager, Tessa, worked it out. She's been up all night going over all the London records. And this morning, she shouted at the ferry company until they gave her Lizzie's travel details.'

I said, 'Are you sure?'

'Am I sure that my manager could bully a ferry company into divulging confidential information?' Kate replied. 'Positive. We need to get to Scrabster now. They're waiting for us.'

Everything after that was a blur.

One of the ferry terminal men must have filled the tank with petrol, because Kate drove us there in my van. Totally illegal, of course, Kate driving uninsured, but I think she made a judgement call – I was in no fit state.

On the way, paranoia took over. This was all a ploy to arrest me again. Lizzie would be at the port, pretending to be afraid, garnering everyone's sympathy.

But now he's here. Tom is here.

I'm running, tarmac rushing under my feet.

My son.

My boy.

Tom is tiny, walking beside a short, female police officer. He looks tired. Frightened. But he's safe.

I'm blubbing like an idiot.

'Tommo. *Tommo*.' Now I'm on my knees, pulling him into my arms, clutching him tight. 'I never stopped looking, Tom. I never gave up. We'll always be together now, Tommo. Always.'

We're both crying now. Sadness for time lost. But also relief. Happiness. Smiling through the tears.

'I didn't know, Tom,' I tell him. 'I didn't know what she was doing. I fought tooth and nail to get you back. They didn't believe me. I never stopped looking.'

Tom's crying too. 'I'm sorry, Dad. I'm sorry for what I said.'

'It doesn't matter.' I shake my head. 'She did the same thing to me. Told me things until I believed her. I've been searching for you every minute, Tom. I would have done anything to get you back. Smash down doors. Kidnap you. Anything. I was about to jump into the water and swim to the Shetland Islands.'

'Steady on,' says the tall policeman. 'Let's not champion law-breaking.'

I lift Tom into my arms, drawing myself to full height. 'When *your* child is stolen by an abusive partner and everyone says *you're* the crazy one, *you* tell me what you'd want to do.'

'He's got a point there, Darren,' the policewoman says.

Kate

'Have you been drinking my Nespressos?' Tessa accuses, cheeks even redder than usual. 'I've only got three left. There were five when I last looked.'

I don't look up from my computer screen, but I nod. 'I needed some caffeine or I would have fallen asleep at my desk. I'll buy you a new box at lunchtime.'

'I should think you will,' says Tessa. 'They're expensive. I knew you'd be on the coffee, sooner or later. It'll be wine at lunch next, mark my words.'

And I believe her. The nervous breakdown is in the post.

'Did you come straight here after the drive back from Scotland?' Tessa asks.

'Yes.'

'And Tom Kinnock made a full statement? A video interview?'

'Not yet, but he will,' I say. 'We don't need it, anyway. The police found medication in the mother's bag. Heart medication. Malaria tablets.'

'There'll be a court case, then. A lot of work.'

'I know.'

366

'Just make sure you don't leave anything out,' says Tessa. 'I've known parents to walk away from a prison sentence before. And some of them even get custody of the child again.'

'Yes. Yes, I know. I'll make sure it's locked up tight.' I look up at her. 'Thank you. For going above and beyond. We'd never have got Tom back if you hadn't made that phone call.'

I feel Tessa's heavy, slightly awkward hand on my shoulder. 'You went above and beyond too. More than above and beyond. Listen, well done you. We see a lot in this job, but medical child abuse ... well, I mean, it's very unusual. I had two journalists on the phone this morning, wanting me to explain it. I told them I didn't understand it myself. I've never come across real-life Munchausen syndrome by proxy.'

'They call it Fabricated or Induced Illness these days.'

Tessa waves the comment away. 'Makes no sense to me whatsoever.'

'She liked being in control,' I say. 'The power and the attention. It's a personality disorder. A type of psychopath. She probably had an awful childhood herself.'

'Shocking that so many social workers missed this,' says Tessa, fiddling with her Nespresso machine.

'Not really. Who had time to look into it properly?'

'You did. Ignored the paperwork and did your job properly. How many nights' sleep have you missed now? Look, do you want another one of these Nespressos, then? I'm just making a cup.'

Tessa has never offered to make me a hot drink before, let alone from her precious Nespresso machine.

I see this as a breakthrough in our working relationship.

I manage a worn-out smile. 'Yes, that would be great.'

'Don't worry about getting me some more – I've got an emergency stash under my desk.' Tessa winks. 'I imagine the newspapers will be mounting a furious attack on social services. Demanding to know how this could have been missed for so long. I mean, it was all there. The constant hospital visits. Unexplained seizures. Physical injuries.'

'Lizzie was a very good liar. She sold a better, more believable story – that she was the angelic mother, obsessed with Tom's health and wellbeing. And she manipulated a confession out of Tom – don't forget that.'

'But surely someone should have noticed something fishy about her.'

'I don't blame the other social workers,' I say. 'We barely have time for a cup of tea. Not enough funding. Not enough staff. If Tom hadn't had a moment of courage—'

'You did a decent job.' Tessa gives me another clumsy pat on the shoulder. 'Listen, maybe all the court business won't be as bad as you think. Getting the kids to stop protecting their parents – that's the hard part. And you've done that, haven't you?'

'Yes. It looks that way.'

'Awful, awful woman. Bring back hanging. Pure evil is what she is.'

Sometimes, I wonder if Tessa is right for this job. Social work isn't black and white, good and bad. But on the other hand, her no-nonsense outlook has probably saved her from a nervous breakdown.

And she did just offer me one of her Nespressos.

Maybe there's hope for us yet.

Olly

'Okay, buddy?' I fasten Tom into his coat, hanging his new bag around his shoulders.

Tom admires it in the hallway mirror, grinning in his school uniform.

Tom and I live in a new house a few roads from his school. It would have been too disruptive to move him again, so I moved instead.

'Thanks, Dad. I love it.'

It's a Marvel Action Heroes rucksack – I bought it for his first day back at school after the holidays. Apparently, Transformers is 'for babies' now.

I'm in danger of spoiling him, but that's okay. And I don't hear Tom complaining.

Tom has *shot* up over Christmas. Like the tomato plants on our windowsill. Just growing and growing. He's a completely different boy, tall and strong. Good food, exercise and no medication, that's all it took.

'Come on then.' I take Tom's hand – he still lets me do that. 'Let's go. We don't want to be late.'

There was a time when I couldn't hold Tom's hand. Couldn't see him, talk to him, tuck him in at night. You can't imagine how it felt. I was in hell. Now, every day is like my birthday.

'Are we walking?' Tom asks. 'Or going in the camper van?' He loves the camper van.

'The camper will be a bit hard to park today, Tommo. They're still doing those roadworks.'

'*Please.*'

I glance at his little face. 'Oh, all right then. First day back. What do you think your new teacher will be like?'

'Hopefully nicer than Mrs Dudley.' Tom gives me a mischievous grin.

I met Mrs Dudley at the court hearing. She'd left Steelfield School by then. Voluntarily, according to her. But we all know she was pushed.

The headmaster was sacked and may face a prison sentence.

In court, Mrs Dudley was asked to give evidence about Tom's erratic school attendance, lateness and the fact he was often tired, pale and hungry.

I remember Lizzie was always a nightmare with time, either ridiculously early or hours late. So it was no surprise to hear she repeated this pattern with Tom at school. Early some days, very late on others.

When I think what could have happened to Tom ... But that's a dark road, and I try not to go down it.

During the hearing, I was obsessed with justice. Justice against social services who lost records and mixed up reports, and the doctors who misdiagnosed and ignored. Justice against the police, who gave me a restraining order based only on Lizzie's testimony and self-inflicted wounds. Justice against the family-court judge who let Lizzie walk away with my son.

Justice against Lizzie herself.

Lizzie Nightingale, a wolf in nurse's clothing.

Of course, I'm not absolved from blame. I was so caught up with the romance I didn't see what was right under my nose. Lizzie over-medicated me, drugged me up, made me see things, hear things. I became so aggressive, angry and depressed, I hardly knew myself. But even in my darkest moments, I never hurt my wife or child. It was all a figment of Lizzie's imagination.

In my clearer moments, I suspected something was wrong. But mostly, I had no clue. Not until it was too late.

Tom and I still see a counsellor together to help us make sense of things. We go every Friday, then head to McDonald's (Tom's choice) for a Happy Meal with chocolate milkshake.

It's tough, the counselling. Emotional. Very tiring.

A lot happened that Tom needs to talk about.

During the last session, Tom said Lizzie put menstrual blood on his dressing gown to make it look like he'd had a nosebleed. He saw her doing it in the toilet, but she convinced him he was seeing things. And she gave him three different tablets one morning – the morning he attacked the little girl in the playground.

Tom knew the tablets made him feel bad. He tried to get rid of them, bringing medicine bottles into school, giving the tablets to Lloyd and throwing the empties away at the back of the school field.

My medicine bottles, as it turns out. Painkillers I'd been prescribed.

Things like that are very, very tough for me to hear.

We talk about me as well and how angry I am with Lizzie. Years of mood swings and paranoia – all at her hands.

But I don't only blame the meds. Seeing yourself through someone else's eyes is a real wake-up call. The illusion of Lizzie

I created … no one else did that. I'm a hopeless romantic, all my friends say so. When I meet a woman, I think she's perfect.

I have a new girlfriend now and she doesn't take any of my rubbish. She tells me to cut it right out if I try to put her on a pedestal. Which is better. More real. Tom likes her, but we're taking things very slowly.

Sometimes, Tom will ask about his mother.

'She's mentally ill,' I tell him. 'She's gone somewhere to be helped.'

Lizzie is at a secure mental health hospital. Her delusions are so severe. Even in court, she insisted she'd done nothing wrong. Whether she can really be helped … I don't know.

The only thing I know for certain is that I am now truly awake. Wide awake. I see my blessings as clear as day: Tom, Tom, Tom.

I help my little boy into the camper van and buckle him into his booster. It's a beast, this seat. Huge. The most expensive one in the shop with safety notices plastered all over it. I've turned into one of those cotton-wool parents.

'Excited to be back at school?' I ask Tom as I start the engine.

'*Really* excited.'

I think: *You're the bravest little boy I've ever met.*

'Who did you miss most over the Christmas holidays?' I ask, putting the car into gear and pulling out.

'Jake.'

'What about Pauly? Little Dennis the Menace? The one who drew felt-tip all over the carpet on our Christmas Eve playdate?'

We both laugh.

'I still like Pauly,' says Tom. 'But he is a bit crazy. Jake's my new, new best friend.'

Tom knows I like Pauly. That little boy has issues, make no mistake about it. But I like him. Tom and Pauly were like magnets once upon a time. Two little boys with messed-up mothers. Pauly helped Tom see things more clearly. That mothers aren't always perfect. And that Tom could trust Kate Noble. So he probably saved Tom's life, one way or another.

Mine too.

I'll always look out for Pauly and his brothers. But perhaps it's for the best that he and Tom are drifting apart.

'Tell you what.' Our camper trundles down the street. 'Why don't you see if Jake wants to come round after school? We can do cinema in the camper van. Popcorn. Watch stuff on the laptop.'

'Can I, Daddy?'

'Yeah, why not?'

Tom grins.

I smile at the windscreen, turning the camper past groups of kids in blue school uniforms.

They've renamed Steelfield: it's now Kipling School after the children's author. I think they wanted to get rid of all those negative associations. There were a lot of scandalous stories going around after the headmaster was sacked.

Actually, I like it round here. Coast just twenty minutes down the road. Climbing centre nearby. Lots of woodland walks. I work in the bedroom and have just sort of let go of London life.

Tom's school is changing now the old headmaster has gone. Parents are allowed to come and go as they please. No more bars on the windows or chains on the gates. The kids are a lot freer. It's a happier place.

Turns out, the headmaster was cheating like nobody's business. Altering tests, getting rid of badly behaved kids during

OFSTED inspections, blackmailing pupils not to tell. He even opened SATS test papers and briefed staff on what to teach.

According to the staff, Mr Cockrun ran a police-state. Filming everything. Having records made about the tiniest little thing, and then using the information to blackmail staff and children alike.

Terrible.

Some parents have removed their children now the school has lost its outstanding status, but I don't care about any of that stuff. It's just image, isn't it? The main thing is that Tom is happy.

Tom and I go to church on Sundays. It's for the social side, mainly, but I keep an open mind to a higher power after the police found my son on the ferry, minutes before it was due to leave.

We see Kate Noble at church most weeks with her husband. He's a lot of fun, Col. Not what I expected. He likes a drink.

I'm meeting new people – the girlfriend being one of them.

Most of the staff at school know what Tom's been through, and the new headmistress has been amazing, putting lots of support in place.

These days, I spend as much time with Tom as possible.

We go outdoor swimming. Bodyboarding. Rock climbing. And on Kate's recommendation, I'm reading him *The Chronicles of Narnia*. He loves it.

The doctors thought Tom could have liver problems, but the last tests showed everything is normal. A clean bill of health.

Tom is so fit and healthy now, tearing around the place, climbing, jumping. Maybe we'll go snowboarding next year.

Every moment with my son is a privilege.

I always knew it.

Now I'll never forget.